DANGEROUS LOVERS
RVantaire

Printed in the United States of America.
First printing edition 2021

Pecan Tree Publishing
Hollywood, FL 33020
www.pecantreebooks.com

ISBN: 979-8-9855014-1-4 (Paperback)
ISBN: 979-8-9855014-2-1 (E-Book)
Library of Congress Control Number: 2022900917

Front cover design by Glenda Antonio
Interior and eBook design by Charlyn Samson
Author photo by Jonas Stefon, Stretch Life Visuals, IG: @stretchlifevisuals

Pecan Tree Publishing
www.pecantreebooks.com

New Voices | New Styles | New Vision –
Creating a New Legacy of Dynamic Authors and Titles
Hollywood, FL

Dangerous Lovers

RVANTAIRE

Contents

CHAPTER 1

Coming Back for More

Every time I have sex with this man, I ask myself, how did I get here? Is my self-esteem so low that I am willing to sell my soul? Why do I keep coming back to him when I know that nothing is going to change? I'm not going to lie; one reason he keeps pulling me back in is the sex. Oh Lord, this man deserves an Oscar for the things he can do! His passionate kisses set my face on fire. His touch shoots electricity through my body. But soon after we were done, the guilt and shame hit me. I want to die. I tell myself it will be the last time I sleep with this man, the last time until he calls - again.

CHAPTER 2

First Encounter

The first time I met Michael was at The Ellington Jazz Club on Bourbon Street. The Ellington is the spot to hang out with my girls after a challenging week. As regular customers of the club, we do not have to wait in line. Tonight's costume party is on fire. The club appears smaller tonight. The oversized ghosts and witch balloons hanging from the ceiling cover the high ceiling. The animated ghost decorations and the witch cauldrons on each table made the club feel gothic. You couldn't move without bumping into someone.

I look fierce in my schoolgirl uniform and thigh-high boots. Nadine is so predictable in her police uniform. She pins her real detective badge on the uniform to make it official. Well, the uniform is not what her department ordered. With her ass hanging out in that mini skirt and her boobs are standing to attention. Misha dresses a little more conservatively to balance out our costume. The nun makes her look older than she is. Sara is in her biker's outfit. As soon as we get to our regular table, Nadine climbs on a chair to get the waiter's attention. Sara holds on to the chair and yells, "Girl get off the damn chair before you bust your ass and embarrass us." Nadine did not pay Sara no mind. She screams our usual waiter's name, Eduard's until she gets his attention.

He rushes over, mortified, trying to help Nadine off the chair. She pretends that she's about to fall, Eduard quickly catches her.

Nadine's boobs brush against his chest. She loves torturing the poor boy. Rumor has it that he's gay, but Nadine doesn't care. She takes pleasure in torturing him. To rescue him, I ask about the drink special. He uses the opportunity to escape from Nadine's grip. He pulls a pad and his pen from his apron and smiles as he announces, "Tonight, to honor the occasion, we have the Witch's Heart cocktail. It's made with apple brandy, grenadine, homemade blackberry shimmery liqueur, and powdered dry ice."

"Oh, that sounds good. I'll have that." Sara looks at me and rolls her eyes,

"Well, I don't want no Witch's Heart, so I'll have what regular folks have a screwdriver." With my nose flared, I gave Sara a blank stare. Nadine asks for the Apple Martini, and before Misha can place her order, we all scream, "rum and Coke." She raises both of her middle fingers toward us, which makes us laugh harder.

Eduard shakes his head as he writes our orders. He leaves to place our orders with the bartender. I forgot to add a couple of bottled water with our drink orders, so I squeeze my way to the bar to order. As I waited for the bartender, a group of guys was having a not-so-private conversation about why monogamy should be legal. In a vampire costume, a tall guy comments, "Man, the more flavor, the better."

His compadre wearing army attire replies. "Man, you're crazy. Wait until you find the one. All that shit you're talking about now will go right out of the window."

Listening to their conversation makes me wonder how many men feel the same way as this joker. Finally, I got Eduard's attention. I ask that he add a couple of bottles of water to my bill. As I'm about to leave to walk to my table. The vampire asks, "Are you a good schoolgirl or a bad one?"

With a disgusted look, I reply, "Not your kind of flavor." The nerve of that asshole, after making a statement like women ain't shit, then turnaround and tried to flirt.

Minutes later, Eduard came with our drinks, and Nadine could not wait. She grabs hers and guzzles it down as if it's water. She squeezes her way to the dance floor. We all know once Nadine gets one drink in her, there's no telling what she's going to do. Between her high-stress job as a detective and her husband dying in a car accident, hanging with the girls is the only time she has to let her hair down. We grab our drinks then look in Nadine's direction. How could she move her butt cheeks that fast while her weapon stayed strapped underneath her dress? Some of the guys tilted their heads, trying to get a better look. Nadine is of average height and weight until she turns around; all you see is that butt. Nadine did a split, and all you hear is OHHH! I cringe when she tries to get off the dance floor.

The wood dance floor is decorated with black and gray balloons. Some are floating in the air, creating a mirage. Thunder-like applause around the dance floor when Nadine finishes dropping it like it's hot. In typical Nadine fashion, she bows then walk off the dance floor to our table.

Misha claps and asks, "Girl, who taught you how to dance like that?"

Before Nadine answers, Sara chimes in, "Girl, you know she used to be an undercover stripper."

With her hands on her hips, while rolling her neck, Nadine replies, "Bitch, I was a damn good one too."

"We see, that's the reason you almost bust your ass on the dance floor," I shout.

Nadine curls her lips, then replies, "You just jealous because you, Jasmine, my darling, cannot handle all of this." As she turns to show me her full butt. As we are taking jabs at Nadine, a familiar voice startles us.

"Can I buy you, beautiful ladies, a drink?" He asks.

I turn around to see who's the generous host. Oh, it's the joker who was talking about the more flavor, the better.

I reply with a quick tongue-lash, "You don't think that we can buy our own drinks?"

He smiles with a smooth baritone voice. He comments, "I am positive that you can buy your own drinks, but mine will taste sweeter."

Everyone at the table started laughing. He ignores my objection, signals the bartender, then commends, "Can you please put the next round of whatever the beautiful ladies are drinking on my tab?" He turns and walks back to the bar.

"What an arrogant bastard," I comment.

"Bitch, why are you always so mad at the brothers?" Nadine screams. "He was nice enough to walk over and offer us a drink. All you had to say was thank you."

I roll my eyes and give her the finger. She did not hear the conversation I had heard earlier. From what I saw, the vampire costume suited him well. He is a bloodsucking, narcissistic jackass who I have no patience to entertain.

As the night progresses, I am intrigued by Duke Ellington's portrait hanging on the wall. It reminds me of home. Mère used to play Duke's music on the piano, and Pawpaw would sing his heart out while twirling me around. I missed them both. I wished they were still alive. Mostly I miss Pawpaw and his silly jokes.

I got lost in the memories of my parents when a voice snapped me back to the noisy club. The vampire man is sitting at my table and begins talking about Duke Ellington. With a blank stare, I say, "I am not your flavor." I walk away before I cuss him out. I made my way to the dance floor as people were cheering, clapping, high fiving each other. Curious to see what's all the fuss is all about. I squeeze my way to the front of the dance floor. Nadine is on the floor doing the snake with her ass showing in the air.

Sara and Misha were standing on the other side. Sara almost knocks the onlookers out of the way, rushing over to me.

Angrily she waves her hand in the air, "Nadine is drunk and out of control. We need to get her off the dance floor before she goes viral on social media."

Misha, who's been quiet most of the evening, replies, "She has had too much to drink Jazz. We need to get her out of here."

Nadine started raising her dress as the men cheering louder.

"Yes, it's time to get her out of here," I agree with the ladies.

We push through the crowd and try to shield Nadine. Sara takes off her jacket and puts it around Nadine's shoulders. Nadine shoves

Sara to the side and begins twerking. A man in a Frankenstein mask grabs Nadine from the back and starts humping her. I look around for reinforcement. Security is nowhere to be found. The vampire rushes over asks if I need help. I gladly say yes. He signals his friend, who was wearing army attire for help. Before Nadine could realize what was happening, the army guy swoops her up while the vampire pushes the guy who was humping her back. Without skipping a beat, vampire man and army man headed to the door. Misha rushes outside to get the car while Sara and I stay with the men.

Nadine is screaming and kicking, "Put me down, you son-of-a-bitch. I'm not ready to go yet."

Jerome, an ex-military bouncer with biceps big as a sledgehammer, screams, "Hey, put her down." As he approaches the man who's carrying Nadine over his shoulder.

Feeling that things could escalate, I jump in front of the bouncer, then announce, "Jerome, everything is cool."

His face softens once he realizes it's me. Jerome clears the path allowing us to get out of the club quicker. Misha is already in the front waiting for us. She jumps out, runs to the other side to open the door. Nadine continues pounding on the poor man, "I'm gonna fuck you up, put me down," she continues with her abuse.

With care, the man put Nadine in the car. Sara gets in the back with her trying to calm her down. My face was flush with embarrassment. I thank the guys and regret that I was so nasty to the one in the vampire costume.

CHAPTER 3

Michael's Attempt

Sitting at the bar looking at everyone in their costumes makes me realize, people of New Orleans know how to party. I've only been here for a year since I moved from Chicago. A three-eyed witch is sitting across from me is staring as if she's trying to enter my soul. I quickly turn my attention to my buddy Cobby who's talking trash, busting my balls about my lifestyle.

Cobby comments, "Michael, I am telling you, there's nothing better than to find that someone special to spend the rest of your life with."

I want to get him riled up, so I reply, "Man, who says I want to spend the rest of my life with anyone?"

Cobby takes the bait. He takes a big gulp of his drink, then says, "My brother, all of these women you're sleeping with will haunt you one day. And when the day you meet someone and want to settle down comes, karma will follow you."

To piss Cobby off, I reply, "The more flavor, the better."

To my right is this fine woman trying to get the bartender's attention. She's wearing a schoolgirl outfit. I turn my attention to her, shooting my shot. I ask, "Are you a good schoolgirl or a bad one?" If looks could kill, call me a corpse.

I brace myself as she looks straight in the eyes and says, "Not your flavor."

My jaw dropped as I watched her walk back to her table. I wanted to challenge her more to see where it could go.

"Damn, she is fine," I say to the bartender.

He smiles, "Sorry buddy, she is out of your league. She and her girlfriends have been coming here for years, and none of the brothers dare to approach her."

"Why is that?" I ask.

He leans over, then replies, "Because before they can say two words to her, she shuts them down."

I never back down from a challenge. I decide to walk over and introduce myself to the ladies. They look like a friendly group. What can be so hard about introducing myself and offering to buy drinks for the ladies? I stop for a second to collect my thoughts, clear my throat, then announce, "Hello ladies, this table looks like it's having more fun than the rest of the club. Can I buy you ladies' drinks?"

I did not realize I committed an abominable sin with that question. The schoolgirl turns around, her eyebrows creased up, then replies, "we can buy our own drinks," then turns her back to me.

With a quick rebuttal, I reply, "But mine tastes sweeter."

She turns back to face me with a disgusted look in her eyes. She comments, "Why don't you go and bother some other table with this weak ass smack."

Damn, she is tough. Ignoring her tongue-lash, I signal their waiter, then say, "Please put the next round of whatever the ladies are drinking on my tab."

With my wounded pride, I walked back to the bar. Damn! The bartender was right. She's going to be a challenge. I adjust my seat so that it faces her table. The bartender laughs as he refreshes my drink, "I told you." Through the night, I keep my eyes in her direction, watching her every mood. Plotting how I'm going to make my next move.

"Earth to Mike," Cobby yells as he snaps his finger.

I ignored him, keeping my attention on the table where the ladies were. Damn! I must get her number.

Cobby notices that I have not been paying attention. He says, "brother, you always scheming on how to get the ladies. you're sick!"

We both laugh as he continues, "I cannot wait until one of these ladies got you hooked and make you act right." Cobby slaps me in the back of my head.

Cobby realizes that he's not getting anywhere with me. He grabs his drink then walks over to another table where his friends sitting. Usually, I would be offended, but I don't care because my mind is wonderfully occupied with her.

The bartender refreshes my drink and asks, "still dreaming, huh?" As he tilts his head at the ladies' table.

Everyone at her table made their way to the dance floor except her. She's mesmerized by the portrait of Duke Ellington hanging on the wall. I seize the opportunity to go back and talk to her, tell her something about The Duke, hoping that will open the door slightly. My legs feel heavy as I make my way to her table. I sip on my whiskey to chase the jitterbugs in my stomach. Why was The Duke's portrait so fascinating? Clearing my throat to get her attention makes her jump from her trance.

"I am sorry. I didn't mean to scare you." I move to sit beside her. "Did you know he started playing the piano when he was seven years old?" I continue.

The puzzled look on her face made me realize she didn't know who I was talking about. I pointed at the portrait. Her face relaxes a little.

I continue with more fun facts about The Duke. "Do you know how he got the name Duke?" Another blank stare. I state, "Well, his friends gave him that name because he always dressed and acted like royalty, hence the name Duke."

"Oh, by the way, my name is Michael." I extended my hand to her.

With an aggravated look on her face, she replies, "I don't care what your name is, as I said before, not your type of flavor." With her drink in her hand, she turns and walks toward the dance floor. A chill comes over me, watching her walk away. What is it about her?

I didn't even get her name. This is going to be more challenging than I thought. After getting rejected twice, I walked over to where

Cobby and his friends were sitting to lick my wound. I am sure that I will see her again and I need to bring my A-game the next time.

The dance floor is Poppin. As I make my way to see what's going on, I notice the schoolgirl is looking left then right as if she's looking for someone. I rush over to see what's going on. I tap her on her shoulder. She turns around with a frantic look. She asks, "Can you help me with my friend?" As she points to her friend on the dance floor doing the snake. Oh! That's what all of the commotions were about. I signal Cobby to come over to help me. I explain the situation to Cobby, and he swiftly moves to action. Cobby is 243lbs, six-two all muscle. He swoops the lady over his shoulder as I make way through the crowd.

This is the perfect opportunity for me to get to know a little bit about schoolgirl. Once Cobby and I put her friend in her car, I decided to follow them to ensure they arrived safely at their destination. Luckily, her friend doesn't live too far from me. Once they arrive at their destination, I park my car and ask if they need help getting her in the house. The one in the biker's outfit signals me to come over and help. I'm on a mission to win schoolgirl over. I guarantee she will see me again.

CHAPTER 4

At The Club

We arrive at Nadine's home. She is passed out in the back seat. It's going to take all of us to get her inside. I didn't realize that vampire man had followed us to Nadine's house. Okay, this dude is beginning to creep me out. He parks beside our car asks us if we need help. I almost say no, but Sara, with her big mouth, replies that we need help. He was too eager to help us with Nadine inside. Once he was done helping us with Nadine, I walked him to the door. Then without skipping a beat, I say, "Thank you for your assistance. Good night."

With an awkward stance, he replies, "I hope to see you again." I just shut the door without responding to his statement.

Sara, Misha, and I got Nadine to bed upstairs. "I will stay with her tonight," I announce.

Sara agrees, "Great idea Jazz. I don't think she should be alone tonight."

In our silence, we share the burden of Nadine's pain. She carries a burden of guilt from the night of her husband's death. That night, Nadine and her husband were driving home after a night out. They had a fight. She lost her temper and threw her phone at him. Trying to dodge the telephone, he veered and collided with another car. He was killed on impact, and the other driver was severely injured. It had been two years since the accident, and Nadine had not come out of that dark space. She almost lost her job as a detective.

Once Nadine was settled upstairs, Sara, Misha, and I tiptoe downstairs to talk. Looking at the pictures on the living room wall reminds me of how fragile life is. In all the photos, Roger is full of life. Pictures when he made captain, Nadine was so proud. Pictures when they went on a cruise. They were so happy. Misha walks into the kitchen to make tea, and I follow her. Misha moves through the kitchen without saying a word. I notice her silence. I walk over and put my hand on her shoulder, then ask, "You're alright, Mish?"

Misha puts the tea kettle down, turns around with tears rolling down her face, and answers, "I just hate seeing how much Nadine is hurting, and there's nothing I can do to help."

Sara walks over and hugs Misha, "You are doing something Mish, you're here, being supportive." Sara wipes Misha's tears and continues, "Nadine knows we love her, and we got her back."

Misha nods her head then goes back to brew the tea. Sara and I move to the living room continue looking at Nadine's photos. Sara picks up Roger and Nadine's wedding photo. She says, "Remember how nervous Nadine was. We had to calm her down."

Sara smiles, which makes me smile too. I remember how happy Nadine was. She kept saying, I can't believe I am getting married. Roger was a gentle giant. Standing at six-five and 275lbs. He adored Nadine with all her flaws. He would have done anything to make her happy.

Misha comes with three cups of tea, hands one to Sara then me. The warmth of the chamomile tea soothes my throat. It's just what I need to help me to sleep tonight. Once Sara and Misha finished their tea, they hugged me good night and left. Putting on an Ellis Marsalis record sitting on the shelf by the record player, I am taken back to my childhood when Paw would play his records all day. Mere and Paw had been on my mind all day. It had been a while since I visited their gravesite. The memories, I ponder, were their way of reminding me that they are still around me. At times I can feel Paw's presence, especially when I am scared.

As I climb the stairs to check up on Nadine, a screeching sound comes from her bedroom. I rush to the door to ensure she's okay. With her eyes still closed in her bed, Nadine is punching the air as if she's shadowboxing. Fearing that she'll hurt herself, I yell, "Nadine, wake up!"

She opens her eyes as she holds her head. She looks around the room, then asks, "Why are you yelling? Where am I?"

"You're home. Are you okay?" I reply.

She stares at the picture on the nightstand, then covers her head with the blanket without saying a word. I climb into the bed, wrap my arms around her, and say, "I got you."

CHAPTER 5

Past Hurt

I was thinking about the vampire man and why I was so mean to him on the way to Nadine's home. It all came down to my father's betrayal. After all these years, I have not forgiven my father for the pain he caused my Mere. Growing up, I saw my father as my hero. He could not do anything wrong. He was perfect in my eyes. Born in Lafayette, Louisiana, he was the eldest of four. His parents were sharecroppers. He worked many jobs to put himself through college. That's where he met my mother. My mother came from a middle-class family in Baton Rouge. She was sophisticated and very artistic.

My parents got married right after college. Three months later, she was pregnant with me. My father decided to join the military and was deployed to Germany when my mother was twelve weeks pregnant. I was born in my father's absence. I think he felt guilty because when he came back, he spoiled me rotten. Papa was a giant in my eyes, although he was of average height with beautiful caramel skin. I was his princess, and he was my king. We were inseparable. I was daddy's girl. It was so much fun growing up with a daddy in the house. My mother would play the piano, and daddy would sing while swirling me around. Louis Armstrong's "What a Wonderful World" was his favorite. Papa and I had a special bond that I think Mere was jealous of. She would get mad at my papa when he let me get my way. Mere did not play. Standing five foot four with smooth chocolate skin, daddy could always make her laugh.

He would tease her "Adèle laissez les bon temps rouler."

She would respond, "Gustave, Let the good times roll is not the answer to everything." The pitch of her voice would increase an octave, the madder she was. Then daddy would tickle her until she cried, "Ça suffit." I would join in the fun.

I missed those days. I missed my parents. Not sure why the portrait of Duke Ellington reminded me so much of my childhood. My parents were not perfect, but they were full of love for each other.

The night was quiet once Nadine fell asleep. The anniversary of her husband's death was close, and I knew that she was hurting.

I know a thing or two about heartaches. My world came crashing down when daddy got sick with leukemia and was hospitalized. It was devastating seeing daddy suffer. The light in his eyes disappeared. His clothes no longer fit his frail body. He could barely stand on his own. I spent most of my days with him. I would go straight to the hospital after school so that he was not alone. During one visit, daddy was sitting on the edge of the bed, looking defeated.

He said, "I have something to tell you. I'm afraid that I am not going to last any longer." He started slowly, his emotions making his words slow and steady. "You and your mom bring so much joy in my life. You are my world."

With his frail hands, he reached over to pull me to sit beside him. I could tell that he was struggling to say what he wanted to say to me. Watching the oxygen machine rising mirroring daddy's breathing, he spoke through a labored breath, "What I am about to tell you is going to break your heart, and your mother is going to be devastated."

"Daddy, whatever it is, Mom, and I can handle it. We love you," I assured him.

As he continued to fight for breaths, tears escaped from his closed eyes, "I have another family living in Arizona."

Chills invaded my body. I rubbed my arms to warm up. At first, I thought I misunderstood what he said, or the medication made him confused. "Paw, we're the only family you have."

This time with his eyes wide open, he repeated his words, "No, sweetheart, I am not confused. It's the truth."

My heart sank. I did not want to believe that my hero, my king, had a secret family in another state. The news was too much to bear.

"How? When? We were always together except when you're away for work," I pleaded.

And here I thought that I was the only child. It was a lot to process for a sixteen-year-old. I was numb. I could not speak or move from the bed. I finally mustered enough strength to run out of the room and went to the hospital chapel to cry.

Later that evening, Mom sensed something was wrong when she picked me up from the hospital. She asked if everything was okay. I did not dare tell her that daddy was a liar, and I hated him. During the ride home, Mom tried her best to cheer me up. She even tried to tell me some of daddy's jokes.

I could not take it any longer. I blurted out, "Mom, Daddy told me that he has another family in Arizona, and he was lying to us all those years."

Mom abruptly stopped the car in the middle of the street and asked, "Are you sure you heard him, right? He probably was medicated and didn't know what he was saying."

"That's what I thought, Mom. I told him that he was confused. He assured me that he was not, and he was telling me the truth," I pleaded with Mom. The cars behind us were blaring their horns to alert my mom to drive. "I hate him. He is a liar and a cheat. How could he do this to us Mom?"

I could not stop lashing out, and in the middle of my rant, Mom slammed on the brakes again, jolting me forward. She pulled over to the side of the road and stopped the car.

"I know you're hurt right now, but I will not allow you to disrespect your father. Do you understand?" My mother rebuked me though I could see her eyes glossing over. We stayed silent for what felt like an eternity. Mom finally spoke with a shaky tone. "I am sorry that you are hurting. There must be an explanation. I will speak with your dad and get to the bottom of this. He loves you. You're always going to be his princess."

He would disappear for months. When we thought that he was on an assignment, he visited his other family in Arizona. How could he do this to me, to my mom, who gave up everything to be with him? Her family disowned her because of him, and all this time, he was lying to us.

I did not want to visit my dad after the news. I could not face him. Mom told me that I had to see him keep him company. During a visit, dad gave me his family's information in case I wanted to meet them. I was not interested in a family reunion. Weeks later, dad passed, and I had to call them to let them know. They were aware of Mom and me. I have three brothers and two sisters, one of which is two months younger than me. This man had two women pregnant at the same time. I hated him more because he had the decency to let his other family know about us, and we had no idea of their existence.

Mom said nothing about daddy's transgression from the day I told her. She tried her best to act as if everything were okay, but I could see the pain in her eyes. I went with her to the funeral home to make the final arrangements for dad. Mom picked a light blue casket. Blue was dad's favorite color. He always said that blue is a symbol of serenity, divinity, and wisdom. His military buddies would officiate the service. Mom wanted me to read the eulogy. I told her that I did not think that I could do it. And asked her to have one of his friends deliver the eulogy.

On the day of the funeral, daddy's second family was sitting in the back of the church. I recognized them from the picture daddy showed me when he was in the hospital. Watching daddy laying in the casket made this nightmare real. The church was packed with his military buddies and members of our community. I did not cry during the funeral because I was too angry at him. The rest of the day was a blur for me. My mother was distant, as if she was dead inside. She had to deal with the pain of her husband's death and his betrayal at the same time. How could he do this to us? To ME, his princess? Weren't we good enough? Was it my fault? My father's sin left a void in me. As a result, I never trusted men. My past romantic relationships were filled with betrayal, lies, and hurt.

CHAPTER 6

While doing my weekly grocery shopping, I'm trying to decide if I want green or yellow apples when a voice comes from behind me comments, "You know the green apples are great for juicing."

I turn to see who's offering the unwanted advice. The voice sounds familiar, but I don't recognize him.

With a puzzled look, I ask, "Are you talking to me?"

He laughs then replies, "You don't remember me, do you?"

I frown, "I am afraid, I don't know who you are."

He's trying to convince me that I have seen him before. He continues, "I was at the club during the Halloween party when your friend needed rescuing."

That night did not end well for us, so I replied, "I am so sorry, you will have to be more specific. There were so many people at the club that night. Most of them wore costumes."

He smiles, "Yes, I wore the vampire costume."

That's all he needed to say. It has been three weeks since my first encounter with the vampire man at the club. I'm surprised he remembers me. Suddenly, the produce aisle becomes smaller.

I reply, "Oh, the flavor man." This time I laugh.

He frowns. "Hopefully, you will be nicer to me than you were during our last encounter." I laugh again to hide my embarrassment. Then he replies, "With a beautiful smile like that, you should be ashamed of yourself for being so mean. You should smile more often. the world would be a better place with a smile like yours."

I must admit the brother is smooth.

He insisted, "Let's start from the beginning. My name is Michael Kane, and what is your name, young lady?"

Looking down, ponder for a second before I respond, "I am Jasmine Banks. My friends call me Jazz, but *you* can call me Jasmine."

He takes my hand, expecting him to shake it. Instead, he brings it to his lips and plants a soft kiss. I quickly pull my hand from him, trying to compose myself. I must admit he looks better than in the vampire costume. He's wearing these sexy pair of linen shorts and a button-down shirt. He seems taller, too, six feet. I didn't notice how smooth his dark chocolate skin was at the club. In the daylight, I can see all his features, not too muscular, a sexy well-trimmed beard, and well-manicured hands. The brother takes excellent care of himself. He hands me his card as I walk away.

He stops me, "Don't you think that it is rude for me to give you my number, and I don't have yours? What if I fall? Who will rescue me in this big store?" We both laugh.

I give him my number while thinking, he's a persistent little bugger, and we part ways. I finish my shopping then head home. As I'm getting ready to turn in for the evening, my phone rings. I roll my eyes looking at it. It's no other than Mr. Smooth Operator himself. I purposely answer with a tired tone, "Hello."

He replies. "Oh, I'm sorry. Did I wake you?"

"Who is this?" I ask, knowing damn well who it is.

"It's Michael. Michael Kane. The guy from the supermarket." Sounding defeated.

"I'm sorry, Michael. Can I call you back another time?" I ask.

I knew that I wasn't going to call him back or entertain his foolishness.

Later in the week, my phone ring, and I'll be damn if it's not him. I put the phone on the kitchen counter as it rang. Finally, it stops, and I continue with my task. I walk around the kitchen counter to grab a plate to put my Cajun take-out on. The phone rings again. This time I answer, "Hello, this is Jasmine."

"Hello, Ms. Jasmine! I have been waiting by the phone for the callback you promised me." The first thing out of his mouth is foolishness.

Letting out a deep sigh, I reply, "Well, why didn't you call me back if you feel you needed to talk to me?"

He replies, "Well, a lady should always keep her word. You said that you were going to call me back, and I took your word for it." I guess he senses my annoyance. Michael quickly changes his tune, "But, I am happy that you answered, even if it is days later."

I get the feeling that this joker is not going to give up. So, I pour myself a glass of red wine and get comfortable on my couch with my dinner. Hopefully, it will be quick, and I can go back to my dinner. The conversation starts with a typical question. "Why are you single?" This question gets on my nerves as if being single is an illness.

I roll my eyes and reply. "Must I have a reason for being single?"

"Oh! No need to be defensive. I was just wondering. A beautiful woman like yourself should have plenty of suitors," he quickly replies.

"Again, who is to say that I don't have many suitors? Maybe I have not found a man that can challenge me spiritually, intellectually."

As I'm about to finish the sentence, he cuts me off, "And sexually." The fool laughs at his joke. I didn't even entertain his tasteless joke.

"I don't need to ask you if you're single because you like variety." Using his own words against him.

Michael laughs then says, "Okay! I need to explain that comment. You did not hear the whole conversation, madame. My buddy was hassling me about finding someone to spend my life with. I made that statement to get him off my back."

Not trusting his explanation, I ask, "I'm sure you have lots of flavors in your circle, so what do you want from me?"

"I'll answer the question over dinner." Evading my question.

I must give this man his prop. He is smooth. I wanted to cut this conversation short, so I agreed to go to dinner. He comments, "I know this nice Cajun restaurant on Eastern Bay called Chuck & Dive. We can meet there Saturday at 8pm."

I didn't tell him that I knew the owner of the restaurant. Before we end the call, he comments, "I am counting the hours until I see you again Jasmine." I end the call, wondering what I've gotten myself into.

Saturday comes quick. I've been on dates before; I don't understand why tonight is any different. I lay out several outfits. The green dress makes me look like a leprechaun; this one is going in the donation box. Why am I so nervous? The pants suit is too business-like. Don't want to be too rigid. It's just dinner Jazzy, get a hold of yourself. Aww, the fitted jeans will go perfectly with the red pumps. This is it. It takes me two hours to get ready. I decided on fitted jeans and a silk wrap-around top. Compliment with my favorite red pumps.

I arrive at the restaurant while Michael's chatting with the valet attendant. My heart skips a beat when Michael and I make eye contact. He walks over to open my door. He greets me with a beautiful bouquet of autumn roses. He takes my hand and hands the keys to the attendant. The cool autumn breeze caresses my face as we enter the restaurant. It has been a minute since I visit the restaurant. I try to avoid anything that reminds me of my paw. The open space was illuminated with drape chandeliers. The red- and orange-colored drapes created a beautiful sunset silhouette. It's odd to see a New Orleans funeral possession painting hanging on the wall. There are paintings of women flashing their boobs with beads hanging on their necks. As the host directs us to our seats, the Cajun spices tickle my nose. The joie de vivre of New Orleans is all around the restaurant. The host shows us to our table. Jack, the owner, notices us the moment we sit down, with a serious look on his face. He sits between Michael and me, turns to Michael, and puts a bit of edge in his voice as he demands, "What are you doing with my wife?"

Michael's face becomes stern as if he's ready to throw down. Before this man starts throwing punches, I reply, "I'm sure Marjorie wouldn't appreciate you taking another wife while you still married to her." I point to the beautiful, tall, slender lady at the bar.

Jack laughs, and Michael's face relaxes. I introduce Michael to Jack then say, "Jack Michael is from Chicago. I don't believe that he ever ate Cajun food before."

Jack slaps Michael on his shoulder and says, "Well, my man, you're in for a treat. I'll be right back."

Jack hops off the table and makes his way to the kitchen.

Michael looks in Jack's direction and says, "Happy fellow."

I smile and reply, "Jack and his wife are good people."

"How did you know them?" Michael asks.

I pondered the question for a minute and decided to give Michael the shorter version, "He and my dad served together in the military. After Jack retired, he and his wife opened the restaurant."

The gentle giant, that's what I call Jack, comes back with a bucket full of crawfish. His face lights up as he plops the crawfish on the table.

With a suspicious look, Michael asks, "How do you eat these things?"

Jack and I let out a loud laugh. Jack replies, "Okay, pretty boy, I will teach you how to eat crawfish." He hands Michael a bib and says, "This is for you not to mess up that pretty shirt of yours."

I stay quiet and watch how Jack is taking pleasure in busting Michael's chops. Jack continues with his instructions as he picks up a crawfish to show him how to handle them the right way. "What you do is you gently twist the tail with your thumb and index finger. The shell will break free from the meat. You pull to separate the head from the tail, suck the juice out of the head. You eat the tail meat and repeat." Jack slams the shell and the crawfish head on the empty tray, then turns to Michael and teases, "You think you can handle that, city boi?"

Feeling challenged, Michael reaches for a crawfish and says, "Challenge accepted."

The poor guy tries to follow Jack's instructions, but the crawfish slips out of his hand and hits his nose. I almost spill my drink laughing so hard.

Jack throws his hands in the air and says, "Chere, why did you bring this city boi to my restaurant?"

I put my hands up to mimic Jack and reply, "Oh, I did not bring him here. He suggested the restaurant to me."

Michael did not look happy that Jack and I were laughing at his expense. He picks another crawfish and says, "Y'all going to eat your words after I am done with this bucket of crawfish." He points to Jack and me as determination covers his face. He tries again, and this time the meat slips out of the tail. Michael eats the flesh and sucks the head of the shellfish. Just like Jack, he slams the shell on the tray and says, "In y'all faces."

Jack and I start clapping. The young couple that's sitting next to us starts clapping too. Before you know, the whole aisle where we're sitting is clapping.

Michael rises and takes a bow, and says, "Thank you! Thank you!"

Jack shakes Michael's hand and shouts, "Drinks for everyone on this aisle. And Michael, thank you for being a good sport."

Michael's face lightens a little. He even smiles while shaking Jack's hand.

"Okay, let me take your orders. I'll send the waiter out with drinks and alligator tails as the appetizer." Jack recommends.

I can see the relief in Michael's face when Jack left to place our orders. I take the opportunity to find out more about this relentless man who doesn't back down from a challenge. I ask, "What made you move down South? To New Orleans at that?"

He gives me a wicked smile, "To meet a beautiful lady and to ask her out to dinner."

I must admit, the brother has a great word game. I smile back and reply, "Or to run away from your crime sprees. You ran out of places to hide the bodies in Chicago?"

His facial expression changed. He did not respond. As I was about to ask another question, the server put our appetizers on the stable disrupt my thought.

In between bites, he asks, "Have you ever wanted to live anywhere else?"

Waving my hands in the air while looking around, I reply, "This has always been my home. I cannot think of living anywhere else but NOLA." I take a bite and continue, "Don't get me wrong, it has its flaws. Racism is still very much alive here, but it also has its beauty."

Michael frowns, then says, "Yes, I've encountered a couple of good ole boys while driving around New Orleans."

I look at him straight in the eyes, "I'm used to the foolishness of the true South, but NOLA is my home. I love it here. We have the culture, the food, the music, not to mention the diverse history."

He seems satisfied with my answer. He replies, "Well, Ms. Jasmine you must show me New Orleans so that I can fall in love with it as well."

I'm not sure why this man thinks I will see him again, but I smile cordially anyway.

Jack comes out with a tray of Hurricane drinks, the house specialty. He serves us first, then hands out drinks to the other customers in the aisle. I love the Hurricane, so I take a sip and savor the taste.

Michael picks his up and asks, "What's in it?"

I answer, "Bayou silver rum and other select rums mixed with fruit punch. Trust me, a sip of this will give you the southern comfort you're looking for."

He looks at me suspiciously and replies, "Southern comfort, huh?"

He sips his drink then gives me a nod of approval. I smile at him. There's an awkward silence between us. I'm not sure what to ask next.

To break the silence, Michael asks, "Do you have any siblings?" His question hits me in the gut. In a lower tone, I say, "I thought I was the only child up until I was sixteen." With a serious look, he says, "How so?"

I'm not in the mood to rehash the past; I simply say, "It's a long story."

"What about you? Do you have any siblings?" hoping to put the focus on Michael.

"I'm the only child from my mother's side. As for my father, I never met the man and don't know if I have siblings from his side." As he shifts from his seat.

I sense that he too has daddy issues, so I change the subject.

"What's your favorite genre in music?" I ask.

Michael's eyes light up. "Music is a way the universe communicates with my soul. It's not so much the genre but how particular music makes me feel."

Oh! The brother is deep. Let me see where he's going with this.

"Have you ever thought why is that when you need energy, you will listen to fast-upbeat music," he continues, "or when it's a rainy day, you'll listen to slow tunes."

I never thought of it that way. He is on to something. "Okay! I guess that's why you shouldn't listen to sad songs when you're depressed or lonely." I chuckle.

The server brings our entrees to the table. Jack knows what I like, and I assume he recommended a shrimp etouffee, a traditional NOLA dish for Michael, and my Gambo serves with brown rice. The food is delicious as usual. Jack made an excellent choice because Michael likes his etouffee

After dinner, Michael suggests that we stroll by the water to walk off the food we ate. The moon shines over the water creating an illuminous silhouette. The night is perfect. The crisp autumn air makes me shiver. Michael takes off his jacket and puts it over my shoulder. His cologne sends me over the moon. He pulls me closer and says, "Thank you for agreeing to have dinner with me."

I quickly step back and whisper. "This was impressive!"

We come upon a gazebo by the lake decide to sit and continue our conversation. Wanted to know more about why he decided on New Orleans. I ask again, "Why did you move from Chicago to NOLA?"

He pauses for a few seconds, then replies, "I move to New Orleans to start a new life."

"Do you have family here?" I continue with my inquiry.

He laughs, then frowns, "No, I don't have family here, but I have a buddy who lives here."

Why do I get a feeling there's more to this man's story?

"Why did you decide to join the military?" I turn to face him.

He pauses once again, "After my mother died, I was angry and lost. The military gave me the discipline I needed to be a man. The military allowed me to travel the world."

"Wow! Traveling the world sounds awesome. I know people who don't even own a passport, let alone travel to other countries." I reply.

He shifts position and asks, "Do you own a passport, Ms. Jasmine?"

In a sarcastic tone, I reply, "I am not on the no-fly list, Sir! Yes, I do own a passport."

He laughs then says, "Point taken Ms., Jasmine."

It's getting late. I have meetings early tomorrow morning. I think it's time to end this date. I hand Michael his jacket. He looks at me, then the jacket, and asks, "Are you tired of me already?" as he flashes his smile. His eyes squint when he laughs.

"I have an early meeting tomorrow. I have to go home and prepare for it." I explain. Michael helps me up from the bench. We walk toward the front of the restaurant and hand the valet attendant our tickets. Minutes later, the attendant pulls my car upfront. Michael tips him as he opens my car door

"It was a pleasure, Mr. Kane. Especially watching you losing to a crawfish. That was epic." I let out a chuckle to express my amusement.

Michael laughs too, "I am happy that I was amusing to you and your boyfriend Jack. For the record, I didn't lose to the crawfish." We both laugh again.

Before closing my car door, he asks, "Can I follow you home to make sure you make it home safely?"

Surprise by his request, "Or I can call you when I get home." Clearly, Michael did not want the night to be over. I agree to have him follow me, but he is not going to my house after one date. He closes my car door, and off I go.

Thirty minutes later, I arrive home. I realize Michael is right behind me, parking his car. I go into panic mode. Should I kiss him on the first date? What do I do if he wants to kiss me? Michael comes around and opens my door. What if this man is a terrible kisser? We reach my apartment; it is clear neither of us is sure what to do. There's an awkward silence,

"This was nice," I say as he brushes the hair away from my face.

Michael moves closer and whispers in my right ear. "Can I kiss you?"

I did not expect the question. Without saying a word, I turn my cheek so he can kiss me there. He hesitates, then plants two soft kisses on both cheeks and lifts my chin with fingers. The third kiss on my lips. He whispers good night and walks away.

No, this man did not just kiss me on the lip then walk away. I am dumbfounded by his cockiness. I slowly open the door, processing what just took place.

Minutes later, the phone rings, it's Michael.

"I enjoyed your company, Jazz." He sounds so sweet on the phone.

"You're not as bad as I thought you would be," I tease.

"Well! In that case, you wouldn't mind going out again." he quickly asks.

I don't know if I should go on a second date with this man. Although I had a few laughs. His comments at the club still linger in the back of my head.

I have to find an excuse. "Oh! I am busy with a project. I am not sure I can find the time to go anywhere."

"You gotta do better than that. You just admitted that I wasn't that bad," Michael counters

"Yes, I did! But—"

"But what?" he pleads. I hear a slight rise in his voice as he dares me. "You're not afraid now, are you?"

"Why should I be afraid?" I rebut.

"Then you shouldn't have any problem with going on a second date,"

This man is not going to take no for an answer, so I offer a concession. "I'll look at my schedule and promise to let you know." As I'm taking off my shoes. I feel a little giddy after hanging up with Michael. I quickly dismiss the thought and call it quits for the night.

CHAPTER 7

Michael's Bragging Rights

I decided to check in with my buddy Cobby after diner with Jasmine. Honestly, I just want to brag. I dial his number, he answers on the second ring with a grunt, "What's up fool? Why are you calling me?"

Looking at the car's clock and noticed it was two in the morning. I reply, "Sorry pop, I didn't realize the time, and I know you need your beauty sleep."

He grunts again. I did not wait for him to say anything else. I say, "I had dinner with a beautiful lady tonight."

With an annoying tone, Cobby replies, "Fool! Why do I care who you had dinner with?"

I laugh, "Remember the beautiful lady who turned me down at the club, the one we helped with her drunk friend?"

Cobby lets out another grunt to express his impatience. I continue with the story, "We went out to dinner tonight. I was not disappointed."

In an alerted tone, Cobby replies, "Man, why don't you get your shit together before you go and mess up someone else's life?"

I inhale then ask, "Why do you have to rain on my parade?"

Cobby responds, "Because we've been down this road before Michael. You meet a woman, mess with her head, then you want to cry foul when she goes psycho on you."

Snapping my fingers, I reply, "Speaking of Psycho, I swore I saw Mona in the club that night. There was a three-eyed witch who was staring at me all night."

Cobby laughs, "Man, your mind is playing a trick on you. You wouldn't be alive if she followed you to New Orleans."

He's right. Everyone wore costumes at the party. It was my imagination. I ended the call with Cobby.

I admit I've made mistakes in the past with the ladies. I can't explain it. Jasmine caught my attention at the club. I cannot get her out of my mind ever since I saw her at the club. It wasn't a coincidence that I ran into Jasmine at the grocery store. I had to see her again. My love life has been a tragedy. Cobby seems to think that I am this heartless son-of-a-bitch. If I get a chance with Jasmine, I will do everything in my power to make it work. It will not be like the other times when I lied and cheated my way into a relationship.

CHAPTER 8

Just a Question

Michael and I talked every night. There were nights I fell asleep while on the phone. The sexiest thing in a man is his mind. I looked forward to our conversations. Not too many people I could stay engaged in a deep conversation with for hours. He often expressed the same sentiment.

In one of our heated debates, Michael asks, "What's your position on polygamy?"

"I don't know much about it to have an opinion," I reply.

I am curious to know his thoughts, so I ask, "Are you part of a religion that practices polygamy?"

He lets out a nervous laugh, then responds, "No, I am not part of any religion, nor do I practice polygamy." He continues, "But I am intrigued by the openness of it."

I can hear the crackling sounds as I roll my neck. I comment, "I am not interested in a threesome."

"Slow your row. Ain't nobody talking about a threesome. Although if it is your thing, I'll oblige." He laughs.

Michael pauses, then asks, "What if I told you that I was interested in an open relationship?"

Is this joker serious? With a sharp tongue, I reply, "I think you got me confused with these insecure chicken heads. There's no way in hell I'll agree to some bullshit like that."

Michael reacts to my outrage by simply says, "Don't be mad Jazz. It was just a question."

I didn't care to continue the conversation. I ended the call abruptly. I make my way to the kitchen to make some chamomile tea to calm me down. He called and sent text messages all week. I sent them to voicemail.

It's a beautiful Saturday. The sky is clear, and the sun tickles your skin. I decided to chill on my balcony to get some vitamin D. As I'm about to get comfortable on my lounge chair, the doorbell rings. I am not expecting anyone, so I ignore the door. The person insisted and continuing ringing the bell. Dang, this person is not going away. Might as well see who's at the door. I look through the peephole, and there he is, standing in front of my door, looking like a clown. I crack open the door with my anger all over me, "What the hell you're doing here Michael?"

Michael ignores my question and hands a beautiful bouquet mixture of autumn roses and sunflowers he was hiding behind his back. He pleads, "I come in peace."

I didn't want the neighbors to see this six-foot-three man standing in front of my door, acting like Boo Boo the clown. I open the door wider for him to come in. I take the flowers and walk to the kitchen to put them in a vase.

The kitchen island creates a barrier between Michael and me. He continues looking at me with a stupid puppy face while his other left hand is still behind him. I frown, wondering what this man is hiding from his back. As if he can read my mind, he comments,

"Get dressed. I have a surprise for you." Dangling a picnic basket in front of me.

Still feeling pissed off at him, I reply, "I am not going anywhere with you."

"Oh, come on Jazz, please get dressed. I promise you there's nothing behind the question. Don't be mad." He walks over and kisses me. The kiss softens me up. I walk to the bedroom to get dress.

He looks like a child who's on his way to the ice cream shop. With so much excitement in his voice, Michael explains, "I am going to show you my favorite spot in New Orleans."

This joker just moved to New Orleans, and he has a favorite spot. I am still pissed at this man. I don't care what he said about it was just a question. I think there's a hidden agenda to his question. My heart sinks when we arrive at the Jean Lafitte National Park. The same park my parents used to take me to when I was a little girl. I try my best to hide my sadness, but Michael senses something is wrong.

"Jazz, what's going on? Why the long face?" Michael asks.

Without going into too many details, I reply, "I used to come here with my parents."

"Okay! Do you want to go somewhere else?" He asks.

Squinting my eyes, trying to remember the last time I visited the park. I reply, "No, it's fine. We can stay."

With excitement in his voice, he says, "This place is magical, one of my favorite spots in NOLA."

I can understand why he likes the park. It is filled with beautiful trails and animals. As we get closer to the river, a tall, slim man hands Michael the rope securing the motorboat. I look at Michael as if he has two heads, "Do you know there are alligators and snakes in the water?"

Michael laughs and replies, "Jazz are you afraid? Don't worry; alligators and snakes are not going to bother you. I am here to protect you." He holds out his hand and helps me onto the boat.

Michael starts up the engine, and off we go. It's so peaceful. Listening to the sounds of the distinct and varying species creates a harmonious chorus.

"Wow! The view is spectacular." I take a deep breath as I enjoy the wonder of God's creation. The silhouettes of the trees dancing to the beat of the birds singing along the river.

Michael whispers, "This is where I come to quiet my mind."

The calmness soothes my mood. I'm no longer mad at him. We arrive at our destination and dock at a picnic area. He carries the basket and blankets out of the boat. We settle under a beautiful oak tree. Sitting under this tree with him, I wonder about who he is really is. What does he want from me? And why am I on the fence about getting to know him? He looks so peaceful. I can tell that he is in deep thought.

Gently, I tug on his shirt, "Penny for your thoughts."

With a devious smile, he asks. "Where have you been all my life?"

What a corny question? We both sigh and continue staring at the river without a word. Michael opens the basket, pours two glasses of wine, takes the food out and spreads it out on the blanket.

He hands me a glass and raises his, "Here's to many more outings like this."

Smiling, I raise mine. "Here's to friendship."

He laughs. "I don't need any more friends, missy."

"Oh! Then what exactly are you hoping this is?" I ask.

There's that devilish smile again as he takes a sip of his wine, moves in closer, then sings, "I wanna be your lover, lover."

Wow! He is corny, singing Billie Ocean. "Don't give up your day job," I laugh.

He laughs, "You're just jealous of my beautiful voice."

He hands me a wrap and fruit salad.

"Did you make this?" I query as I bite the most delicious wrap I've ever had.

"No, ma'am, I am not that talented," he put his hands up and looked at them comically.

My mind keeps wandering back to the last conversation Michael and I had. Which raises a red flag. I did not want to ruin the mood, so I stayed quiet. Instead, I ask him about his firm.

Michael explains, "I have six talented CPAs in the firm. It has its challenges, but we are committed to our clients."

"Are you planning to expand?" I inquire.

"I am thinking of expanding, but you know the challenges black-owned businesses go through. The hoops we have to jump through," he explains.

Knowing his concerns well, I agree, "Oh! I know, I am facing the same challenges at the gallery."

Michael asks, "Tell me more about your gallery."

I smile from ear to ear as I respond, "Sara and I have been dreaming about opening the gallery for years."

Before I can continue with my story, he asks, "Which one of your friends is Sara?"

A loud sound comes from my throat out of my mouth. I reply, "Sara is the five feet three firecracker that was pushing my drunk friend off the dance floor."

Michael laughs and comments, "Oh, the feisty one."

I laugh too, because feisty is an understatement when it comes to Sara. I continue with my story, "We want to give local artists a platform to exhibit their arts and music."

"Well, this is the right place for an art gallery for sure." Michael comments.

After our lunch, Michael suggests that we stroll down the river to a secluded spot. He was right. The area is magical. We spend the rest of the afternoon in the boat listening to birds singing, frogs croaking, and the soothing sound of the river. Once again, Mother Nature's spell holds me captive. It feels as if I'm floating to ecstasy. She and I become one.

Michael pulls me out of my spell when he asks, "Are you ready to go?"

I jump up, "I can stay here forever."

Michael hugs me tighter, "Me too."

We head back to the car. On our way home, Michael grabs my hand, "This was perfect."

I was thinking the same thing but did not verbalize it. Michael walks me to my door. Once more, I purposely do not invite him in.

This time Michael did not ask if he could kiss me. He gently brushes his nose against my cheek and sweetly kisses my neck. His lips touch mine, then the kiss becomes a little forceful, takes my breath away. Surprised by the kiss, I step back as to tell him that's enough. He did not persist. Instead, he grabs my hand and kisses it.

He says, "You have a beautiful rest of your day Ms. Jasmine." He turns and walks to his car.

I forgot my phone died when I was out with Michael. I plug the phone into the charger as soon as I enter the apartment. I walk to the bedroom to change, then the phone rings. I did not expect Michael to be calling so soon. I did not rush to pick it up, thinking I'd return his calls when I finished changing. The phone keeps ringing. I drop what I was doing to pick up the phone. It's none other than loud-mouth Sara yelling, "Heifer, where have you been? I have been trying to reach you!"

I am too exhausted to be dealing with Miss Drama Queen. "Bitch! What do you want? My phone was off, and why are you yelling?" I shout back.

In a calmer tone, she asks, "Did you forget our appointment today? We were supposed to meet to finalize the business plan."

"Merde Sisi, I forgot. I'll be right over. I promise." I silently scold myself for forgetting.

Sara and I have been planning to open an art gallery with a flair. Michael's impromptu picnic messed up my schedule. I hop in my car to go to Sara's house to work on the plans. I decide not to tell Sara where I was and, more importantly, whom I was with. Did not feel like listening to her usual lecture of being careful and not trusting any man. She means well. Sara experienced my failed relationships with me.

I know Sara would still be upset. On my way to her house, I stop at Café Beignet to buy her pecan pralines and beignet. That will shut her up. When I arrive at Sara's house, she's already working on the documents on her dining room table. I hand her the bag of good-ies, praying that she will let me slide for forgetting our appointment.

She looks at the bag and rolls her eyes, "Bitch, you think you can bribe me with food?" As she reaches in the bag to grab a beignet. Sara bites the beignet leaving powdered sugar on her face.

I take a napkin from the table, then walk up to her and say, "Will you shut up already. I am here now. Let's get to work." As I try to wipe her face.

She pushes my hand from her face and snatches the napkin from me. She replies, "You lucky you're my girl."

I work on the executive summary and the market analysis. Sara works on the marketing sale and the funding request. Between Michael's impromptu picnic and working on the business plan, my brain is fried. I kiss and hug Sara goodnight after several hours of solid work and head home.

CHAPTER 9

The Secret

It's the girl's night out. Misha complains that she doesn't see me anymore. I make excuses that I'm busy with a new project.

Sara can smell my bullshit and calls me out with her usual, "Bitch please, you probably boning a new man and don't want us to know."

"Mind your damn business. I am grown if I want to bone anyone. It's my business," I was feeling defensive about Sara's accusation.

I want to keep Michael a secret because I'm not sure where this thing between him and I is going, and I did not want to publicize it.

Nadine jumps in, "That's right girl, get you some. Don't mind Sara. She's just hating cause there's no action going on down there."

We all laugh at Nadine's comment. I make a mental note to be sure to spend more time with my girls. I miss their craziness. Crazy was definitely what the whole night was, and I loved it.

When I am supposed to complete all of the paperwork for the gallery, I come down with a cold in the middle of the week. It must have been all that fresh air and all that wilding out with the girls. Michael texts to check up on me. It's something that he does two to three times a day. "What are you up to beautiful?" He texts.

I reply, "Ugghh! This cold won't go away. My head is about to explode."

Thirty minutes later, there's a knock on my door. I check the peephole, and I am surprised to see Michael standing on the other side of the door. He has a habit of dropping in without calling first.

I wince as I open the door, "What are you doing here?"

He kisses me on the cheek and strolls by me, leaving me standing by the door with a dumb look on my face. He has two bags in his hands and goes straight to the kitchen without saying a word. I close the door and follow him into the kitchen. As he unpacks the bags, he says, "Wow, your kitchen looks like one of those professional kitchens on TV. I should be expecting many meals from here."

I can feel the heat rising from my neck to my face, something that happens when I am embarrassed. I reply, "I don't cook. You're welcome to come and cook anytime you wish."

Michael decides not to comment and continues to unpack. I can smell the soup from where I am sitting. Ah, my favorite, Creole tomato brisque. The smell tickles my nose. The other bag has a bottle of organic orange juice, cough drops, and peppermint essential oil.

"The doctor has arrived!" He exclaims.

"Please be a good patient and do as the doctor orders." He pours the soup into a bowl and puts it in front of me. The creamy broth feels so good going down.

"Just what the patient needs," I smile.

Michael smiles back, "Well, thank you for being a good patient."

He pours a glass of orange juice and places it in front of me. He takes the spoon from me and begins to feed me the soup. I know that I keep telling myself that there will be nothing more than a friendship with this man, but I have never felt cared for. It hit me - my daddy! I did not realize tears were rolling down my eyes.

Worrying that he did something wrong, Michael put the bowl down and takes my hands, "Why are you crying?"

"I am not sure why I'm so emotional," I sob.

Michael gently kisses my hands, then my cheeks. Oh my God, what is happening to me? I sob harder. He kisses me softly then the kiss intensifies. I have an out-of-body experience. I don't know what to do. My first reaction is to run, but I remember this is my house, and I'm not feeling well.

This is too much. I say, "I think it's time for you to leave."

Michael gathers his things then leaves. I close the door behind him and sob harder. I'm angry because I can't control how I feel about him. Forty minutes later, my phone rings. It's Michael. I let it go to voicemail. Later, that evening after composing myself, I listen to the voicemail. His voice is genuinely concerned and apologetic. I cry even harder after I listen to the voicemail. Michael called me twice the next day. Instead of leaving a voicemail, he texted me. The text read:

I am so sorry that I upset you last night, especially when you weren't feeling well. I don't know what it is about you that makes me lose all my sense of reasoning. I need to clean up all the mess I created in my life. I will explain when I see you. All I ask of you is to be patient. Once again, I am so sorry for upsetting you. It was not my intention. I am weak *around you, and I don't know what to do about it.*

My jaw drops. I did not realize that he was as conflicted as I am. I did not reply right away. I wanted to process the text and our current situation – the only word that fits at the moment - before I respond.

The next day I reply to his text.:

Michael, I am sorry for my reaction last night. My tears were not for the kiss but for the way it made me feel. We just met, and I don't like where this (whatever is this) is going.

The phone rings seconds after I send the text. I jump, not expecting Michael to call again. After four rings, nervously, I say, "Hello."

Hearing his voice makes me want to run for cover. There's a brief silence before he speaks. "Jazz, I feel bad for upsetting you."

"No need to apologize. Those tears were for my father," I answer.

He sighs, "Do you want to talk about it?"

"My daddy used to take care of me whenever I was sick," I sigh.

Michael lets out a sigh, then replies, "You never talked about your dad. I want to take care of you too."

That's so sweet. Michael wants to be my daddy. I laugh at the idea as I am pacing back and forth in the living room like a nervous teenager. The picture on the piano grabs my attention as I'm speaking with Michael. It's a picture of Daddy and Mom laughing. Finally, I respond, "Michael, I am not sure we should pursue this, whatever this is."

He continues, "Can I ask you a question?"

I hesitate for a second, "Ask away."

"Why are you so conflicted?"

"I am not sure. I don't think we're a good fit," I reply.

It was a lie, the truth is I think whatever this is, is moving too fast, and I am not sure I am ready. This is crazy. The more I want to run away from Michael, the more I want to be with him. I abruptly stop pacing and reply, "Listen, Michael, I need time to sort all of this out."

He lets out another sigh, then replies, "I know you need time to process this, but I think we should keep a dialogue going. I just don't want you to shut me out, Jazz."

My name sounds so sexy coming from him. Hearing him call me Jazz calms me down a bit.

He continues, "How much time do you need?" He rapidly adds, "I am not trying to rush you. I just want to know how long I have to go without speaking with you."

"I am not going out of the country," I muse.

Michael did not know how to take the news. I promise to stay in touch before we say our goodbyes. The call took every ounce of my energy. Although it's the early afternoon, I crawl in my bed and sleep for what feels like forever. My phone ringtone wakes me from my deep sleep. I have got to change that obnoxious bingo ringtone. With my eyes closed, I answer the phone.

"Hello" My throat is dry, and I sound hoarse.

Sara is screaming some gibberish, "Are you on your way?"

"On my way for what?" still sounding confused

She yells, "Wait a minute, why do you sound like you are half asleep? Are you in bed? Why are you in bed?"

My head is spinning. Why is Sara asking all these questions? What day is it? More importantly, what time is it? I glance at my phone and realize that it's Saturday, at six p.m. I jump out of bed, dropping the phone. I can hear Sara screaming on the phone, which flips under the bed. I slept the entire day. Then it hit me! I slept through the preparations for the grand opening of our gallery. Sara and I have been planning and dreaming of opening the art gallery with a twist for years. Promoting young local artists in a bar where people can see the arts with happy hours. The arts illuminated as people vibe. There will be live performances on the weekends. It's perfect for promoting local artists to expose their skills and be recognized for their works.

Now that our dreams are finally coming true, I sleep through the preparations. Sara is going to kill me. I jump in the shower, pull out my favorite jumpsuit and my red pumps, and get dressed; the jumpsuit accentuates my curves in every way. I am blessed with a tiny waist, big boobs, and a semi-big butt. Thank you, Mother Nature, for being generous to me. I grab my cosmetics bag to apply my make-up in the car. I'll wear the bright instigator color lipstick to accentuate my full lips. Zipping through traffic, I finally arrive at the gallery.

Oh, Lord! Sara is standing at the front entrance, greeting our guests when she spots me rushing in. Her face, when she sees me, says I am going to kick your ass. I smile and kiss her on the cheek and rush inside. I can hear Sara's footsteps behind me, ready to interrogate me of my whereabouts. She grabs me by my elbow and stops me in my tracks and

She whispers, "What happened? Where have you been? And why are you late for the opening?"

Sara's questions have my head spinning. Luckily, the rest of the posse comes and rescues me from her wrath. Nadine rushes over and hugs Sara and me and screams

"Congratulations, heifers! I am so proud of you both. This place looks amazing!"

Misha seconds that with a more subdued congratulatory wish.

"I am so happy to have my girls celebrating this milestone with us. I wouldn't have it any other way." As I signal the server to bring the champagne over. I hand a glass to each of the ladies and start with a toast, "I want to thank you for being so supportive of our vision. We couldn't have done it without your input and unwanted advice."

We all laugh at my comment. I raise my glass to toast. Misha and Nadine follow my lead.

Sara rolls her eyes then replies, "Although SOMEBODY forgot that today was the opening."

Nadine and Misha both give Sara a disapproving look dismissing her comment. I choose not to respond; I continue with my toast and tell the ladies how much I love and appreciate all of them.

We raise our glass again. Nadine screams with her loudmouth, "CONGRATULATIONS TO MY GIRLS!"

Misha put her index finger in her ear and says, "Girl, why you gotta be so loud?"

We all laugh and look around to see if anyone is looking at us. I quickly scan the room to see if Michael is here. Nadine and Misha make their way to the bar leaving me with Sara, who is glaring at me.

"I'm so sorry Sisi. I promise to tell you why I'm late." I plead with her.

Sara is my ride-or-die chick, my partner in crime, my support system, and it is fitting that we went to business together. I don't want her to stay mad at me because I'm distracted by Michael's intrusion.

The gallery comes to life with colorful art pieces. The sculpted statues erect on the tables create a realistic view. New Orleans cuisine was on display for the grand opening. There's shrimp remoulade, crawfish mac-n-cheese, pork boudin, and for dessert, we have dixie pecan pie. The room smells great. Some of our friends are walking around the gallery. It looks like everyone is enjoying themselves. The artists are standing by their works to answer questions or offer explanations to guests. I'm not sure what my reaction will be when Michael shows up. I have not discussed Michael with Sara, but I know I will – eventually.

More people are coming in. My eyes are constantly looking at the front door to see if Michael has arrived. I walk over to the bar to get a drink because I need to calm my nerves. I am not nervous because of the opening of the gallery but seeing Michael again. It has only been one day since I told him to back off. What the hell is wrong with me? Why I am getting all bent out of shape for a person

I barely know. As I am ordering my drink, I can feel him standing behind me. I stand at the bar, paralyzed, afraid to turn around.

He whispers my name, "Jazzy."

The bartender serves me my wine. I take a sip before I turn around. Oh! The man looks good. He is wearing a sports jacket with a nice button-down shirt and these slacks. Oh my God, these slacks must have been tailored because they fit him like a glove. I almost drop my drink.

He takes a step back and says with a big smile, "WOW, you look gorgeous." Then kisses me on the cheek. He hands me a beautiful bouquet of yellow roses, which I politely take while composing myself. He takes my hand and ushers me to the corner of the gallery, where it's semi-private. "Are you okay?"

"I am great! My gallery is finally open, and life couldn't get better." I remember something I need to take care of and turn to walk away.

He grabs my arm, "No, I mean you, me, us."

I know what he meant; I just did not want to deal with that right now. I close my eyes, but before I respond, and suddenly Sara is standing beside me, clearing her throat. I look at Michael, then Sara. In an awkward stance, I say, "Sara, this is Michael, Michael, this is Sara."

Sara looks at me, then Michael. She extends her hand to him, not sure what to say, "Nice to meet you."

He takes her hand. "It is a pleasure to meet you, Sara."

Sara comments while looking at me. "Yes, you as well. I am sorry, who are you to my friend?"

"Oh boy, Sara please tone it down." I give her a tense look. I can't blame her. She is very protective of me. She grabs my hand, pulling me away from Michael. I look back at him as Sara ushers me away. I whispered to him, "I am sorry,"

He flashes his sexy smile and says, "It's okay."

Sara asks, "Is this the man who got you so hot and bothered that you forgot your grand opening?"

I offer a quick explanation hoping that Sara will drop it for now. "Remember the guy who bought us drinks when we were at the club?"

She replies, "Oh! The brother's head you chopped off when he offered to buy us drinks. Wait! What is he doing here? And how long have you two known each other?" Sara is pounding me with her million questions.

Brace yourself Jazz, you're about to feel Sara's wrath for not telling her about Michael.

I smile, "Let's get through the night, and I will tell you all about it."

Michael is still standing like a soldier at a post, waiting for me. As I'm about to walk to Michael, the MC (our friend) calls Sara and me on stage to say a few words. Sara was happy to grab the mic to thank our friends and family for their continuous support.

Sara announces in a joking tone, "Don't expect a discount in this gallery just because we are friends and family."

A thunder of laughs explodes around the room because everyone who knows Sara knows she's not joking. She has a great business sense. When it comes to business, Sara is a different beast. As for me, I am the softy. You will win me over with any sap story. That's the reason why Sara and I have been friends for so long because we balance each other. I take the mic from Sara and thank everyone while sharing our vision for the space and announcing what's to come for us. With that, we turn the entertainment back to the stage.

The band continues playing, and everyone hits the dance floor, including Nadine and Misha. Someone grabs my elbow, I turn around, and here's Michael with that stupid grin. He walks closer and whispers, "Dance with me."

I turn to walk in the other direction when he pulls me closer, and that's all she wrote. We were on the dance floor dancing. Wow, the man can move too. I close my eyes and put my head on his shoulder, as we move. My feet never touch the floor. I am lost in the music. I did not realize that the music had ended. Michael had to call my name to bring me back on earth. How embarrassing! I walk off the dance floor, leaving Michael standing with curiosity on his face.

I can't handle him being so close to me, I don't have control over this situation, and it's driving me crazy.

I see Sara's talking with the guests. I wave my hands, hoping to get her attention. She is eyeing me suspiciously as she walks toward me. Looking in Michael's direction than mine, she asks, "What's up with you and Mr. Rico Suave over there?"

I rub my temple then reply, "Nothing is going on. Will you please drop it?"

She sighs, "Don't you give me any attitude Jasmine. I am not the one who almost missed the biggest night of our lives. I am not the one being distracted by the mere presence of Mr. Man."

"His name is Michael." I throw his name at her, feeling annoyed.

Sara takes a step back then continues, "Jazz, this is the biggest night of our lives. You have been looking like you're attending a funeral ever since he walked in here. Do I need to go kung fu on his ass? Let me know. I will drop-kick this fool if he is messing with you."

Only Sara could find humor in this. I hug Sara and tell her that she's right. My mood lightens up for the rest of the night by trying to avoid Michael as much as I can. The night ends beautifully. The guests were satisfied with the opening. Many buy art pieces.

Sara and I stay by the door to wish our guests a good night. I am happy we survived the night. The caterer starts cleaning up as the musicians are packing up their instruments. My head is pounding from the excitement of the grand opening and Michael, not to mention that I am still fighting the cold. I pick up a half bottle of wine to drown in my sorrows.

Suddenly I hear, "Aren't you driving home, young lady?"

Why is he still lurking around? I honestly thought he left since I did my best to avoid him. Annoyingly, I ask, "Why are you still here?" It did not come out the way I wanted to, and his face turned stone cold.

He replies, "You've been treating me like shit all night when all I wanted to do is make sure that you're good."

He is right. I apologize. "I am sorry, I didn't mean for it to come out the way it did. I am tired and have a headache."

Looking worried, he asks, "What can I do?"

I appreciate the concern expressed. I explain, "I have a lot on my plate with the gallery and…."

"ME," he replies.

"Yes, you and other things," I reply.

He takes the bottle from me, "I don't think this bottle is the answer."

He ushers me to a table in the corner of the gallery to sit down. My head is about to explode. I hold my head with both hands and lean on the table.

Sara comes over with her protective tone filling the space, "Are you okay?"

"I'm okay, just a little lightheaded." I wince.

I just did not want to get into it with Sara while Michael was sitting beside me.

"Are you okay to drive home?" she continues with her inquiries.

I reply, "Yes, I am fine to drive."

Sara squints her eyes and tightens her lips, and says, "I don't believe you."

I look at her and assure her that I am fine. Looking at me with a suspicious glare, Sara realizes she's not going to win this battle. She lets it slide but gives Michael the *what the hell are you doing to my girlfriend* look. Sara, my hero, is always ready to fight my fight.

I yell, "Girl go home! I will talk to you tomorrow!" Sara has eyes on Michael as she exits. I shake my head at the thought that Sara, the five-foot-three, one-hundred-and-twenty-three-pound, going toe-to-toe with six feet three two-hundred-pound man. That is one of the reasons why I love and put up with her. She always has my back. I trust her with my life. Sara blows me a kiss as she exits the door. I pretend to catch the kiss and hold it to my heart. She laughs then waves goodbye.

Michael was observing our silly gestures, "You all are tight right?

"Sara is a pain in the ass, but I love her to death. We have been friends for more than twenty years. She has been with me through thick and thin. She is my rock, my defender, my lifeline." I explain.

Michael says jokingly, "Well, I don't like her."

I ask him why because I'm getting ready to tell him about himself.

He replies, "Because I want to be all of that and more to you."

I cannot deal with this man. I did not answer, trying to change the subject.

"You should be afraid of Sara. She was about to go kung fu on you tonight." I threaten him.

Michael lets out a belly laugh, "Is that right?"

"Damn skippy," I laugh and wince. I forgot that my head was hurting.

Michael smiles. "You know she probably can kick my ass; she looks tough. Wait, why did she want to kick my ass again?" He asks.

"Because she thought that it was your fault that I was miserable on the biggest night of my life," I explain.

He looks wounded," Is it true? Am I the reason you were miserable tonight?"

I reply, "I don't know. Things are so confusing for me right now. I have a lot on my plate."

Still looking wounded, he asks, "Would you have preferred that I didn't show up tonight?"

Trying to appease him, "I'm happy you came and had a chance to share this important part of my life."

He reaches over and squeezes my hand, and my body freezes. I am perplexed by how my body reacts to his touch. The server stands by the table, hinting that she needs us to get up so she can break down the table and go home. I get the hint, and I stand up. I forgot that I was lightheaded. I got up too quickly and was about to fall. Michael quickly jumps to his feet and catches me. His overreacting startles the poor girl who's standing beside me. She runs to get me a glass of water. The server comes back with the water. Michael grabs it from her and hands it to me. I look at him to say, "Relax dude," as I take the glass from him. He acts as if I was shot or something. I sit back down for a minute and drink the water.

He exclaims in his overreacting tone, "That's it! You are not driving home by yourself. I am taking you home. You can pick your car up tomorrow."

I raise my hand to object, but he quickly gives me the *"it is not up for debate"* look. I retract my objection and follow his demand. Michael waits until everyone is gone. He takes my keys and locks up the place. He rushes to get his car and helps me in it. I must have been tired because I did not remember the thirty-minute ride to my house. All I remember is Michael picking me up, carrying me inside, and putting me into my bed. I wake up around six-thirty a.m., finding him sleeping uncomfortably on a chair in my bedroom. I look at this beautiful creature sleeping on my chair, wondering what it is about this man that gets me all tingly inside. I tiptoe around him to the bathroom, not wanting to wake him up. I brush my teeth, wash my face, and fix my hair a little. I swear the things we do to impress men is ridiculous.

I try to sneak back into bed, but I'm caught. He opens his eyes and asks, "What are you doing out of bed woman?"

He is so adorable, trying to be the disciplinarian. I smile and say, "Can a sister use the bathroom at her own house?"

He gives me a crooked smile and replies, "Not without my permission."

I laugh out loud and wince; my head still hurts.

He said, "Huh, that's what you get for being disobedient."

He gets up from the chair stretching; as he extends his arms above his head, I'm admiring his full erection. Michael catches me looking and says with a wicked smile. "Enjoying the view?"

My face turns red. I'm blushing from ear to ear. Thank God for my dark chocolate skin because Michael would have seen how embarrassed I was. Michael and I have not discussed intimacy. I know that I am safe and want to make sure that he is before talking about sex. I imagine the conversation would be difficult for both of us. I throw a pillow at him to hide my embarrassment, and he just laughs louder. He makes me laugh too. He walks to the bathroom, pops his head out and asks, "Do you have an extra toothbrush?"

I explain, "I always stock up on toothbrushes because I never know when I am going to have an uninvited guest."

With a raised eyebrow, he asks, "Am I one of your uninvited guests?"

This man is so sensitive. I must be careful when I joke around him. I smile and reply, "No, you just invited yourself to my house."

He is still standing in the doorway with his raised eyebrow without saying a word. I match his stare for a minute just to annoy him. He realizes that he is not going to win this battle. He walks back to the bathroom to look for the brush. Five minutes later, he washes his face, plops on my bed, and plants a kiss on my forehead, and says, "Good morning!"

It takes me a few seconds to respond, making sure he is not sour because of my earlier comment. He flashes a smile. I smile back, then plant a kiss on his cheek and reply, "Good morning."

My kiss was the invitation he needed. He jumps on top of me, pinning me down on the bed. My thoughts were oh boy, this is not going to end well. He kisses me again on both cheeks, then my neck, my ears. I feel the room is spinning. He moves down to my breast line then my mouth. My inside is on fire. The heat intensifies with each kiss. I'm weak. I can't breathe. This is becoming too much.

He has total control of my body. As he starts caressing my breasts, I muster enough courage to tell him to stop. He pretends he did not hear me; he continues with his task. This time with enough strength, I push him off me. He lies next to me, not saying anything. I'm so mad for allowing him to get this far. I have this internal war between my head and my body, and it looks like my body will win.

CHAPTER 10

The Surprise

I speak first, "I am not sure that I want to be intimate because I don't know much about your lifestyle."

His silence puzzles me. I continue, "I cannot afford to catch any STDs for being negligent."

Feeling defeated, he replies, "Okay, I understand." He rises and walks out of the bedroom. As he leaves the room, he stops to say, "I hope you grant me the opportunity to show you the real me."

I lean back in my oversize bed, pull the pillow over my head, and I scream as loud as I can to let out my frustration. I'm both sexually and mentally frustrated. I throw the pillow in the door's direction, not realizing Michael is standing at the door. The pillow hit him on his head, catching him off guard. He looks at me with disbelief and starts laughing, which makes me laugh. His laugh is contagious.

He snaps his finger then says, "Get dressed. I have an idea."

Here he goes with his disciplinary tone again. I will have a conversation with this brother to let him know that I am not the one, as I am getting up to get in the shower. I shower and put on shorts and a t-shirt because I'm unsure where he is taking me.

Michael looks at me, "Although you look hot in these shorts, you might what to change to something else, like yoga pants or something close to that." He raises his eyebrow. "Go change. It's a surprise."

I turn back and change into yoga pants, wondering what he's up to. During the car ride, Michael put on a smooth and sexy jazz tune. Not familiar with the artist, Michael teaches me a thing or two about his repertoire. As I'm about to ask him who's the artist, the car stops. He jumps out of the car, rushes to the passenger side, and opens the door with a big grin on his face. What is he so happy about? He takes my hand, helps me out of the car, and ushers me to this warehouse. I look at him and ask, "Are you taking me to a dog fight?"

He lets out a belly laugh and replies, "Stop being suspicious and trust me." As he gently knocks on the door. This tall older gentleman opens the door and gives Michael a big bear hug. Oh! This is the friend who wore the military outfit at the club.

Still holding my hand, Michael turns to me and says to the gentleman, "This beautiful young lady here is Jasmine."

I extend my hand to shake his. He takes my hand, "It's a pleasure to finally meet you, Jasmine. I am Cobby. Michael tells me so much about you."

He tries to hug me. Michael pushes him, gets in the middle of us, and says to Cobby, "A handshake will suffice."

Cobby shakes his head. "You have not changed a bit, jealous as ever."

Michael did not let me reply to Cobby. He ushers me inside the warehouse. The place is breathtaking. You would have never thought by just looking at the outside. Ahh, the lobby's décor is very feng shui. A sense of stillness is present in the lobby. Reminds me of the calmness I felt at the bayou during our picnic.

Michael explains, "Cobby and I have been friends since we were young."

Funny, Michael never mentions Cobby until now. In fact, Michael and I talk about many things but nothing in detail about his personal life. A petite Asian woman meets us in the lobby and directs us to a private room. The tranquil atmosphere and the aroma of the eucalyptus put me at ease. Once we're in the room, the woman turns her attention to Michael and me, bows down, and addresses us in Japanese. Michael bows and I follow his lead. He responds to the woman in Japanese. The woman hands me a long silky kimono robe and ushers me to a private room to change.

I step out of the room in my robe. Michael is waiting for me in his short kimono robe. The woman stands in front of us and bows, and we both follow her lead. She sprays essential oil in each corner of the room and asks us to take a deep breath. It just hit me that Michael and I are in a private yoga session. The woman softly directs our every move. From sun salutation to downward dog, it feels good to stretch. I get to see a softer side of him. Not only is he intelligent, but he is also in tune. I am not talking about religion. I am talking about finding his Zen and allowing it to take him away. I feel lighter and connected. Yoga was just what I needed.

Thirty minutes later, the woman finishes the session, takes another bow, and ushers us to another room. Another woman was waiting for us. She stands erect with beautiful long legs, blond hair, and big boobs. I can only guess that she is the massage therapist. She hands Michael and me different robes, points us to the changing room and instructs us to strip and put the robes on. I panic. OMG, this is not happening! I did not shave today. I don't want this woman to think that I am an Amazon woman with hairy legs.

I reluctantly comply. I step out. Once again, Michael is waiting for me. We take our seats on the tables; another woman walks over to Michael's table. She was as beautiful as my attendant. I don't know how I feel about that. I'm a little jealous of having this lovely lady touching Michael. He is not my man though. Why am I jealous that a woman is giving him a massage? I quickly shake that thought out of my mind and try to relax. My masseuse brings us a bottle of white wine and two glasses and places them by the small table in the middle. Michael pours a glass and hands it to me, then he pours himself a drink. He raises his glass. "To us."

I didn't want to toast to us, I reply "To good health and friendship."

Michael rolls his eyes and says, "whatever," then takes a sip of his wine.

I chuckle and drink my wine. It tastes familiar. I look at the bottle, and it's a bottle of Pouilly-Fuissé - Maison Louis Latour White

Wine, my favorite. How did the ladies know? He must have called while I was getting ready at my apartment. He planned all of this for me. This man is making it hard to drive him away. Michael's masseuse takes the glasses from us and asks us to disrobe. Michael has no shame and drops his robe on the floor, standing butt naked, then hops on the table. I glance and tell myself this man is fine on every level. He is toned with smooth skin. That butt, oh that butt, I think he did that on purpose so that he could show me what I'm missing. Well, I'm not as brave as Michael, the woman holds the sheet up, and I slip under the sheet so that Michael would not see me. Not that I look bad. I take pride in my body, scars, and all. The ladies begin their massages. It has been a while since I had a massage. The attendant is good at what she does. She loosens every knot in my body. Michael is moaning next to me. Based on that, it was clear his attendant had great hands as well. The woman massages every part of my body. I am floating. It felt extraordinary. I am so relaxed. The ladies finish then exit the room. I pick up my robe, with the sheet wrapped around my body, and slip it on. Michael walks over, still naked, and stands in front of me, taunting me. I am about to lose my mind. What is this man doing to me?

He whispers to me, "How are you feeling?"

I close my eyes, take a deep breath before I answer, "I feel great."

He plants a kiss on my lips and walks back to put on his robe. Why is this man torturing me like this?

He takes my hand, "I have one more surprise for you."

I don't think I can handle any more surprises. He directs me to the shower and removes my robe. I did not contest. I simply let it drop to the floor. He takes off his and turns on the water in the shower. Michael extends his hand to me, and I slowly take his hand, afraid of what is to come. The water feels so good. I allow the water to run down my back. The warmth relaxes my tense shoulders. Michael pulls me closer to rub my shoulders as if the massage therapist did not do a good enough job. I don't know how much I can take of this. My body is on fire, and it is not because of the water. He lathers his hand with eucalyptus-scented soap. I surrender to his touch and let my body go. I lean back. Michael is supporting me with his chest. I can also feel his erection. My body is so weak, I feel like I am going to faint. Overwhelmed with desire, I turn and wrap my hands around his neck and begin to kiss him. My action takes him by surprise.

He grabs my face then whispers, "Are you sure?"

Faintly, I respond, "Yes, I am sure."

He gently kisses me and turns me toward the shower. Michael continues in silence. He washes my body, allowing the water to rinse the soap off. Once he is satisfied, Michael takes my hand and pours soap in it. I assume he wants me to reciprocate. I slowly lather my hands and rub his chest, his stomach, his back. Michael tilts his head back and closes his eyes. He takes a deep breath and lets out a soft moan. I am not sure what is going through his mind. He grabs both of my hands and slowly guides them down to his penis. I use both hands to stroke him. His breathing becomes more robust as I do. Michael pins me in the shower and begins kissing me, more like devouring my lips.

I am about to explode when Michael stops and says, "Not here. I want our first time to be special."

My head is spinning. I cannot believe that Michael is the one who is saying no.

He explains, "I don't want our first time to be in my buddy's place of business."

In my head, I was pleading with him. I don't care where we are. I am about to explode. Why is he punishing me?

Finally, I muster enough courage. "I don't care where we are. I want you."

Michael welcomes the invitation, picks me up and carries me to the massage room. He lays me on the table and begins to plant kisses on my head, moving down to my neck, ears, and chest. He caresses my neckline, moves down to my back. His soft touch brought my body to a frenzy.

Michael clutches my face once again and asks, "Are you absolutely sure that's what you want?"

I am shaking my head frantically, "Yes…. Yes…that's what I want. Stop asking."

I can feel his tongue moving down to my stomach, my navel, then down to my garden. This man knows how to please a woman. His tongue is driving me crazy. Michael skips my vagina moves to my inner thighs, gently nibbling. The nibbling sends an electrical sensation to my head and back to my toes. How does he do that? He moves to my clitoris. His tongue is magic. I am about to explode in his mouth. I can no longer control myself. I let my body take over. I climax in Michael's mouth. He comes up for air and whispers, "sweet nectar." His voice sends chills through my spine. He climbs on top. Looking into my eyes, Michael asks, "Are you ready?"

Little does he know that I have been ready since the day I saw him at the supermarket. I will never confess that to him. I want to keep my good girl image. I shake my head to let him know that I am ready.

As Michael enters me, he asks that I keep my eyes open. He whispers, "I want to see your soul."

It takes me a while to sync with him since I am unfamiliar with his rhythm. After several strokes, we are finally moving to the same rhythm. For a minute, Michael and I have become one. It's like something that I've never experienced before. Each stroke takes me to ecstasy. This is more than a physical. I try to keep my eyes open as Michael requests, but my body is taking over. The feeling is more intense when my eyes are closed. His strokes intensify, and I can feel that he is on the verge of exploding. I get excited at the thought of Michael ejaculating. We release at the same time. It was magical.

Michael kisses me and whispers, "Thank you."

I look at him, "Why, thank you?"

"You just shared the most sacred experience with me."

Then it hit me. What have I done? How could I be so stupid? Why couldn't I control myself? Oh my God, I just had unprotected sex with this man. I start crying.

The sudden outburst startled Michael, "What's wrong?"

I lied, "I am overwhelmed by the experience."

I did not want to tell him that I committed the abominable sin. I also did not want to say this was the last time I would make this mistake. I did not say anything because he went through so much trouble, and I did not want to disappoint him. I got up and went to the bathroom to take another shower by myself. I let the water run over my head to drown my tears. How can I feel this awful after the experience I just had? I am on an emotional rollercoaster. I am crying because I lost control of the situation. I'm angry at myself for allowing it to go this far. I dress quietly and step out of the bathroom. Michael is waiting for me, already dressed. How does he do that? I put on a fake smile to let him know that I was okay. He walks over and puts his arms around me and holds me tight. His arms feel so good. I feel secure in his arms. Even if it is a false sense of security.

He pulls me back and looks at me. "Are you sure you're okay?"

I smile, "Yes, I am more than okay." I know that I'm not okay. I had to assure Michael because he went through so much trouble planning this.

His face lights up, "Now, for my last surprise!"

"What! More surprises? I don't think that I can take any more surprises," I reply.

Michael grabs my hand; he is practically dragging me because he was so excited. He guides me to the middle of the lobby, where a table is set for two with beautiful yellow roses as the centerpiece and multi-colored lanterns. The lobby smells divine. There's no one in the facility but a gentleman dressed as a chef. He walks over and offers Michael and me a drink. A surprise indeed. When did Michael plan all this? The chef serves us my favorite pomegranate sake. He instructs us to the table to take our seats. Michael walks over and holds out my chair.

My curiosity got the best of me, "When did you have time to plan all of this?"

"Last night while you were sleeping. I figured that you needed a little rest and relaxation after the day you had." He explains. He is not that bad. Michael was right; I needed this after the day had yesterday.

He continues, "I asked Cobby to close the spa for the day to set everything up."

"Oh! you that powerful?" I laugh.

He laughs too, "No, it's not power; it is friendship. Cobby and I have been friends for a long time. We served in the military together. Cobby saved my life on many occasions."

I look around the lobby, "Looking at Cobby, I would have never guessed that he owns a spa."

Michael pauses for a second. "There's a story behind Cobby's Spa. Fifteen years ago, while stationed in Japan, Cobby met his wife, Lau Ling. Her parents did not like Cobby very much because he was black. Against her parents' wishes, she married Cobby. Lau's parents disowned her. Life was good for Cobby and Lau. They opened a beautiful spa in Japan. Many dignitaries, people in power would go to the spa to relax. The business was successful. One day two masked individuals came into the spa and demanded money. Lau was in the lobby area greeting the guests when the shooters came in. Lau tried to run, they shot her in the back. She died hours later in the hospital. He loved Lau. He used to call her his saving grace. He was in a bad place after her death. He started drinking. It was awful."

I don't know Cobby yet, but my heart aches to hear such a tragic story. Michael was a little emotional when he was telling me the story.

"Were you close to his wife as well?" I ask.

"Yes, she was a beautiful soul. I was full of rage. She taught me how to meditate and bring awareness of my inner peace." Michael explains.

Curiously, I ask, "What do you mean full of rage?"

He hesitates, "After my mother died, I was mad at the world, and it manifested into rage at times, which got me into lots of fights. Thankfully, I've never got in too much trouble with the law. That's the reason why Cobby suggested that I join the military."

"I would have never thought that you had an anger issue," I explain.

"All thanks to Lau. I was devastated when she was murdered." Michael continues.

Continuing with my inquiry, "Did they ever find the gunmen who killed her?"

Michael continues, "Lau's brother was behind the robbery. He had a gambling problem, and he figured robbing the spa was easy money for him."

"Where's Lau's brother now?" I ask.

Quickly he responds, "Six feet under."

"What happened to him?" I continue with my inquiry.

With his hands up, he offers his thoughts, "I don't know. Karma? They found him at the pier tied up with his gut sliced open. No one ever speaks about it."

"How did you bring Cobby to a good place?" I wondered out loud.

"With lots of prayers and patience. I convinced him to move back to the states. I helped him open this spa in Lau's honor. Hence the name Lau's Tranquility Spa." He extends his arms to show the span of the place.

I look around the spa and think there is a sense of peace when you enter the establishment, the décor, the colors, the setting. It is a sacred place. We were so deep in our conversation that we forgot the chef standing on the other side of the room. Michael signals him to come over with our food. The chef brings two salad plates with Asian mandarin salad served with peanut sauce. For the main course, the chef serves a pan-seared salmon with red Thai sauce. Everything on my plate tastes so delicious. I must have been eating fast because Michael stops eating to watch me.

I stop mid-bite, "Are you okay?"

"Oh, I am fine. I see you worked up an appetite. It must have been all of the work you put in earlier" Michael laughs.

Blushing, "Yes, I am starving after all the work I put in earlier."

Michael reaches over the table holds my hand, "And I love and appreciate all of your hard work."

Squeezing his hand, I smile and say, "Thank you for this. It was very thoughtful of you."

His response warms me, "Jazz, I'll move heaven and earth to make you happy. I just need you to give me a chance to show you how much you mean to me."

Tears are rolling down my cheeks again, but this time they are tears of joy. Besides daddy, no man has ever made me feel so cherished. This man is throwing all the punches to win my heart. Sad to say, he won. Michael notices the tears. He put his napkin down, scoots his chair closer. Without a word, he wipes my tears and plants a kiss on my lips. The kiss melts my heart, and just like that, the tears stop flowing.

"Are you enjoying this?" He asks.

"I am having an amazing time," I reply.

Michael flashes a sexy smile. It melts my heart. He waves to the chef signaling him to bring dessert. The chef comes with two plates and places them in front of us. He uncovers his first, and it's a piece of chocolate cake. I take the cover off my plate, and it's a box wrapped in a beautiful oriental ribbon.

I look up, "What's this?"

Michael looks suspiciously, "Well, you won't know until you open it, Sherlock."

I give him one a don't-be-a-smart-ass look.

He sighs, "Well, are you going to open the box or not?"

I reluctantly open the box. Inside is a beautiful Pandora bracelet engraved with "Our Story Just Begun."

I can feel the tears running down my face looking at this beautiful bracelet. I walk around the table and give Michael a big kiss. He pulls me on his lap and plants another kiss that makes my toes curl. We escape to our own little world for a minute. Cobby snatches us back when he clears his throat, "I didn't mean to interrupt you love birds, but this old man gotta get home."

Michael gets up, pretending that he was mad, throws his napkin on the table, "Well, I can see when we're not wanted."

Cobby rolls his eyes, knowing all this mellow dramatic gesture is just for show. Michael asks him, "Can I at least go and get the car?"

Cobby points to the door while smiling.

"Don't you go and run off with my woman," Michael jokes as he runs to the door to get the car.

Cobby yells, "Oh, I wouldn't think of it."

Both men start laughing. As I am standing in the room waiting for Michael,

Cobby confesses, "I have never seen Michael this happy. You are incredibly special to him. He talks about you all the time."

"Oh, by the way, how's your friend?" Cobby asks.

"Which one?" I reply. Knowing damn well, he was asking about Nadine since he was the one who carried her out of the club that night.

Cobby comments, "The shorter one, she was yelling at your drunk friend." I laugh because I realize he is talking about Sara. "Oh! She's great," I reply.

I used the opportunity to ask him about Michael. I pry a little to see if Cobby will take the bait, "I am sure that I am not the first person Michael brought to your establishment."

Cobby chuckles, "Michael is like a brother to me, and I will give him my right arm if he needs it. He has issues but believe me when I tell you that you're the only one he talks about. I see the way he looks at you. If I am not mistaken, I think the brother is in love."

"Oh, Please, you're exaggerating," I tease

Cobby replies, "I call it as I see it."

I quickly change the subject as Michael walks in.

He gives Cobby and me a puzzled look, "He behaved?"

I reply, "Cobby was a perfect gentleman."

He rolls his eyes, "Well, now I've heard everything. Cobby a gentleman?"

Cobby gives him a playful jab, "You can learn a thing or two from me." Cobby turns to hug me, "It's a pleasure to finally meet the woman who will finally make this knucklehead walk in the right path."

Michael quickly grabs my hand and pulls me out of the door. Cobby starts laughing again.

CHAPTER 11

Juicy Details

The spa was outstanding. During the ride back home, I was processing the day, but more importantly, the conversation Cobby and I had. I still cannot believe that I just had sex with Michael. He probably thinks that he has me exactly where he wants me. I lean back in my seat and doze off. I did not realize we've reached my apartment.

Michael whispers as he gently shakes me, "Wake up sleepy head."

Still feeling drowsy, I explain, "I am tired. I am going to bed. Thank you for today."

Michael walks me to my door and kisses me goodnight.

I pull my shoes off and throw my purse on the sofa. A buzzing sound catches my attention. Michael was rushing me earlier. I accidentally left my phone on the kitchen counter. Twenty-two missed calls, most from Sara, who also left me nine messages, some sounded worried, and some sounded that she was pissed. I pour myself a glass of wine before I call her.

Sara is never shy about expressing her anger. "Where the hell were you, Jasmine? I called and left several messages making sure that you were okay. I was just about to drive to your house to check up on you."

Sara wouldn't let me get a word in. I allow her to vent, "I was scared thinking that Mr. Rico Suave cut you up in pieces and put you in his trunk."

Oh, the ever-melodramatic Sara is at again. I reply, "As you can hear, I am not in Michael's trunk cut up in pieces. I left my phone at the house. That's why I missed your messages. I am sorry that I worried you."

In a sarcastic tone, she asks, "Where were you anyway?"

"Michael treated me to a spa day," I respond, knowing Sara would have something to say.

Sara screams, "Who the hell is this Michael guy? You have given up everything for this guy."

"Wait a minute! Now you're pissing me off. I admit that the last couple of days, I have been preoccupied with Michael, but I have not given up everything in my life for him." I shout back.

Through a deep breath, she says, "I am coming over, and you better spill the beans."

I know exactly what Sara means about spilling the beans. She wants the juicy details from the last two days that I have been away from her. Fifteen minutes later, Sara knocks on my door. I open the door and give her a please-forgive-me hug. She hugs me back and walks straight to the kitchen with the binder we need to work on.

"First things first, let's work on the gallery inventory and then, I will tell you all the juicy details." I wink at Sara, which makes her laugh.

Sara and I triple-check the gallery's inventory, ensuring that we have everything we advertised in the newspaper. It takes us three hours to complete the stock and the final plans for the gallery.

When we are finally done, Sara jumps up, flips her hair, and demands some answers, "Okay, now spill and don't leave out any details."

I laugh at Sara's enthusiasm to know the details of my encounter with Michael. She doesn't even like him. I open the wine cabinet in the kitchen and grab a bottle of wine from my collection. I figure if I am going to need it to relive my day with Michael.

Sara screams, "Oh shit! It's that good that we need a bottle of wine. This must be serious."

She has no idea. Sara has been my best friend forever. I don't ever keep secrets from her. This is one secret I wish that I could. I know how she would react.

I take a deep inhale before I set a disclaimer, "Okay, promise me you won't judge me or get mad."

"Why would I get mad or judge you Jazz, you're grown." She replies in an aggravated tone.

Another deep breath, I continue, "Michael drove me home last night because I was lightheaded. When I woke up, I found him sleeping on the chair."

"Wait a minute, this joker invited himself in your house and decided to overstay his welcome and spent the night?" Sara asks.

I feel that I must defend Michael, "No, Sara, he did not want me to be alone because I wasn't feeling well. He decided to stay to make sure that I was okay."

She replies with a smirk, "I bet he did."

"Damn Sara! Do you want me to tell you the details or not?" I hope the aggravation in my voice was clear.

She replies, "No need to get mad. I was just stating the facts. I'll shut up."

I take a sip of the wine before I continue, "He must have planned the spa day while I was sleeping. Because all he said was get dressed, he had a surprise for me."

Skipping the part that he was trying to get frisky, and I had to push him off. That would give Sara more reason to trash Michael.

Instead, I say, "He took me to this beautiful spa called Lau's Tranquility Spa owned by his best friend."

Sara interrupts, "Oh, I heard of the spa. It's located in a ware-house near the French Quarter."

I scream, "Yes! That's the place. The owner is Michael's best friend, Cobby. The guy who helped us with Nadine the night she got drunk. "When we arrived, I thought, what in the world is this place, but once I was inside, it was magnificent. We got a private yoga session and unbelievable massages. I guess I got caught in the moment, then we…"

"Oh! You did the nasty?" Sara blurts out like a young brat.

In one breath, I explain, "It was more than that. It was more like a connection. It was intense. I have never experienced that type of ecstasy."

Sara is on her second glass of wine when she yells, "You're a freak…OMG! Weren't you afraid that someone would walk in on you?"

I continue, "Michael arranged to have the place exclusively. It was just the two of us and a couple of staff and Cobby, of course. I think he planned it that way."

Sara approves. "Well, I am happy that you finally got some because I was worried that you would go through a long, torturous dry spell." We laugh loudly and touch our glasses together.

I say, "Me too."

It was quiet for a minute. Sara put her glass down and says "I don't like that look. There's more you are not telling me, isn't it?"

I shake my head, "Yes. I am conflicted. My head is telling me to stop, and my heart is telling me to go. I am not sure which road to take."

Sara senses my reluctance. I can tell she's thinking of what to say next.

Sara moves closer, then takes my hands, "I know you went through a tough breakup, and I understand what you're feeling. You're scared, and that's normal. I must be honest with you. There's something about this guy that does not sit right with me." Oh! Here she goes with her psychic ability again. "You are beautiful, intelligent, and talented. You will meet someone who will love and treat you right," Sara continues.

I pour myself another glass of wine, sipping it while pondering Sara's observation. She may be on to something. There were red flags during my interaction with Michael. But I can't help how he makes me feel.

The conversation is getting too heavy. I have to seriously analyze my situation with Michael, then decide. My head is about to explode. We finish the bottle of wine.

I tell Sara, "I'm tired. I want to go to bed."

Sara hugs me good night and says, "Take it slow with Mr. Rico Suave."

I really hate it when Sara calls him that. I'm too tired to argue with her. I simply kiss her good night.

The following day, I was so excited, I could not sleep. I make sure to get to the gallery before Sara. Thirty minutes later, Sara shows up all cheery with two cups of tea. She hands me a cup and says, "Good morning." She asks how I slept as she sips on her tea.

I reply, "I'm so excited about the gallery opening that I did not sleep at all." I was also pondering this mess with Michael and how I think I am falling for him already. Which I did not dare tell Sara.

Once the gallery is opened, there's a constant flow of curious people. Around lunchtime, Michael surprises me with flowers and lunch.

He kisses me and says, "I was in the neighborhood and thought that I should stop by to feed you."

I give him a suspicious look, knowing damn well that his firm is across town. He waves to Sara; she just gives him a dirty look. I can tell she's not too pleased to see him.

Michael laughs, "I don't think she likes me too much."

Trying to defend Sara, "She is like this with everyone. It will take time for her to warm up to you."

Another lie, I know my friend. It takes her a second to decide whether she will like you or not from the first time she meets you. She definitely doesn't like Michael.

He kisses me and says, "Get back to work, you slacker. Will I see you tonight?"

I reply, "I am not sure. I have so much work to do." I am trying to avoid Michael as much as I can. I am not ready to face him again.

The week went by fast. Sara and I have worked twelve hours every day since the gallery opened. I did not see Michael too much except when he dropped by during lunchtime.

It has been two months since the gallery opened. The holidays are around the corner, and things are picking up very well. We've added poetry night on Thursdays. It's packed with local artists and people who appreciate great poetry, varying and engaging art, and strong drinks. All these long hours are taking a toll on both Sara and me. We decide that we need to hire help to give us a break. The next day we posted a wanted sign on the gallery window for a part-time position. Sara and I interviewed several people for the role, no one stood out. The following week a young lady walks in and asks if the job is still available. She looks eager, so I interview her on the spot. I genuinely like her. Her name is Laycee.

"Where are you from Laycee?" I ask.

"I'm from Houston," she replies.

I continue with the questions. "What brings you to New Orleans?"

She replies, "I major in art history, and I thought New Orleans has such rich history. I wanted to move here to start my career."

Laycee is beautiful, tall with long legs. She looks like a runway model. She seems nice, deeply knowledgeable about the arts. I think Sara will like her too. Since Sara is not here, I ask her to come back for a second interview.

The next morning, Laycee shows up thirty minutes early to meet with Sara for her second interview. Sara spends an hour talking with Laycee before giving me the thumbs up to hire her. Laycee is very thankful for the opportunity. She replies, "I will be your most efficient right hand. I promise."

Since Laycee started working for me, Michael and I have seen each other often. We go out on dates as often as our schedules allow us. One night, while on a date, his phone keeps ringing. His facial expression lets me know that whoever was on the other end of the phone, he did not want anything to do with them. He keeps sending the calls to voicemail.

The phone ring one more time. I slam my utensils on the table then comment, "Obviously, this person needs to speak with you; answer it."

He looks at the phone, rubs his head, then looks up. I sense Michael is about to give me some unwelcome news.

He reaches over to hold my hands, "I need to talk to you about something."

With my antenna already up, I whisper, "Just tell me what you need to tell me."

Bracing myself for whatever has Michael so worried. Is he sick? Please don't let it be some incurable disease. I'm not sure I want to know. He moves his chair closer, still holding my hands, and just when he is about to tell me the news, the phone rings again. He seems visibly annoyed. He excuses himself and walks outside for more privacy. I wait at the table feeling like an idiot, wondering what's going on. I watch Michael pacing, waving his left hand and rubbing his head as he talks on the phone. His facial expression intensifies. I'm racking my brain thinking of a million questions. What is it about this call that has him so upset? Who is he talking to? What was he trying to tell me earlier? I decided to stop torturing myself and wait for Michael to tell me what he needed to say. A few minutes later, Michael comes back and is so apologetic. He tries to explain the phone call. I'm too hurt to care.

I was no longer in a festive mood. I ask Michael to take me home. When he arrives at the apartment, he asks, "Can I come up? I would like to explain the phone call."

I see that he wasn't going to drop it, I reply, "Just for a few minutes. I have to catch up on some work."

Michael goes straight to the kitchen and asks, "Do you have anything stronger than wine?" Luckily, Misha had given me a bottle of Rhum Barbancourt straight out of Haiti. I point to the direction where the bottle is sitting. Michael grabs two glasses out of the cabinet and begins to pour the Rhum. I open the refrigerator and take the orange juice out, knowing that I cannot drink this five-star Rhum straight. Michael sips his with a surprising look; he says, "This is good. It's smooth. You have to get me a bottle of this."

Feeling anxious, I reply, "Michael, you did not come up here to talk about Rhum. Please tell me what you need to tell me."

Michael pauses, then takes a deep breath, "I moved to New Orleans to get a fresh start. I made lots of stupid mistakes and hurt lots of people," Michael continues as he makes his way to the living room. "I've dated many women, and with that came lots of complications." He takes a deep breath, "I have a six-year-old son in Chicago. His mother wouldn't let me see my son."

I ask, "So, when were you going to tell me that you had a son? You don't think it's something that I may need to know!" Feeling crushed by the news. I take a seat on the couch to better process the information.

He pleads, "Jazz, I have been waiting for the right opportunity to tell you about my son. I was afraid that you may not want to hear it."

His statement hurt, "You think that I am that shallow if you tell me that you had a son, I wouldn't want to be with you?"

He rubs his head, "No, Jazz, I don't think you're shallow at all. It's more complicated than that."

I yell, "Then uncomplicate it for me! From where I am standing, it feels like there's more to the story! If it is you have a son, you had a life before you entered my life!"

Michael starts pacing in the living room, "She gave me an ultimatum. In order for me to see my son, I have to remain in a relationship with her."

I explode, "What kind of bullshit is this? Let me get this straight, you mean to tell me that you're entertaining the idea of staying in a relationship with this woman although you don't want to."

He replies, "I love my son very much and don't want to jeopardize the relationship."

The heat from my face is rising. I scream, "WOW! You must really think that I am stupid. Get out of my face with this bullshit."

In a calmer tone, he replies, "I don't think you're stupid Jazz. I just need you to understand."

I pause for a second, then ask, "So, she wants you to move back to Chicago to be with her for you to see your son?"

Michael rubs his head again, "Yes, that's what she wants. But I think she may be in New Orleans. I am not hundred percent sure."

I jump up from the couch, "Wait, what do you mean you think she may be in New Orleans? Do I have to worry about any drama, Michael?"

He gently touches my shoulder then replies, "You don't have to worry about any drama. I promise you; it will not come to that."

The news hit me like a brick. This joker has been lying to me for months. I thought of what Sara told me earlier, getting involved with Michael might be a dangerous thing. It sounds like this woman is a hand full, and frankly, I don't have the energy to go against Michael's crazy baby mama.

The more Michael tries to explain the phone call, the angrier I become. He's insulting my intelligence with all the excuses as to why he maintains that relationship.

"Jazz, you have no idea what this woman put me through. She is not stable.," he explains.

I yell, "That's a good indication for you to stay away from her."

I don't want to come across as a jealous chick, so I back off. The more Michael pleads for me to see his side, the more I see him as a narcissistic, womanizing, selfish son-of-a-bitch.

"This is too much. I can't do this right now. Please leave," as I fling the apartment door open.

He tries to reason with me, "Jazz please, you have to understand I was trying to protect you until I get this situation under control."

I yell, "Get the fuck out of my apartment!"

Michael stops for a second when he realizes that I'm serious. Finally, he walks out while he whispers, "Good night."

The door makes a loud bang as I slam it behind him.

CHAPTER 12

Blast from the Past

Instead of going home, I decided to go and talk to Cobby because he is the only one who can help me sort out this mess I am in. I arrive at the spa just as Cobby is about to leave. "Going somewhere old man?" I shout.

He flexes and replies, "Oh, I got your old man." I love busting his chops just as much as he likes to bust mine.

"What are you harassing me for?" Cobby asks.

I respond with a sense of urgency in my voice. "I need to talk to you man."

With a concerned look on his face, Cobby replies, "Is it about Jasmine?"

I don't know how to answer that without going into details, so I just nod to say yes.

He lets a big sigh out and says, "Come in my office. We can talk over this bottle of whiskey I've been saving."

Cobby pulls out a chair for me to sit. He then walks around his desk, pulls a drawer open, and takes the whiskey out and two glasses. Before I say anything, I take a swig of the whiskey to calm my nerves. Cobby looks at me and says, "It's that bad?"

I signal him to pour me another shot. This time I just hold the glass as if I am protecting the drink. Without knowing where to start. I just blurt, "I think Mona followed me to New Orleans."

Cobby almost drops his drink. Shocked, he asks, "Are you sure? How does she know you're in New Orleans?"

I reply, "Remember I told you that I thought I saw her at the club that night. I brushed it off, thinking that it was just my imagination."

Cobby takes a sip of his drink then asks, "How can you be sure?"

"I am not sure, but lately, she has been calling me, dropping hints that she's watching me," I explain to Cobby.

He frowns and says, "If that's the case, you have got to tell Jasmine."

"Speaking of Jazz, while we were out tonight, Mona kept calling non-stop. Finally, I had to answer to make her stop. I decided to tell Jasmine about my son. She was not happy that I waited this long to tell her." I explain.

Like a father chastising a son, Cobby replies, "Can you blame her? Jasmine is a nice person. If you keep playing games, you'll fuck it up just like every other relationship you had."

"I don't need a preacher right now, man. I need my buddy right now," I blurt out. He is right though; I don't want to mess things up with Jazz.

Cobby continues, "Mike, before anything gets too serious with Jasmine, fix your shit. If it's true Mona followed you here. You know you'll be putting Jasmine in harm's way."

I take a sip of the whiskey before I respond, "I don't know for sure if Mona is in town. She keeps dropping hints that she knows where I am and what I'm doing at all times. I told her that she was bluffing."

Cobby asks, "Is the restraining order still valid?"

This drink is not doing its job. My head is about to explode. I thought I left all of this shit back in Chicago. All I want to do is start over and live my life in peace. My wish is to live it with Jasmine. I respect her too much to have her caught up in my mess. The issue with Mona is much deeper than just not seeing my son. I have to get in front of this before it gets out of hand.

Cobby realizes I am no longer listening to him. He slams his glass on the desk and yells, "Mike, are you listening?"

I guzzle the last sip of the whiskey, plop my glass on the desk then leave. I can hear Cobby calling my name, but I don't respond. I have to find out if Mona is really in New Orleans and keep her away from Jasmine.

CHAPTER 13

Tug-of-War

How did I find myself in this predicament? The logical thing to do is to tell Michael to go fuck himself and lose my number. My heart, the traitor, is saying, "you've been bitten by love, and there's no way my logic is going to win this fight."

For the next couple of days, I bury myself in the gallery. I avoid Michael's calls and texts. We added another event on Friday nights called "Grown and Sexy Night" and book local jazz bands and create a platform to discuss grown folk's business. Our guests consist of relationship experts, family therapists, sex therapists, financial advisors, and others. Friday nights, promoted and managed by Laycee, have become immensely popular. Laycee has total autonomy to select the topics for the forum discussion and the band.

Sara notices that Laycee follows me around like a lost puppy. In Sara's distinct way, she comments, "It's peculiar that Laycee takes an interest in you."

I dismiss her comments because Sara is suspicious of everyone. I try not to judge. I will trust first and wait until the person betrays, then remove myself from the individual. Laycee has indirectly become my assistant. She is like the sister that I never had. She comes to my apartment to watch movies on weekends. She asks me for relationship advice. Not that I am an expert in the subject matter. But I do my best to advise her from my perspective.

One weekend while watching television, Laycee confesses that she left her hometown to get away from her abusive boyfriend.

She explains, "When I found out that I was pregnant with his child, he became angry and stated that the baby was not his. I must have slept with some other guy. He beat me until I passed out. After my baby was born, I had to work two jobs to support myself and my son."

I admire her courage. The more Laycee tells me about her life, the more I want to help her. I say, "I commend you for leaving." Laycee's eyes get watery as if she's about to cry. I walk over and hug her and say, "You're not alone. Anything you need, don't be afraid to ask me."

Laycee replies, "I have no family nor friends in New Orleans."

My heart aches for her; still holding her, I reply, "We are your family now."

She breaks free from me and chuckles, "I don't think Sara likes me very much."

I assure Laycee that she doesn't have to worry about Sara.

After the baby mama announcement, Michael would show up at the gallery to take me to lunch during lunchtime. I would decline his invitation. When he calls, I send his calls to voicemail. He leaves messages or texts that I do not respond to. One day Michael shows up to the gallery, walks straight into my office with a picnic basket, and says, "Lunch."

He hugs me, then replies, "Since you've been ignoring me, I brought you lunch that way you have no choice but to eat with me."

I push past him, "I don't have time for your bullshit today."

He pleads, "Jazz, please I need you. It has been hell the last couple of weeks. Besides Cobby, you're the only person that I can count on."

I reply, "I don't care; just leave me the hell alone."

With his hand clenched, "What do I have to do? I am at your mercy," he continues.

"Michael, I don't have time for your bullshit lies. As you can see, I am swamped." Waiving my hand around to show how busy I was.

Instead of leaving, Michael sits at my desk, "I am not leaving here until we have a conversation. I am sorry Jazz; I don't want to lose you. I am trying extremely hard to clean up the mess I left in Chicago."

I can feel the three lines my forehead forms when I am livid. I reply, "I was not part of your life in Chicago, and I should not be part of your mess either."

Michael ignores my protest, crosses his arms, and stares.

I sigh, then reply, "Say what you have to say, and then leave."

He replies, "No, we're going to have lunch, have a conversation like civilized people, and then when I'm good and ready to leave, I'll leave."

I notice a smirk on his face. I just roll my eyes and sit down. He starts taking the lunch out of the basket. It's two sandwiches, apple pie with water.

I look at him, "Who told you that I was hungry?"

With a devilish smile, and comments, "Jazz, you are always hungry."

I flip him the finger then grab my sandwich.

Michael looks at me with a smile, "I miss you!"

I ignore his comment. I take a bite out of my sandwich. He smiles, "See, I know you very well." He teases.

I reply, "You better shut up or get out of my office."

He explains, "Jazz, I am sorry I did not tell you sooner. It's more complicated than just my son. I moved to get away from her."

"What about your son?" I ask.

"She refuses to let me see him." He answers with sadness.

After a second pause, I reply, "I am sorry that you're going through a tough time. I am, really. Still, I need to distance myself from you and your drama."

Shaking his head, he comments, "Jazz, I cannot do this without you. I understand that you may not want to be with me, but please don't give up on me."

I frown, "There's nothing I can do for you Michael. It's just like you said, clean up your shit, and leave me out of it."

Michael rubs his head, "I would rather have you in my life as a friend than not have you at all. I can't do this without you."

He put his sandwich down as if he had lost his appetite. I did not have much of an appetite as well. I drop mine on the desk. We just stare at each other without a word. The room becomes colder all of a sudden.

Michael finally breaks the silence, "I have an appointment with a client nearby. I have to go. Can I come over tonight to finish our discussion?" He asks.

With a side-eye, I respond, "You must be out of your mind, thinking you can invite yourself to my house."

He walks over to my side of the desk and tries to kiss me. I turn my face, so he'll kiss me on the cheek. He whispers goodbye. A few minutes later, Michael comes back into the gallery visibly upset.

With a concerned look, I ask, "Did you forget something?"

He clenches his fist," Someone slashed two of my tires."

I am now alarmed. Why would someone slash two of his tires in broad daylight? More importantly, what kind of people does he have in his circles devious to do something that devious?

I ask, "Should I call the police?"

Shaking his head, he replies, "It's not necessary."

I am suspicious about why Michael is taking it lightly. Why didn't he want to call the police? It's an act of violence. Someone meant to slash those tires. Maybe he knows who did it and did not want the police involvement. He's on the phone with a towing company when Sara walks into the gallery with the same alarming look as Michael.

She walks up to me and starts with a million questions. "What's going on? Why are Michael's tires flat? Were they slashed?"

Overwhelming with all of her questions, I take her hand and drag her to the office. I explain, "Michael told me that he has a baby mama. He thinks that she's in town but not sure."

Sara jumps off her chair, loud enough for Michael to hear, "Jazz, are you crazy? Why are you even considering getting involved in this mess?"

I roll my eyes before I respond to Sara's statement. "I am not considering anything. I've already told Michael that I didn't want anything to do with him," I explain.

The towing company finally arrives. Michael steps outside to speak with the man. I follow Michael to hear what story he's going to tell the man. Sara stays at the counter, watching the drama unfold. Where did Laycee disappear to?

The guy looks at Michael's truck and shakes his head. He asks, "Damn man, who did you piss off?"

Michael tenses up to show he's not pleased with the man's comment. Michael barks at the man, "Just fix my damn tires so I'll be on my way."

The man put his hands up then replies, "Sorry man, my bad, I didn't mean to upset you." As he pulls two new tires from the back of his truck.

Michael ignores his comment, then turns and walks inside the gallery. Like a curious child, I follow Michael inside. Michael rubs his head and keeps pacing back and forth as he keeps his eyes on the man changing the tires. I walk past Michael, go to the bar, and grab two bottles of water. I hand him a bottle. He whispers, "You have something stronger?"

I look at this joker and say with all the attitude I can muster, "You're lucky you're getting this bottle of water."

Not pushing his luck, he takes the bottle and guzzles the water down. Sara is peering through the office window, watching our every move. Michael returns to pacing the floor, mumbling.

Feeling the tension growing from my head traveling to my neck and shoulders, I feel that Michael owes me an explanation. So, I ask, "Is there a reason you don't want the police involved?"

He pauses once again, rubs his head, "Yes, but I have to be sure about something."

As I'm about to ask my next question, the mechanic enters the gallery, sweaty like he just ran a marathon. I grab paper towels and hand them to him. I don't want his sweat drops all over the floor. With his clipboard under his arm, he takes the towel and wipes his face. Once he's satisfied, he flips a couple of pages then explains,

"The tires were in bad shape. I replaced them with two new ones. Please sign here, and you're good to go."

With a sour look on his face, Michael grabs the clipboard from the tow man, looks over the papers. He signs the last page, hands it back to the mechanic and grabs his keys. The mechanic nods his head as he exits the gallery.

Michael walks closer then says, "Can I see you later?"

Sara, who was watching from the back, walks closer, stands behind the counter, and continues eavesdropping. She comes around the counter and says, "No, she will not see you later."

Michael ignores Sara's comment and continues to address me. He asks, "Can you walk me out?"

As we walk out the door, Sara yells, "Don't be stupid, Jazzy!"

Michael shoots Sara a dirty look and asks, "Why is she always so nasty?"

I reply as I lead him outside, "I don't blame her. I don't even like you right now!"

He stops as if he were hit by a train, "You don't mean that."

I snap, "The hell I don't."

He pleads, "Jazz, I promise you this will be over soon. I just need a little more time to clean this up." He sounds like a broken record.

My gut tells me that there's more to Michael's story, and he's not upfront with me.

To be on the safe side, I explain, "Until you get your shit together, don't call me nor stop by the gallery or my apartment."

After my statement, I walk back to the gallery. The warm tears run down my cheeks. I wipe them away because I don't want Sara to see me crying. As I enter the gallery, Laycee is standing at the bar. Strange, where was she when all of the commotions were happening?

Annoyingly I ask, "Where have you been?"

Laycee cocks her head to the side. With a weird facial expression, she replies, "I'm on my period. I went to the drugstore."

Sensing Laycee is lying, without a word, I walk past her into the office.

Sara is looking at me with crooked lips, "What the hell are you getting yourself into?"

I lean over my desk, holding my head. Sara notices how stressed I am. She walks around the desk and hugs me. That's all it takes. A flood of tears come rolling down my cheeks. Through my sobbing, I ask, "Why am I letting myself be tortured by this man's baggage?"

Sara replies, "Do you want me to kill him?"

I let out a faint laugh, then reply, "Hold the assassins for another occasion." We both start laughing.

I'm not sure how long Laycee has been standing in the doorway of our office eavesdropping.

With an innocent look, she asks, "Is everything okay Jazz?"

Not wanting to go into too much detail with Laycee, I reply, "Yes, I am fine. I just have a headache."

I decide to go home for the rest of the afternoon. On my way to my car, I notice a note on the windshield. I panicked, thinking the crazy person who left slashed Michael's tires left me a threatening message. As I approach the car, I notice the handwriting. It's Michael's, it read:

"Jazzy, I am so sorry that I am not able to give you a straight answer about what is going on. I am trying to protect you from all of this drama. Please be patient with me. I need you in my life. I know that I need to clean up this mess I made before you give me another chance. I will make it up to you. I promise. Forever yours."

He did not sign his name, but I know his handwriting. I crumple the note and throw it away. Reading the stupid note makes me upset. I don't know exactly what he's protecting me from. I've told Michael that I do not want to see him anymore. I did not care to know. When I arrive home, I check in with Sara to tell her that I'm home safely. I pour myself a glass of wine, replaying today's scenario in my head while sipping on my Merlot. I decided to go to bed early, hoping tomorrow would be better.

It's three a.m. when the alarm company calls to say that it appears that there was a break-in and that the police were notified and on the scene. I call Sara at once; she confirms she received the same call. I quickly pull on my sweatpants and a shirt and race to the gallery. As I pull up, Sara is talking to the police. I park the car right in front of the gallery. My jaw drops, seeing the extent of the damages. The windows are shattered, and broken glass is everywhere. The front door is off the hinges. It looks as if someone ran their car through the gallery. One officer opens a black box and begins to dust the front door for fingerprints. The younger officer is talking with Sara as I make my way in their direction.

I wave my hands around the room and ask, "What happened?"

The young officer offers some insight, "It appears that someone threw rocks through the windows or tried to take access the building by yanking the door from the hinges." As he points in the direction of the front door.

The officer surveys the gallery to make sure it's safe to enter. Looking around with his flashlight, he ensures us it's safe to enter. As we enter, my eyes scan the gallery to assess the damages. Sara walks over to the bar and notices the word "BITCH" painted all over the counter. Art pieces are ripped off the wall and tossed on the floor throughout the gallery. I am horrified. Sara and I worked so hard to open the gallery now some vindictive person wants to destroy it. The instruments are scattered around the stage.

In an impatient tone, the young officer asks, "Do you ladies have any idea who might break in and vandalize your gallery?"

I have my suspicion, but I'm not ready to divulge that information until I speak with Michael.

Sara shrugs and replies, "I am not sure who could have done such a thing, but rest assure when I find out, I will kill them."

I whisper in Sara's ear, "It's probably not a clever idea for you to make a statement like that in front of an officer."

The officer raises his eyebrow, "Let us do our job, ma'am."

Oh boy, this officer doesn't know who he is talking to. Sara replies, "That's right officer, do your job."

The officer shifts his weight on his right foot as he addresses Sara, "Ma'am, I'm going to need you to calm down."

I take Sara's hand and ask if she can continue assessing the gallery and taking an inventory while talking to the officer. Sara looks at the officer from head to toes, sucks her teeth, turns around, and walks to the back.

I turn to the officer with an apologetic tone to continue with his questions. In a more relaxed manner, the officer continues, "How long has the gallery been open?"

I answer, "Less than a year."

He continues with his interrogation, "Have you ladies received any threatening calls or experienced any disgruntled employees?"

I reply to the officer's question, "We only have one employee, and she has been wonderful."

I also let the officer know that we had not received any threatening phone calls. He wraps up his questions, gives me his card just in case I remember anything. The older officer who was dusting the door for prints interrupts the conversation with an abrupt grunt, "It's going to be difficult getting a good fingerprint, with so many people coming in and out of the gallery."

The younger officer replies, "Well, it was a shot."

He turns around and walks out, leaving me with my mouth open. Instead, I ask the older officer, "So that's it. Nothing else can be done?"

"Look," pointing his chubby index finger at me, "These types of break-ins are difficult to prove. Call your insurance and file a claim. That's the best advice I can give you." He turns around and follows his partner.

CHAPTER 14

The Break-in

The clock on the wall reads five-thirty a.m. When the officers left. Sara and I decided the gallery should remain closed until we finish cleaning up. Thank goodness we have insurance. We need some reinforcement to help with the cleanup and board up the busted windows and the door.

Sara and I start picking up the broken glass in the front when all of a sudden, she snaps her fingers and exclaims, "I have a theory about who might have broken into our gallery."

"Brace yourself Jazz, Ms. Conspiracy Theory is going to layout the who-done-it," I reply.

Sara continues, "I think it's a competitor." She waves her arms around in her dramatic fashion.

I haven't said anything to her about Michael's baby mama or the real possibility that it was her. I, however, entertain the idea it might be Michael's ex or present girlfriend. I don't know what to think. Michael is hiding something from me, and now he indirectly involves me in his drama. All kinds of questions are running through my head. Questions like, how did she find out about me? Am I in danger? Now, I am pissed and scared. And, I have put Sara in danger too. I need to speak to Michael. It was early, but I did not care. I need answers. I call Michael to ask him which one of his females is fucking with me. He answers on the third ring.

With a groggy voice, he answers, "Jazz is everything okay?"

With an unforgiving tone, I respond, "Someone broke into the gallery and trashed the place."

Suddenly, he sounds awake and alert, "What? When? How? Are you okay?"

I yell, "How the hell am I supposed to be, okay?"

He dismisses my question and replies, "I am on my way."

Before I can protest, he hangs up. Twenty minutes later, Michael shows up with Cobby in a pickup truck with tools. Cobby greets me with a big hug and a cup of tea. He has always been nice to me. Michael trails behind him, almost knocking Cobby over to get to me. His possessive tendency gets on my last nerves.

He hugs me and whispers, "I am so sorry you're going through this."

I back away from him and ask, "Is it the same person who slashed your tires earlier? The person you did not want the police involved about?" Michael did not respond, and it pissed me off. "Is this your baby, mama's doing?" I yell.

Sara rushes from the back to see what the ruckus is about. She sees Michael and starts attacking him.

Sara is in full attack mode. "What the hell you are doing here?"

Michael did not know what hit him. He did not know whether to answer me or answer Sara. He kept looking between Sara and me.

Cobby quickly intervenes. "We will sort out who has done it later, but for now, let's clean up to get the gallery running." He squeezes my hand as he ushers me toward the front of the room. He confesses, "You know Michael is miserable without you?"

I give Cobby a stern look and reply, "I don't want to hear this right now. It's because of him that I am in this predicament."

I know Cobby is looking out for his boy but being miserable is none of my concern.

Cobby continues to defend Michael, "He is trying hard to make amends and trying to be a better person."

It's annoying that Cobby is defending Michael. I cannot deal with this right now. I walk away, leaving Cobby standing in the middle of the gallery.

I continue picking up the glass in the front alone. I need this time alone to really assess it is worth getting in bed with Michael and his issues. I am furious with Michael; nevertheless, I'm happy to see him. My addiction to this man is dangerous. He walks over to me as if he knows what I'm thinking.

He whispers, "I miss you, Jazz." I just look at him as if he is crazy. Michael continues, "I'm dealing with some fucked up shit, I want to turn to you, but it will not be fair to get you involve in my shit."

I would have helped him regardless. I'm still processing this whole predicament I am in.

I try one last time, "Michael, do you think your ex-girlfriend trash my gallery?"

He pauses and asks me to sit down. I take a deep breath, sensing that whatever he has to tell me is serious because he has a way of rubbing his head whenever he is stressed. I sit down, and he pulls a chair to sit across from me.

He begins with a deep breath, "Back in Chicago, I dated this young lady named Mona. We dated for three years. She wanted a committed relationship, and I wasn't ready to commit to anyone at that time. Things got weird. She became very controlling. I could not spend time with friends. Every time I turned around; she was there. I broke it off, and this was when things started to get really complicated. She created a fake page on social media announcing we got married. She posted photoshopped pictures of us on our honeymoon and tagged all my friends and colleagues."

"What kind of twisted woman do you go to bed with? How many crazy women you're dealing with?" I ask.

Michael ignores my question and continues," I was not aware of what she had done until Cobby called me, and he was upset about the fact that I got married without inviting him."

I understand why Cobby would be upset. If Sara had gotten married without my knowledge, I would have killed her. I stay quiet as I listen to Michael's story.

"I thought Cobby was joking until he sent me the link to the page. I demanded that she take the page down, or I was going to report her to the authorities," he explains.

So, from what Michael is telling me, it may be his crazy baby mama who's harassing him or trashed the gallery. But then again, she's in Chicago. How many women is he involved with? OMG! Now, I understand why he asked if I was down with a man who dates multiple women. Why didn't I go with my gut feeling from the beginning?

Michael continues, "When she refused to take the page down, I had to file a complaint to have the page shut down. I called friends and colleagues and told them that the page was fake, and I did not get married. She was enraged that they took the page down. She would show up at my office to make a scene. One day she showed up with bruises on her face, and she claimed that I physically abused her."

Wow! This bitch is crazier than I thought. I remain quiet and let Michael continues.

Michael shifts in his seat as he is telling the story. He continues, "She keyed my brand-new Mercedes. She slashed my tires. I eventually had a restraining order issued against her."

I wonder what could have driven her over the edge. Was Michael playing her? What lies was he feeding her?

Finally, I ask, "What led her to be that possessive? Did you promise exclusivity, and she found out you had other women?"

"How could I have made it clearer to her? I told her that I was not ready for a committed relationship," he confesses as he attempts to reach for my hand.

I reply, "See, that's where you were wrong. I am betting money; although you stated that you didn't want a meaningful relationship, you two did things like a couple would have done, right?"

He looks confused, "Yeah, how else would we have acted?"

His ignorance annoys me. I comment, "Why is it men are quick to tell women they are not ready for a meaningful relationship yet expect us to act like wifey? That gray area cowardice breaks lots of hearts. You wonder why women become bitter. You'll be afraid of a commitment then have the nerve to get mad when another man sees our value."

Michael continues with his BS, "Although there was a restraining order against her, the harassment did not stop. One day she broke into my house, installed a crib, and put baby clothes in my spare bedroom."

Okay, this woman was creative and crazy, I thought.

Michael goes on, "When I got home, she was in the bedroom breastfeeding a doll. I honestly never realized how deranged she was. I called the police, and she was arrested for violating the restraining order. That's when Cobby suggested that I leave Chicago."

I reply, "I was right when I said that you were running away from something."

He rubs his head, "Yes, you were right. I was too ashamed to tell you then. It seems my past life has caught up with me."

Well, damn! How many women did this dude piss off in Chicago? First, it was his baby mama. Now, this deranged doll breastfeeding bitch. He can sense my apprehension. He grabs my hands and pulls me closer.

He confesses, "I didn't want you to worry; that was the reason I didn't tell you."

I pull away from him, "It is too late now! This deranged woman found out about me, and now I am a target."

He replies, "Jazz, I will do everything in my power to keep you safe."

I ask him, "How is that possible? She has an advantage. She knows who I am. I do not know who she is. How am I supposed to feel safe when my gallery was vandalized?"

I hope the camera was able to capture an image of the person. Michael tries his best to appease my worries. I am more concerned now that I do not know this batshit crazy lady. Oh, my stomach, I think I am going to get sick. I rush to the bathroom to throw up. Michael follows me into the bathroom to make sure that I'm okay. He helps me in the stall, holding my hair while stroking my back. I clean my face and step outside, leaving Michael in the bathroom.

It's already mid-morning, and the gallery still is not completely clean. We need reinforcement. I call Misha and Nadine, update them on the break-in, and ask for their help. Misha is already at work but promises to come by after she's done. Nadine says she's on her way with her "boy du jour." Nadine has a new boy toy every week. Hey! I ain't mad at her. Men do it all the time. Why can't she do it too?

I realize that it's Laycee's day off, but I think it will be okay under the circumstances. She sounds asleep when she answers, "Hello, Jazz, what's going on?"

I explain, "Laycee, I am sorry to call you so early on your day off. There was a break-in at the gallery. I need your help cleaning up before we can open."

She takes a deep breath, "Are you okay? Do the police know who did it?"

I reply, "It's too soon to know. The police are going through the security footage and hope that they'll be able to identify the person."

She sighs, sounding a little more relaxed, "I don't think the footage will be helpful."

Puzzled by her comment, nevertheless, I ask, "Are you able to come and help us with the cleaning?"

She replies, "I have to make arrangements for my son. I will be there as soon as possible."

The sun started to peek its head out. Feeling overwhelmed, I need to get out of the gallery. I walk by Sara and Cobby, who are in a deep conversation. I walk right by them to go outside. My head is about to explode. I keep asking myself over and over. How did I get here? Why am I allowing this man to drag me down with his drama? I walk across the street to the neighborhood coffee shop to get a cup of tea. It's early, so the regular customers have not arrived, which means I can quietly drink my tea and sit by the window facing the gallery. I am a regular at the café. I just say, "good morning."

The perky young cashier asks, "Your regular Chai Latte and a pain perdu?" I give her a faint smile and shake my head. "Yes."

I wish I had her energy this morning, but this thing with Michael has taken all my energy. The café is small but inviting. The tables are set on both sides of the room, creating an isle in the middle.

There are three booths in the back, which I like for privacy. I take my usual seat, the booth facing the gallery. Looking at the gallery from the café looks like a hurricane struck it. I have an eerie feeling that the storm is not over. Michael steps out of the gallery looking in each direction. My guess is he is looking for me. He reaches in his pocket, pulls out his phone, looks at it, and pulls it to his ear. Observing the coffee shop, I watch him pacing back and forth, rubbing his head, and using his fist, illustrating his anger with whoever is on the other line. I have never seen Michael this upset. The young cashier brings my order to the booth. I slowly sip my tea while observing Michael pacing up and down the sidewalk. I take one bite of the pain perdu, though I have no appetite. I just drop it on my tray and drink the latte instead. I need to head back to the gallery because we still have lots to clean up. I finish my tea then step out of the café. Michael notices me across the street. He takes a deep breath as a sign of relief and crosses over to meet me. He looks worried.

"Jazz, I don't think it's a wise idea for you to walk around alone." He pleads for me to think cautiously.

I give him a puzzled look, "I just went across the street to get tea."

He is still looking around as he ushers me back into the coffee shop. Now, I am worried. I ask, "Michael, what's going on?"

I sense Michael knows something, and he is not telling me. He continues ushering me into the café.

I stop in the middle of the café then yell, "I am not taking another step until you tell me what is going on!"

By then, customers are coming in to get their morning coffee. The few customers that are in the shop turn and stare at us. Embarrassed, I walk back to my regular booth for privacy. Michael follows me.

With a lower voice, I ask, "Who was on the phone?"

With a stunned look on his face, he takes a deep breath and rubs his head

I ask him again, "Was it your ex, Chantae?"

In a deep breath, Michael replies, "Yes. And I think she's close by."

My antenna senses danger. I'm looking around from the window as if I know what his ex looks like. My hands started to shake.

Michael grabs my hands, "I won't let anything happen to you. I will do everything to protect you."

I pull my hands away from him and ask, "How can you protect me from this maniac?"

He senses that I am scared. Michael tries to put his arms around me. I push him away, causing a loud thump. The young cashier rushes over and asks, "Ms. Jasmine is everything okay?"

I say, "I am okay. I was just leaving."

With a suspicious look, she walks back to the counter. Nosey customers are looking in our direction as well. Just as I'm about to leave, Michael attempts to hug me. I push him to break free. He only holds me tighter refuses to let go. I pounce on his chest while screaming, "Let me go, you lying sack of shit."

By now, the customers are on high alert. A man has his phone out and asks, "Do you need me to call the police, chère?"

I realize then that I'm making a scene and scaring the customers. Without a word, I run out, making my way to the gallery. Michael follows me outside, trying to calm me down. This time I surrender. I did not have the strength to fight him off. I let the flood of tears break free. He keeps whispering, "I am sorry for all of it."

I have to get back to the gallery to help Sara and Cobby with the cleaning. I muster enough strength to pull away from Michael. He tries to follow me to the gallery.

I stop him and yell, "You've done enough damage for one day. Stay the hell out of my life and my gallery."

There's nothing I can do about this predicament. As I enter the gallery, Sara comes running to meet me, "What the hell happened?"

With tears in my eyes, I tell Sara, "One of Michael's exes is stalking me."

"What the hell do you mean one of his exes? And how do you know this?" Sara asks.

I didn't' want to get into it, but Sara has the right to know, "From what Michael tells me, he thinks his ex-girlfriend followed him here from Chicago."

Sara replies, "Are you sure? You think there's more than one person?"

In one breath, I reply, "Yes. He also has a baby mama."

Cobby comes around to see what's going on. He looks at me and opens his arms. I oblige and run to him. I just let the tears just fall as he hugs me.

Cobby whispers, "I am so sorry that you're in so much pain. Don't worry about the gallery. I will help you with the cleanup and have it re-open in no time."

Sara put her arms around me, "Don't worry, I got you. We are in this together."

The tears will not stop flowing as they try to console me. I thought Michael left after I told him to stay away; instead, I see him standing in the doorway, watching me crying my eyes out in Cobby's arms. His eyes were fixed on Cobby. Sara turns and sees Michael and walks over to him to unleashes her wrath. Her anger pushes her body up, so she is poised on her toes, trying to look Michael directly in the face, "You shit-faced liar. It's your fault the gallery was destroyed."

In any other circumstance, I would burst out laughing at the sight of Sara's barely over five-foot-two self, trying to go toe-to-toe with a man a whole foot and an inch taller than her. But I don't. She's feeling everything I was, and she was fierce.

She yells, "Haven't you done enough?"

Michael did not back down from her verbal abuse. He shouts back, "Sara, I am not here for your shit. I just want to make sure that Jazzy is okay."

Oh, she went in, "Are you stupid? Does she look like she is doing fine? What else do you feel the need to do?"

I did not tell Sara the latest news, that one of the crazy girl-friends may be watching us as we speak. Michael looks for me to rescue him from Sara's wrath. He brought it upon himself. I just give him the evil eye.

Michael shakes his head and tries to walk past Sara to get to me. She jumps in front of him, jabs him with both hands in his chest, and yells," She doesn't need you, Get the hell out of here!"

Michael looks at me to see if I agree with Sara's demand. I glance at him to let him know hell yeah, I agree.

Cobby jumps in and replies, "Mike, your being here is not helping the situation. I'll drive you home. It'll give you a chance to think about your next move."

Michael was about to contest. Cobby gets in his face and says, "Listen man, you should go home. NOW."

Michael holds his hands up, then exits the gallery. Cobby follows him out of the door. I collapse on the floor and start sobbing. Sara helps me off the floor and to the chair in the corner to sit down.

CHAPTER 15

The Confrontation

I was sure of one thing, leaving Jazz and Sara at the gallery by themselves, knowing that Mona might be watching the gallery was not smart or safe. This nightmare will never end. I did not tell Jazz how far Mona could go to get what she wanted. Cobby realizes that I'm in deep thought. I'm sure, like me, he's trying to figure out how to handle this situation.

Cobby yells while driving, "Michael, you have got to tell Jasmine the truth."

I reply, "Cob, it's more complicated than that."

With aggravation in his voice, Cobby says, "Dammit Mike, uncomplicate it. I told you to clean your shit up. Now you got Jasmine in the middle of this shit, which she doesn't deserve."

"Mona is in New Orleans," I confess to Cobby.

Cobby hits on the brake, causing my head to hit the dashboard, "Fuck man, why did you have to brake so hard?" I scold Cobby.

He replies, "Your crazy ex is here, in New Orleans." As he pulls over on the side of the road.

I step outside the truck, holding my head as if I'd been hit by a brick. The morning sun has already peeked its head. It's hard to breathe, not because of the humidity, but because I'm going to relive the horrible torment Mona put me through. Cobby steps out of the truck and walks to the passenger's side. With a defeated look, I say, "I don't know why Mona is doing this."

Cobby's jaw is clenched. He says, "Well, for starters, you will accept some responsibility for her actions and reactions. Mike, you will never be free from this until you look at yourself in the mirror and see the part you played in this tragedy."

I reply, "I tried to reason with Mona several times before I moved. She is insane."

He crawls back in the truck, slams the door to make his point. I don't understand why he is mad. If anyone should be furious, it should be me. He says, "Man get your ass in the truck and let me take you home."

I explain, "Cobby, I did not know Mona was crazy before I got involved with her."

Cobby just grunts and stays silent for the rest of the drive. My head is throbbing, so I decide to stop talking too. We arrive at the house, and Cobby finally speaks up, "Open the door Mike, I want to show you something."

I look at him with a confused look and ask, "What do I have in my house that you need to show?"

In an impatient tone, he says, "Open the damn door."

I open the door and Cobby pushes his way into the house. Standing in the living room, he asks, "Has Jasmine ever come to your house Mike?"

I'm not sure where Cobby was getting, so I reply, "No, but…"

Cobby cuts me off and says, "And you want to know why she has not been in your house?" He walks to the glass bookshelf and grabs a picture from a shelf.

I did know how to answer that. Cobby gets closer to my face holding a picture of my ex-fiancée. His actions hit me like a brick. He says, "That's right, Chantae. How long has she been dead? You have not taken responsibility for her death."

My chest got tighter. I push past Cobby, walk to the kitchen to pour myself a drink. I can't believe Cobby wants to accuse me of not taking responsibility for Chantae's death.

I met Chantae in college in Chicago. She was timid and sweet. I approached her, thinking this was another girl I could add to my collection. She would be just like the others, a temporary fix. I was wrong about her. Chantae was driven, intelligent, and independent. She reminded me of my mother. After dating for two years, I realized that I could spend the rest of my life with this woman. She was the drug I needed. I decided to ask her to marry me. This was when all hell broke loose.

I was lost in my thoughts and did not realize Cobby was talking or yelling at me about something. To shut him up, I point to my glass, then ask, "Do you want a glass of this rum?"

He shakes his head, "it's too early in the day to be drinking man."

"Well, more for me." I pour another drink and guzzle it down.

This drink serves as a painkiller. I walk over to where Chantae's picture as I say, "I loved this woman, Cob. I did not think that I could love anyone like that. Especially after my mother's death. I was so mad when Mom died."

Cobby takes a seat in the living room. He shifts uncomfortably in his chair and says, "I remember man, you were a mess when your mom died. But Mike, how long you're going to be mad at her for dying?"

I roll my shoulders to release the tension and reply, "Cob, my mother's death could have been prevented if she wasn't so stubborn."

Cobby flexes his chest as he's about to speak, "Mike, you can't keep using your mother's death as an excuse for your behavior."

I take another gulp of my drink, not because I need it but because I want it to prevent me from hitting Cobby. I walk back to the kitchen to get the bottle of rum. This time I did not use the glass. I bring the bottle to my mouth and take a big gulp.

Cobby continues with his attack, "You need therapy for your mommy issues."

This time I could not contain myself. I explode, "Man, fuck you! Where the hell do you get off saying that I have mommy issues?"

Cobby stands in the middle of the living room and yells, "No, Mike fuck you for being so screwed up that you can't see the pain you're causing the people who love you."

He picks up Chantae's picture once more and says, "Exhibit A, this woman loved you, and what did you do? You went and fucked her sister and got her pregnant."

"Oh, that's a low blow, even for you Cobby," I scream.

Still holding Chantae's picture, he walks to the kitchen and puts the photo on the counter. "Have you ever wondered t if you weren't so selfish, Chantae might still be alive?"

Without thinking, I pick up Chantae's picture and slam it on the counter, causing the glass to shatter on the floor and counter. "You don't think that I live with the guilt of Chantae's death every day? Who the fuck are you to judge me on how I live my life? I loved Chantae."

Cobby shouts back, "Mike, you know nothing about love even if it slaps you in your face."

I take another gulp to stop the knife that Cobby keeps digging in my wound. I reply, "You think I wanted her sister to get pregnant? How did I know that Mona was crazy enough to tell her sister about our affair?"

"Dammit Mike, stop playing the victim and accept your role in this," Cobby replies, hearing the frustration in his voice.

His words have me hot. I decided to school Cobby. I reply, "You don't know what the hell you're talking about. You don't think that I live with the guilt of Chantae's death every day. She killed herself in my apartment." I take another gulp from the rum before I continue, "If I did not sleep with her sister, she would still be alive."

Cobby's face softens a little before he replies, "Mike, I know how painful it was for you. Man, you need to go see a therapist. And don't tell me this bullshit that black people don't go to therapy. That's the problem. Y'all walk around with unresolved hurts and trying to function."

Shaking my head, I say, "I don't need a damn therapist."

Cobby throws his hands up as a sign of surrender, "Then you will always be in the predicament you're in now."

He turns around to showcase the apartment, then he says, "Take a look around this apartment and tell me if you don't see anything wrong. You have your dead fiancé's pictures all over your apartment. Oh, why does Jasmine never step foot in your apartment?"

Cobby stops and looks at me, "And you don't see the need to see a therapist." He picks up his keys that were on the kitchen table and comments, "Well, I can see there's no getting through you. I'm going back to help the ladies with the gallery. You do what you want."

Cobby slams the door behind him. I pick Chantae's picture up from the shattered frame, and with the rest of the rum, drag myself to my bedroom.

Usually, I would welcome the bright sun shining through my room. Today I'll trade the windows for blackout curtains. Chantae looked so happy in the picture. I took that picture while she was sitting under a tree, smiling while the sun caressed her face. She committed suicide two months after the photo was taken.

Chantae's death shook me to the core. I never met a woman like her. She was fierce, kind-hearted, independent, sexy as hell, and most importantly, she loved me despite my flaws. She reminded me of my mother. After my mother's death, I swore that I would never get too close to women. It was different with Chantae. She could see right through my bullshit, kinda like Jazz.

It was a mistake sleeping with Chantae's sister. It really didn't mean anything. She was jealous of Chantae and wanted to get back at her. I did not even know she was pregnant until Chantae confronted me. It was a different kind of betrayal. I did not know how to fix it.

Chantae confronted me in my apartment when she found out that I slept with Mona. The hurt and disgust in her eyes made me feel like the scum on the earth. It was a rainy night. She showed up with wet hair, bloodshot eyes. I knew she'd been devastated. Still, I was alarmed because I'd never seen her in that state.

She stood in the living room, shivering. She removed her hand from her coat pocket and handed me a sonogram picture. With a confused look, I asked, "What's this?"

She answered, "This is your baby."

My face lightened up, thinking that Chantae and I were going to have a baby. I asked, "We're having a baby?" As I rushed to give her a hug. She held out her hands in front of her stopping me from getting closer.

I was confused. Why was Chantae acting so strange? She just gave me the happiest news. The woman that I love was pregnant. She should be happy. Instead, she's rambling on about her sister.

"Chant, you just told me that we're going to have a baby," I was trying to figure out what she was talking about.

She let out a long deep breath, then replied, "You and I are not going to have a baby. You're having a baby with my sister." Tears rolling down her face, she asked, "Why my sister Mike? You could have had any woman in Chicago. Oh wait! Correction, you had every woman in Chicago. To make matters worse, she is pregnant with your child. How do I compete with that?"

I was speechless. I could see how disappointed and hurt Chantae was from the revelation. I tried to explain, "It was a mistake Chantae. It did not mean anything. I did not mean to hurt you. I love you."

I could see the anger in her eyes. She walked over, slapped me, then said, "You're disgusting. You don't give a damn who you hurt. As long as you got your fix." She moved closer then yelled, "I can't help you with your mommy issues. I am done. You and my sister deserve each other. I hate you." She stormed out.

CHAPTER 16

Strange Girl

Laycee enters the gallery from the back door. Assessing the gallery with a shocked tone, she says, "Oh My God! I did not know how serious the damages were."

I reply, "Thank you for coming on your day off to help with the cleaning."

With a faint smile, she says, "That's at least I can do. You've been there for me when I needed help. Anything you need, I am here for you."

Sara suggests that I go home because I'm too upset. I protest, "I am fine Sisi. I just want to keep busy. I want to help with the cleanup. Besides, I want to stay busy to keep my mind off Michael's new revelation that his crazy girlfriends are after me."

Laycee replies, "I am so sorry you're going through this."

She seems genuinely concerned. I reassure, "Laycee, you don't have to worry. You still have a job here. Minor vandalism is not going to stop me."

Sara insists that I go home and rest. Laycee is standing in the doorway with a strange look. Finally, she says, "You don't look so well. I can take you home if you don't feel like driving."

I politely decline Laycee's proposition, "I'm okay to drive home, but thank you."

She quickly replies, "It's not a problem. Besides, you don't look so well. I wouldn't want anything to happen to you on your way home."

Sara thought Laycee driving me home was a safer move. I feel bad leaving her to clean the gallery, but I am an emotional wreck. It's better that I go home.

During the drive home, Laycee seems concerned. Glancing at me, she announces. "Why would someone destroy the gallery? Do the police know who did it and why?"

I refrain from telling her Michael's revelation.

It's sweet that Laycee is worried about the gallery. Trying to appease her concern, I offer, "The police are investigating, and I am sure we will know something soon." I opt to change the subject, not wanting to bring myself down. "How's your son settling in the new apartment?"

She smiles, "He loves the apartment, especially the park across the street."

I called in a favor from my former landlord to help Laycee get the apartment. She was so happy when she moved a few blocks from my apartment. We reach my apartment. Laycee offers to come up to make me tea. I wanted to be alone, but I didn't refuse her kind gesture. She walks upstairs straight to the kitchen. She made me a cup of chamomile tea with honey. There's something about tea that speaks to your soul. This is just what I needed. I feel lightheaded, so I walk to my room to lay down, expecting Laycee to take the hint and leave. To my surprise, she follows me to my room, which I think is strange. Laycee has visited my apartment, but she never goes into my bedroom. Another red flag. She has been acting odd since she found out about the break-in.

I turn to her and explain, "Laycee, I am tired, and I just want to go to sleep. Thanks for driving me home."

Standing in the doorway of my bedroom with an awkward look, "Is this your boyfriend?" She asks.

Funny, I never really noticed the picture on my nightstand until she pointed it out. Michael and I took that picture on our fourth date. He surprised me by framing it and sending it to me with a box of chocolate with a card that read

Looking forward to many more memories with you!

I thought that was a sweet gesture. Laycee scratches her throat. I must have drifted for a few seconds and did not realize that she was still talking. Michael has that effect on me.

I reply, "It's someone I was seeing."

I figure if I answer her question, she will leave. She heads to walk over to pick up the frame. I got a little short, "Laycee, I am tired. Please leave."

With a smirk on her face, "I am so sorry, I did not mean to upset you. I'll leave for you to rest."

I walk her out then close the door behind her. As I'm making my way to the bedroom, my phone ring. I glance over and notice it's Michael. I let it go to voicemail because I did not have the energy to speak with him. He did not leave a message, but he called right back. It doesn't look that I'm going to get any rest. I answer the call.

Michael did not even let me say hello. He quickly says, "Please don't hang up."

I reply, "What the hell do you want?"

Michael replies, "Cobby told me that you were not feeling well. You went home."

I made a mental note to cuss Cobby out the next time I see him.

I'm exhausted, and I don't want to deal with him, "Michael, I am fine. Please STOP calling me."

I end the call. Not even one second passes, the phone rings again. This time I did not say a word.

I hear Michael take a deep breath, "Jazzy, can't you understand that I can't leave you alone even if I want to?"

I ask him, "Why can't you leave me alone? Don't you have enough women in your life? I just want to be left alone."

I can feel the raging heat surrounding my face. I didn't give him a chance to reply. I hung up the phone mid-sentence. I pour myself a glass of wine before I crawl into bed with a throbbing headache. The sun is shining outside. I close the curtains in my room to have total darkness.

I fall fast asleep. I'm awakened by a loud noise. I jump up, try-ing to figure out where the noise is coming from. It takes me a few minutes to realize that someone's banging on my door. Now my adrenaline is running high. I grab the baseball bat that's in my closet. I rush to the door with it in hand, ready for action. I swing open the door, ready to confront whoever is on the other side.

As I'm ready to swing the bat, Michael yells, "Jazz, it's me."

With a surprised look, I ask, "What the hell are you doing here Michael?"

He grabs the bat from me, walks in, and puts it down on the coffee table. Standing in my living room, his body tense, he states, "Jasmine, you are the most stubborn, infuriating woman I have ever known."

I yell," Listen, you son-of-a-bitch, how dare you come in my house acting like you have no sense! Have you lost your mind?"

He cuts me off, "Yes, I have lost my mind the very first day that I met you."

I did not expect that response.

He continues, "I have always dated multiple women. It was always clear to them that I wasn't looking for exclusivity." Michael rubs his head as he paces in the living room. "Since I met you, all I wanted is to be with you and you alone. The truth …" He stops, rubbing his head again.

I reply, "The truth is what?"

He walks over and takes my hand and leads me to the couch. He continues, "The truth is that I am in love with you."

This revelation hit me like a brick. I did not know how to respond.

Michael continues, "I have made lots of mistakes when it comes to relationships. Now, I am dealing with the consequences of my mistakes. It's not fair to you because you are in the middle of my mess. Jazzy, believe me, I am trying to clean the mess I've made. I should have straightened up shit before I got involved with you. I know that now. I thought that I could handle it."

I have no energy to respond to Michael's confession. He continues, "I never meant to jeopardize your business or your safety. I promise you; I will take care of it. I just need you to be patient with me and be safe."

CHAPTER 17

The Lies

I'm still on the "I'm in love with you" statement. I stop listening to the rest of his conversation.

"Did you hear anything I said Jazzy?" He asks.

I shake my head, yes, but I lie. As he's about to continue. I hold my hand up to stop him from speaking. I explain, "I want to believe you, I do, but my instinct is telling me to run."

He looks confused, "What exactly don't you believe in what I am telling you?"

I realized Michael never directly told me if he sees other women. This is his opportunity to come clean. Not sure if I really want to know the answer, but I ask anyway, "Are you seeing other women?"

He rubs his head and asks that I take a seat. Now, I regret asking the question. He starts, "My mother raised me as a single parent. My mother was a gentle soul. She worked hard to take care of me and everyone else who was in need. Mother was also a proud woman. No one would know when she was hurting. Growing up, I can't remember ever seeing my mother sick or in bed because she wasn't feeling well. One day Mom passed out while cooking. I called my neighbors for help. They took her to the nearest hospital for observation. The doctors said that Mom had a large tumor, putting pressure on her brain, causing her to blackout. Mom complained of headaches, I begged her to go to the doctor, but she said she was okay. She just needs rest. Mom did not have health insurance. She died due to the complication of the brain tumor. I was devastated when my mother died. She was my world, my everything. I was never the same after her death. I was angry at my mother for leaving me. My mother's death plays an instrumental role in my relationships. I did not fully dedicate my heart to anyone. To answer your question, yes, I dated multiple women. I know that I hurt a lot of women. I made a mess of my life and theirs."

Michael's revelation is too heavy for me to process. But this is my opportunity to find the underlying cause of this, so I continue with the questions. "How do I know it's not the same thing you are doing to me?"

He replies, "I don't know what it is about you Jazzy, you make me want to be a better person. You make me think that I can have a better life and, to be honest, there's no other woman who ever made me feel this way. Cobby even commented that I would be stupid to let you go. He is right. I am not stupid Jazzy; I see us growing old together. I just need time to fix this mess I made of my life."

Once again, my heart said just give him a chance, but my logical sense said don't do it. He will only bring you pain and misery.

I ask, "How much time?"

His eyes widen with disbelief. He rushes over to the couch, grabs my face, and kisses me. I hesitate for a minute because I'm still processing Michael's confession. He kisses me again, and this time I respond. That's the invitation he needed. Michael pulls me closer and kisses me with passion. How I've missed this sensation. I am about to pass out with his kiss. I wrap my arms around his neck and respond to his kiss. Michael picks me up and carries me to my bedroom. He gently puts me on my bed and begins to kiss me, caressing my breasts over my t-shirt. He unbuttons his shirt while he keeps his eyes on me. I love watching Michael undress. He takes loving care of his body, and it shows. I run my hand over his chest and his six-pack. I keep moving my hand up and down his chest. He loves it. I sit up on the bed to heighten my height as I start kissing his neck, his earlobe, one of his sensitive spots. I can hear him moaning already.

He holds me tight for a minute. "I miss you so much," he whispers.

That's the ammunition I needed. I forcefully kiss him, my way to tell him that I missed him too. I plant soft kisses on his chest, his nipples, his other sensitive spot. He allows me to finish undressing him. I unzipped his pants and let them drop on the floor. He lifts his foot one by one to step out of his pants. Taking a deep breath once again, admiring this man's physique. I can see his erection through his sexy boxers. He stepped back for me to admire the artwork.

Michael says jokingly, "You like?"

I bite my lower lip, feeling like a little girl in the candy shop. "YES!" My voice rose several octaves.

He drops his boxers and replies, "Well, come get some woman."

I leap off the bed then jump on his arms, nearly knocking him over. Good thing he is strong. He catches me, throws me on the bed, climbs atop of me as we laugh.

Stopping suddenly, he frowns for a minute, then he replies, "I am really sorry."

I put my finger to his lips to shut him up. Michael obliges and kisses my finger, my palm, then my breasts. He moves to my belly button, then my inner thighs. He is driving me crazy. He continues with his assault as he gently bites my inner thighs. He moves toward my sex; I tremble with desire. This man knows how to please me. He knows all my hot buttons. I grab the pillows as he continues tickling my clitoris with his tongue. I hold his head to direct his movement. I'm about to explode. He pauses and says, "Not yet."

He retrieves his pants from the floor and pulls out a condom. He put it on. With a devilish smile, he says, "Are you ready?"

I've been ready, so I shake my head yes as I brace myself. Michael gently pushes forward. I inhale, accepting what is to come. I have an out-of-body experience every time Michael and I make love. It is not something that I can explain. His slow rhythm makes it easier to fol-low his every stroke. His strokes deepen as he moves faster. We erupt together intensely. It was glorious. Michael lies still on me, trying to catch his breath.

Finally, I say jokingly, "Get off me. You're too heavy."

He looks down, rolls his eyes, and says, "Oh, NOW I am too heavy?"

Laughter fills the room. Michael rolls to the other side of the bed. We stare silently at the ceiling without a word to each other.

Finally, I break the silence, "Just because we had sex doesn't mean that I am not still pissed."

He pulls me close and rests my head on his chest, "I know, and I promise things will get better." He kisses my forehead then wraps both arms around me.

We both must have been tired from our sexcapades because we were sleeping when a loud bang came from the parking lot. Someone's car alarm is going off as well. I peek through my bedroom window and notice a shadow. I can't quite make out if it is a male or female. It's just a silhouette of the person with a baseball bat running away from Michael's car. I yell out for him to wake up. He quickly jumps up with a confused look and asks, "What is it?"

"Someone is around your truck with a baseball bat."

Fully awake, he yells, "Call the police and stay inside." He put on his pants and sprints out of the bedroom. I grab my phone and dial 911. I'm walking behind Michael. He turns around and yells, "Stay here," as if he is scolding a child.

A monotone male voice came on the line. He answers, "911, what is your emergency?"

I was talking really fast. I reply, "Someone just broke my boyfriend's window."

The word boyfriend startled me. I noticed a slight grin on Michael's face when he heard my words. I am not sure why I called him that. I will have to deal with that later.

The operator asks, "Is the perpetrator still around?"

I answer in a panicked tone, "I saw someone running away from the car when the alarm went off."

With no sense of urgency, the operator asks, "Are you able to identify the perp?"

"No!" I reply. "I couldn't tell if it was a male or a female."

The operator announces, "The police are on the way."

I hang up the phone with the operator and try to follow Michael outside.

"I thought I told you to stay inside!" Michael yells.

I explain, "You're going to need me if we need to throw some blow. What if it's more than one person?"

He replies, "That's exactly why I want you to stay inside."

I walk right past him. Michael had no choice but to follow me outside.

"You are the most stubborn person I have ever met," Michael hisses through his teeth.

I ignore him as we walk toward the truck to investigate. Whoever did this is terribly angry. They spray-painted the word "revenge" in red on Michael's truck. There's a brick sitting on the driver's side. A folded piece of paper is attached to the brick with a rubber band. His tires are slashed again. I'm mortified that a person would go to this length to get back at Michael.

Curiously, I say," There's a note. Let's read it."

Michael quickly grabs my hand, "Don't touch anything. Let's wait for the police."

As we are waiting for the police, I ask, "Is this your ex-girlfriend?"

He quickly responds, "I don't know Jazz."

Just when he's about to explain, a patrol car pulls up beside us with the spotlight shining on us. Michael and I walk toward the car as both officers get out of the patrol car. Ironically, it's the same officers that responded to the burglary at the gallery.

The younger officer addresses us first. His name is Officer Ortiz, according to his badge. Officer Ortiz looks like he just came out of the academy. He is tall with dark hair with a slender physique. Officer Broussard, the older officer, looks like he is ready for retirement. He is short, bald, and with a full mustache.

Officer Ortiz asks, "What the problem here?"

Michael answers, "Someone vandalized my truck."

Both officers turn around to look at the truck. Officer Broussard takes out his flashlight and walks toward the vehicle to investigate while Officer Ortiz asks. "Do you have any idea who would have done this?"

We both look at each other. I respond, "We think it's his ex-girlfriend."

Officer Ortiz pulls out his notebook and continues with his inquiries, "Do you know where I can find this person?"

I look at Michael while I cross my arms and say, "Yeah, do you know where I can find her so that I can go and kick her ass for trashing my gallery?"

He is doing that thing when he is stressed, or his back is against a wall. Michael rubs his head and begins to pace.

Officer Ortiz impatiently asks, "Sir, what's your ex-girlfriend's name, and do you know where I can find her?"

I can see that Michael did not want to answer the officer's question. Now, I'm pissed because he is hiding something.

I turn my back from Michael to face the officer. I reply, "Her name is Chantae, and according to Michael, she must have followed him from Chicago."

The officer addresses Michael again while the other assesses the truck, "Sir, is this correct?"

Michael said, "No, not exactly."

Now, I am hot. I turn to Michael and yell, "What you mean, not exactly?"

Officer Ortiz senses that I'm about to go off on Michael. He turns to me and states, "Ma'am, can you please go stand over there while I get this sorted out?" He points to the front of the apartment.

I did not want to go anywhere until this lying bastard came clean.

The officer asks me again, but this time in a stern tone, "Ma'am, please go and stand over there while I question the gentleman. I will come over to take your statement."

I walk away like a spoiled child throwing a tantrum. I stand in front of the apartment building with my hands folded, still pissed at Michael.

Observing from afar, Michael appeared more open to talking to the officer after I left. Officer Ortiz did not make eye contact. He was writing in his notebook as Michael is talking. What the hell is Michael hiding from me? I am going to get all his secrets revealed

TONIGHT. I am not going to put up with his bullshit any longer. In my head, I am conjuring a plan to get Michael to open up and tell me what he is hiding. I want to know what he meant when he said "not exactly" when I explained to the officer about his ex-girlfriend. He better not be sleeping with her still. I wanted to march across the parking lot and demand answers from him, but I did not want to risk getting arrested. I stay in front of the apartment like an obedient dog waiting for my master to summon me.

Forty-five minutes later, Officer Ortiz walks across the parking lot to come to speak with me. My arms are still crossed when he addresses me. He asks the usual questions, my name, date of birth if I live in the building. I reply in a harsh tone, "Jasmine, and yes, I live here." I realize that he is just doing his job. So, I tone it down.

When I tell him my name, he looks up, "Are you the same Jasmine whose gallery was broken into?"

"YES! The same," I responded, frustrated yet trying to remain professional.

He looks back in Michael's direction then asks, "Do you think both incidents are related?"

In my head, I reply, what do you think, Sherlock? But I tone down my sarcasm as I respond, "I seriously think that his ex-girlfriend is behind this."

He continues, "Have you seen this ex-girlfriend before?"

I reply, "According to Michael, she followed him from Chicago. I was not aware of an ex until the break-in at the gallery. I don't know what she looks like, and frankly, I am afraid because she knows where I live. She knows more about me than I know about her."

He was silent for a minute while writing whatever he was writing in his notebook.

I interrupted his thoughts by asking him, "Is there any development on the break-in at the gallery?"

Officer Ortiz holds his hand up to stop me in mid-sentence and replies, "No development yet. The case was transferred to Detective Jules Boudreau."

I thought to myself, a detective. "When can I speak to Detective Boudreau? As you can see, this is serious."

Officer Ortiz hands me the detective's number and states that the detective will contact me. In other words, don't call him. I'm upset because of this officer's nonchalant response. My life is turned upside down by a psycho, and I can't do anything to protect myself. This woman can be anyone I meet every day, and I wouldn't even know who she is.

To make matters worse, Michael is protecting her. He must have a picture of her. I am going to demand that he show me a photo of her tonight. This is bullshit. Instead of protecting me, he is protecting her identity.

Officer Ortiz is still writing in his notebook when Officer Broussard walks over and says, "I couldn't lift any prints from the truck."

I look at both officers and think, what a waste of time. I should have listened to Michael and stayed inside. Now, I am so angry, I can explode. I left the men in the parking lot and went up to my apartment. It's already eleven p.m., and I'm exhausted. More importantly, I'm pissed at Michael, the officers, and myself. Sitting on the couch waiting for Michael to come up, I rehearse the list of questions that I will ask him. I need to calm myself down. I need to make tea. While in the kitchen, the door opens. I brace myself because the shit is about to go down. He comes into the kitchen; he looks like he is about to explode. He sits on the stool rubbing his head.

I ask," Do you want a cup of tea?"

Timidly replies, "Do you have anything stronger?"

I gawk at him without saying a word. My facial expression says it all. He settles for a cup of tea.

I pour a cup and walk back to the living room to sit on the couch. I figure the kitchen has too many knives. It's better if I am in the living room. Michael follows me in silence and sits across from me. He knows that he is in trouble. He knows not to sit close to me. I purposely stay quiet to create an uncomfortable atmosphere.

After a few minutes, Michael finally says, "I am so sorry for all of this."

I respond with an innocent gaze, "What do you mean?"

I know what he meant, but I want him to elaborate on his statement.

He replies, "For all this drama."

I reply sarcastically, "What drama?"

Michael puts his cup down and tries to assess my mood, "I understand you're upset, and you have every right to be."

I stop him from speaking further. And say, "Michael, I am tired of your bullshit. I can't do this. You say you want to be honest, but instead, you are hiding shit from me. You are more interested in protecting this bitch of a psycho of yours instead of being truthful. You and your psycho girlfriend have caused me stress and anxiety. I am afraid of going anywhere without looking over my shoulder." I can hear my voice getting louder, and my face is getting hotter. "To make matters worse, you don't even want to tell me about this woman. Are you still sleeping with her?"

Michael attempts to come closer.

I jump up, "Stay the hell away from me. I am tired of your lies and bullshit."

He stops in his tracks. He doesn't know what to say or how to react. I walk up to him and yell, "Who the hell is this woman, Michael? Why is she targeting me?"

Michael tries to answer, but I keep pushing with more questions. "Are you still having sex with her? Is that why she is so angry?"

He grabs me by my shoulders, which makes me angrier. I punch him and continue pounding on his chest with a closed fist.

"JAZZY!" he yells as he grabs both of my hands. "I can't tell you anything about Chantae because she is DEAD."

What? Wait, did I hear him right? I pull my hands from his grip and stand back. "What did you say?"

He looks me dead in the eyes and replies, "Yes, Jazzy you heard right. Chantae is dead. She committed suicide in my living room two years ago."

This is too much for one person. I don't know if I can handle this emotional rollercoaster. I take a minute to process what Michael just told me. I'm numb.

I muster enough strength to speak. "Who was the person you were speaking with in front of the gallery earlier?"

He looks surprised to realize that he is caught yet in another lie. Michael tried again to take a step toward me. I held my hands in front of me to let him know not to come any closer.

He quickly said, "Jazzy, I can explain."

"I don't need your explanation," I yelled. "Why do I even bother trying? You are nothing but a lying bastard."

Michael makes another attempt to reach for me. I take another step back and scream, "Stay the hell away from me. In fact, get the hell out of my apartment!"

I walk to the front door and open it wide to let him know that I'm serious. Michael stands in the middle of the living room not sure what to do.

I walk back, get in his face and yell, "Get the hell out of my house, you lying sack of shit!"

I'm livid. I hate Michael for lying to me, for putting me through this predicament. More importantly, I hate him because I love him. Michael finally walks out but tries to speak while standing outside. I slam the door then walk to my room. I cry out to let out the pain I'm feeling. The betrayal is too much to bear. I have so many questions. What did I get myself into? How did I allow this man to enter my life and not seeing the red flags?

I need to speak to someone. I know that it's late, but I need my girl right now. I call Sara and ask her to come over because something could not discuss over the phone.

Twenty minutes later, Sara shows up at my door and says, "Girl, what happened? You look as if a train just ran you over."

I roll my eyes, "You have no idea."

We both walk to the kitchen for us to get a drink. I open Sara's favorite red wine and pour us a glass.

"Are you okay?" She asks.

I pour more wine into our glass and ask her to sit down. She gives me an exhausted and worried look and sits at the kitchen tool.

I take a sip before I start talking, "Michael was here."

She rolls her eyes and replies, "What did he want?"

I announce, "While he was here, someone vandalized his truck."

Sara exclaims, "What? Jazz, this is getting out of hand. You need to stay away from this guy. I know that I am the last person to give you relationship advice, but this is dangerous."

Sara is right about giving me relationship advice. She's also right about my relationship with Michael. It's getting dangerous.

Sara asks, "Why was Michael here anyway?"

I ignore her question and continue, "We were in the bedroom when I heard a loud noise, and a car alarm was going off. When I looked through the window and saw a shadow running away from Michael's truck."

Sara inquires, "Did you see the person's face?"

"No, just a shadow. According to the police, the same person or people who vandalized our gallery may be the same person who trashed Michael's truck."

She rolls her eyes again when I mention Michael's name. "Do you think it's the same woman who created the fake page of their wedding?"

I take another sip to give my brain a second to regroup. "That's my initial thought."

Sara asks impatiently, "Well if it isn't her, then who is it? This man has more than one psycho stalking him?"

I reply, "I don't know. Maybe it's his baby mama."

"Wait, a baby mama? He has a child? When did you find out about this?" Sara's nagging voice grows more prominent with each question.

Oh, here we go, I reply, "I did not want to tell you because I know how over the top you are with drama. I feel responsible and ashamed that we're in this predicament."

Sara yells, "The hell you're responsible. Michael probably lied and manipulated those women, and they finally caught up with his bullshit, then snapped!"

I totally agree with Sara. I sensed that Michael had not been totally honest with me. Look how he conveniently left out that his ex-girlfriend committed suicide in his living room.

Sara continues with her rant. "He probably toyed with their emotions, tells them that he loves them, they invested themselves in that son-of-a-bitch."

I reply, "I just know what Michael tells me."

Sara continues bashing Michael. I stay quiet because I know why she dislikes Michael. She dated a guy for seven years. He mistreated her, physically abused her, cheated then dumped her. Michael reminded her of her ex minus the physical abuse.

Sara advises, "We should have Nadine do a background check on him."

That's not a bad idea, I thought. I refill our glasses once more to finish up the bottle. Sara takes a big gulp of the wine then continues with her rant. I needed to bring her attention back to, "Focus, I am not done with what I need to tell you."

She stops and thinks for a second, then says, "Wait? What? There's more to the story?"

"Regrettably, it gets worse," I reply.

Sara takes another gulp of her wine and braces herself.

I continue, "This morning, when I went to the coffee shop to get tea while you were talking with Cobby. I noticed Michael had an intense conversation on the phone. He looked like he was livid with the person on the other end. He walked over to the coffee shop to speak to me. I assumed whoever he was speaking with was his ex. I asked him if it was her on the phone, he said yes, but he refused to tell me any more details."

Sara jumps off her seat, "I bet you this bastard is still sleeping with her. Jazzy, we need to find out who this trick is and have a woman-to-woman talk. And if that doesn't work, let's beat the shit out of her New Orleans style."

I tell Sara to slow her roll. She's always ready to beat someone's behind. I continue with the story, "This evening, when the officer was taking our statements, Michael was uneasy about speaking in front of me. The officer had to tell me to go stand in front of my apartment another for Michael to feel comfortable to speak."

Sara replies, "So this bastard is hiding something."

I shake my head to let her know that her assumption is correct.

She looks up, "Well, did you ask him?"

I pause. I can't even verbalize what Michael told me earlier.

Impatiently she yells, "Well, spit it out."

I close my eyes, fearing Sara's reaction, "Michael told me that his ex, Chantae committed suicide in his apartment in front of him."

Sara drops the wine glass, and it shatters all over the kitchen floor. She asks, "What did you just say? Well, damn, how many women Mr. Rico Suave was involved with"

I explain, "Yes, I had the same reaction when he told me."

She interjects, "He failed to tell you such an important detail?"

I comment, "Michael keeps saying that he just wanted to protect me and promises to keep me safe."

Sara says, "Well, that rules her out, may her soul rest in peace." She, humorously, makes a cross sign across her chest. "Then who is it?" I roll my eyes at how dramatic she can be.

I reply, "I am not sure."

Michael tells me that he wanted to clean up the mess he made in his life and be patient. I am not sure if I am patient enough to deal with all of this drama. I did not answer Sara's question. I just shrug it off, and then I deflect by shining the spotlight on her. "I noticed that you're getting cozy with Cobby."

Her eyes widen. I put my glass down slowly. I tease Sara, "Oh shit! Someone has you smitten already."

Sara is grinning from ear to ear as I dig deeper. "I can use the distraction, so spill the beans."

She jumps up and sits on the kitchen counter like a high school girl. "Cobby asked me out."

I clap my hands and jump with excitement. Cobby seems like he is a good guy. She has been through so much in her last relationship. I am happy that she is finally catching a break. He seems nice.

"After you left the gallery Cobby, and I talked for hours as if we knew each other for a long time." Sara's voice got louder.

Sara's over the moon. She's always put the chariot before the horse when it comes to relationships. She falls too hard and too quick.

I offer my advice, "I am happy for you but take it slow."

"Girl! Do you think Cobby is a player?" In her dramatic tone.

"Nah girl, Cobby seems to be a great guy, very attentive, much more emotionally mature," I reply

We both know that I am talking about Michael.

Sara shakes her head, "Hopefully, he is not a lying whore like your man."

Sara gets under my skin hearing her talking about Michael this way. My first reaction is to come to his defense, but too much has happened for me to even try. Instead, I put on a fake smile and continue sipping on my wine.

The Price

Sara senses my apprehension. She walks over and gives me a hug and says, "I am sorry for what you're going through Jazz. I am with you all the way. Even if we have to shank someone."

I laugh, "Girl, why do you always want to shank somebody?"

In a serious tone, Sara asks, "Have you figured out what you're going to do regarding Michael and his ex?"

My heart skips a beat just from hearing his name. I wish that it was as easy as to get Michael out of my life for good. I am so conflicted between his lies and what he is telling me. After tonight, I feel that I don't know this man. Every day he is revealing his true self to me.

Releasing a deep breath, I admit, "I don't know what I am going to do. I just want to find out who is stalking me, stalking us, and try to get to the bottom of it."

Sara replies, "Now that we know that his ex-girlfriend Chantae is dead, it has to be another one of his chicks."

I snap my finger. It startles Sara, "I just remember, Michael told me that he has a six-year-old son with another chick, and she wouldn't let him see the son."

Sara looks at me, "Jazzy, why the hell are you staying involved with this man?"

Ignoring her question once again. I continue, "Michael and I were on a date one time. His phone kept ringing. I got pissed and told him to please answer the phone. He explained that the person who was on the phone was his baby mama who was blackmailing him to be with her, or she wouldn't allow him to see his son."

Sara looks in disbelief, then she replies, "Are you some kind of special stupid? Who are you? He knows who is harassing you! His shit followed him from Chicago to New Orleans. Doesn't that tell you something Jazzy? You're smart, think, please."

This was getting too much. Michael's manipulation is unraveling in front of me as Sara breaks it down. I feel stupid for falling for his bullshit EVERY TIME. I burst into tears once more because this is getting ridiculous. Whenever I want to take one bold and loving leap into Michael's arms, I find out he is playing me for a fool.

Sara hugs me and replies, "The curse of a woman in love. We lose the power of reasoning. We all fall victim to love my dear." Her comment makes me cry more. She continues as she rubs my back to soothe me, "I am sure you are not the first, and you will not be the last." She decides to make us tea; knowing a good brew always makes me feel better. Sara looks at her watch and says it's already two a.m. She confesses, "Girl, I didn't come here to spend the night with you." She gathers her things and makes her way to the front door, then pauses, "Are you going to be, okay?"

I tell her that I will be fine, but I know it's a lie. Sara hugs me one more time and tells me that she loves me. With a faint smile, I reply, "Right back at you."

I walk back to my bedroom and notice my phone on the nightstand. I had eight missed calls from no other than Michael and two from Laycee. Speaking of Laycee, I will have to talk to her about her behavior earlier. I know that I took her under my wing, but she is crossing the line. She made me uneasy earlier when she came to my apartment. Well, I have too much on my plate. I will have to deal with Laycee another day. I listen to my voicemails and skip over Michael's messages. His voice irks me. I hit delete on all of his messages without listening to them. Laycee left a lengthy message apologizing for earlier and assuring I was okay. She said that she cared about me and did not want anything to happen to me. What the hell did she mean that she didn't want anything to happen to me? I am tired, my head is throbbing, and I don't want to deal with her foolishness.

I fell asleep as soon as I hit the pillow. I dreamed that I was tied to a tree (not sure who tied me to it), circled by many angry women. I could not see their faces because they all wore masks. They were carrying torches and walking toward me. I noticed Michael from afar. I screamed for him to rescue me, but he acted as if he did not know me. As the women got closer, I screamed louder. Michael simply stared. He never came to my rescue. The women drew closer. I woke up sweating. My heart was racing one hundred -miles-per-minute. Before I realized it, it was time to wake up to go to the gallery.

My headache is worse than before I went to sleep. I take a cold shower to wake me up. I make my way to the kitchen to make breakfast and realize that my fridge is empty. My routine has changed since Michael entered my life. I would do laundry midweek, my grocery on the weekend, prep my food for the week, and get my work week ready on Sunday afternoon with enough time to relax and enjoy a glass of wine. Now, I don't even know what day it is most of the time. I lose track of time easily. Come to think of it, this man brings more chaos in my life than peace. I finish my tea and make my way to my car. There's a note on my windshield. My heart jumps. I hope that it's not a threat from one of Michael's crazy bitches. I reluctantly remove the note from the windshield and open it. It was from Michael and read:

Jazzy, my heart aches to see you in so much pain. More importantly, I know that I am the cause of all the pain you are enduring right now. No amount of sorry can make up for what you're going through. I know there are many unanswered questions, but I promise you I will explain everything to you. I just need a little more time to sort things out. Jazz, I meant it when I told you that I want things to work out between us. I want you. I need you in my life more than you can realize. I hope to hear from you soon.

Michael

I rip the note with such rage and open my hand so the pieces can escape my grip and fall on the ground. Michael is delusional if he thinks after his lies that I am going to run back to him. I cannot believe the nerve of him to ask me to be patient. I have been more than patient with his ass. My patience got me nothing but more lies and manipulation. My heart starts to race, and my face is getting hotter. I take a few quick breaths to calm myself down.

I am relieved that I'm the first to arrive at the gallery. I need more time to put on a smiley face for the customers and Sara. I am impressed by how quickly Cobby and Sara have the gallery up and running. They did a fantastic job fixing the broken window and counter. The gallery looks like when it first opened. I have to call Cobby to thank him for helping to get the gallery ready. I am thankful for Cobby's friendship. Today is crucial because I am meeting with a new artist this morning. I have an hour before the gallery opens, giving me time to review the artist portfolio and look over the proposal to ensure that I've covered everything.

The front door sensor went off, and I froze. I have been jumpy ever since the gallery was burglarized. I'm relieved that it's Sara.

She is shocked to see me in the gallery. "Oh! I didn't think that I was going to see you here today."

I reply, "I am meeting with the new artist this morning and wanted to review his portfolio."

"Oh, yes," she snaps her finger, "With all of the drama, I forgot about your meeting."

I feel guilty. I know that it's my fault that we're in this predicament. Sara's girlfriend spidey senses and the look of discomfort on my face signal my uneasiness. She smiles softly and changes the subject. She looks around and comments, "The gallery looks great."

Agreeing with Sara's observation, I reply, "Cobby did an excellent job."

Sara looks at me, "Huh, Cobby wasn't working alone. Michael came back and practically spent the whole night getting the gallery ready for today."

Wait, how did he get access to the gallery? When did he come back? It must have been after I kicked him out of my apartment last night. This man makes it impossible to stay mad at him. I will call Cobby to thank him and tell him to thank Michael for me as well.

After about an hour, a very well-dressed gentleman walks in. He walks over and introduces himself as Theo Caldwell. His milk chocolate skin tells me he knows how to exfoliate. His dreadlocks are neatly in a ponytail. He is tall and medium built. The brother walks with such charisma he seems that he's gliding as I usher him to my office.

"Theo?" I inquire as I stand to greet him. "It's a pleasure to meet you. Can I offer you some tea or coffee?"

He flashes a beautiful smile and says, "Tea, please."

Laycee happens to be walking by the office. I flag her to come in. I introduce Theo to Laycee, "Theo, this is Laycee, our assistant."

He stands up and extends his hand to Laycee. She seems mesmerized by his charm. He says, "It's a pleasure to meet you Laycee." As he takes her hand.

Laycee replies, "The pleasure is all mine." Sounding energetic.

I feel that her behavior is inappropriate to the client. I ask, "Laycee, do you mind getting two cups of tea for Theo and me."

Laycee shoots me a look as if she's annoyed. I take a deep breath then give her a crooked smile while making a mental note to talk to Laycee regarding her attitude lately.

She turns to Theo and says, "I look forward to working with you." She exits the office, making her way to the bar.

I take the opportunity to ask Theo a few questions to get to know him. "Where are you from Theo?"

He takes a deep breath before he answers, "I am a native of New Orleans, but I travel around. I was an army brat."

"Is that so," I reply

He continues, "My father was in the military. I lived in France, London, Germany, Japan, and China. I speak eight languages."

I am impressed. No wonder he speaks, and dresses so refine. I would have taken Theo for an English gentleman because of his stance and the way he articulates.

I ask, "What made you return home?"

He explains, "New Orleans always brings the best out of me. It's my first love. I have a spiritual connection with the city. Although I travel around the world, my best inspiration comes from New Orleans."

I continue with my questions, "How do you pick your subjects to paint?"

He smiles, "My subjects choose me. My arts speak to the reality of the world."

I reply, "I love that the fact that everyone who sees your paintings can find common ground."

Theo and I talk for three hours. I explain the terms of our agreement, and he agrees to the terms. I am happy to have signed our first client.

Laycee comes back with the tea. She serves Theo a cup then leaves mine on the tray. I am dumbfounded by her rudeness lately.

I pick my cup of tea and say, "Welcome to the team Theo."

Theo askes. "Will you have dinner with me to celebrate our partnership?"

"I think it's a great idea, my partner and I would love to take you out to dinner to celebrate," I reply

He looks at me, "Oh, you misunderstand me. I am asking you out to dinner."

It takes me a minute to process what Theo just implied. Oh, hell no! This man is asking me out on a date. What is wrong with these men? I'm screaming from the inside, but I keep it cool, calm and collected outside. I politely decline his invitation. I explain to him that I want my relationship to remain as an agent and client.

With a disappointing look, he replies, "I understand. I apologize if I stepped out of bound."

Not to make our first client feel rejected, I reply, "My offer still stands. My partner and I would love to take you out to dinner or lunch to celebrate."

Theo pauses for a second, then replies, "I would love to be accompanied by two beautiful ladies for dinner."

I extend my hand, "I look forward to collaborating with you ."

He holds on to my hand a little longer than I care for. Finally, he responds, "The pleasure is all mine."

I walk Theo out of my office into the gallery and give him a quick tour.

I call Sara to come out to the front to introduce her to our new client. "Sara, this is our new client Theo. Theo, Sara is my business partner."

He kisses Sara's hand while she's looking at me. I shrug my shoulders. Sara quickly pulls her hand from his and replies, "I am thrilled that you have joined the A-team."

Theo responds, "I have no doubt that this partnership will be a great one. Looking forward to seeing you tonight for our celebration."

Sara looks at me with her wide eyes and says, "Tonight? Celebration?"

I committed Sara to have dinner with this man without checking with her. I forgot that tonight is her date night with Cobby. Crap, I don't want to go out to dinner with Theo alone.

"Will you excuse us for a second?" Sara asks. She practically drags me into the office.

Before she can get a word out, I quickly say, "I forgot about your date with Cobby. Otherwise, I wouldn't have committed. Can you reschedule the date?"

Sara crosses her arms as she walks toward me, "Have you lost your mind, Jasmine?"

I see that there's no winning this fight, so I quickly reply, "I'll go to dinner with our new client without you."

She steps out of the office and joins Theo, who's waiting by the bar. "I apologize that I cannot make it to dinner due to prior arrangement." She turns to look at me, "But I am sure you will be well cared for. Jasmine will take diligent care of you." She walks away, leaving me with Theo in an awkward position.

Theo speaks first, "We can reschedule the celebration if it is too awkward for you."

I explain, "It will not be necessary. I will text you the place and time."

He replies, "I look forward to hearing from you." He kisses my hand, then turns and waves goodbye to Laycee as he exits the gallery.

For the rest of the day, I work on the line-up for the month. I call all the local artists who want to be included in this month's live performances. I'm happy that everyone confirmed. Excited to have the gallery open again, I did not realize that it was lunchtime already. I step out of the office to see what Sara is doing for lunch. She's smiling from ear to ear while holding a beautiful bouquet of roses. I stand in front of the counter to get her attention. She hands me the card to read. It's from Cobby, of course. He wrote: *A beautiful bouquet for a lovely lady. I look forward to our first date tonight, C.*

I am so happy for Sara. She deserves a good man in her life. I instruct Sara in a motherly tone, "He seems to be a great guy, don't scare him off on your first date."

She snatches the card from me and pretends that she's upset, "I know what I am doing. Besides, Cobby doesn't look like the type that scares easily."

I agree. It would take a lot to scare him. I demand that Sara calls me with every detail.

She looks at me with a smart-ass grin, "Every detail?"

I reply, "Heifer, I don't want to hear about your freaky shit." We both laugh, then I say, "Just let me know if he's a perfect gentleman and when is the second date."

Sara replies, "Okay! because I was going to give you details to make your toes curl."

I playfully smack her in the back of her head and say, "No sex on the first date."

She comments, "I cannot promise that. If it comes to it, you want me to turn it down because of society's rule."

Well, Sara does not follow anyone's rule, so I let that subject rest. Sara returns to her tasks. I step out to get lunch. As I'm about to cross the street to the coffee shop to get a sandwich, someone yells out my name. It's Laycee. I don't have the energy to deal with her right now. She looks unhinged. Something is going on with her. Ever since her little debacle in my apartment, she has acted weird, and today is no different.

I say, "I'm about to grab lunch across the street. Can it wait until I get back from lunch?"

She replies, "Can I join you? I want to apologize for my behavior earlier."

I want to have lunch alone, but she is persistent, so I agree. We walk across the street together. As we enter the café, the cashier gives me the side-eye. She remembers me from making a scene in the middle of the coffee shop. I was embarrassed that I went off on Michael like that in public. That is not my style. I order a crawfish salad with a bottle of water, and Laycee orders a tuna sandwich. I pay for the food then walk back to my regular booth in the back. She takes a bite from the sandwich then pauses.

I pause too and ask, "Is everything okay?"

Laycee puts her sandwich down and replies," I'm having an issue with my baby daddy."

I have tried not to pry in her personal life too much since I am her employer. Although she seems to be highly interested in my personal life, especially my love life. I wanted to draw the line without appearing cold.

She continues, "My son is six and has only seen his father twice."

I feel sad for her, but I do not comment. I let her vent.

She explains, "He has not supported his son since he was born."

I don't know why she's telling me this. What did she want me to do? Go grab her baby daddy by the balls and make him do the right thing. I am annoyed by this girl, but I try my best to listen. She just moved to New Orleans and doesn't have anyone.

Finally, I ask, "Where's the father?"

She replies, "He moved to New Orleans before my son was born. He was the one who suggested that I move here to try to work things out."

I ask, "Well, what happened?"

Laycee responds, "Once I moved, he told me that things are not working out."

My blood's boiling. What kinda man is this person? Why would he tell her to move to work things out and turn around and dump her? I did not ask Laycee those questions, but I'm upset that men have the luxury to be deadbeat dads, and women must pick up the slack. No wonder men are messed up emotionally. It starts with the decisions parents make.

Laycee complains, "I did not want to move here. My family is in Houston. I have no one here. My relationship with my baby's father was rocky. I thought if I followed him, we would work on our relationship. Moving to New Orleans was supposed to be a fresh start."

Women fall for that trap every time. If we are in a rocky relationship, having a child will be the answer to fix our relationship. When things do not get better, we become bitter and take it out on our children. We waste our time and energy with someone who's not interested in being in a committed relationship. We think that we are tricking the man into staying with us, but we hurt ourselves. If a man is afraid of commitment, it doesn't matter how many children you pop out of your coochie for him; he will not stay. I decided not to offer any advice to Laycee for the moment. I did not want to come across like I was judging her. Right now, she just wants someone to listen. Her issues take my mind off my mess.

Tears are rolling down Laycee's face. I reach across the table and hold her hands. Thinking that my gesture will make her better. She cries harder.

She confesses, "I feel so stupid. I fell for his lies. Now he doesn't want anything to do with my son or me."

Now I understand her attitude was not toward me. She's just going through a rough patch. Attempting to console her, I sit next to her, put my arms around her and say, "I'm sorry for what you're going through. You're smart. You will survive."

Laycee replies while wiping her tears, "Jasmine, thank you for listening to me. You're all I have."

Although she can be annoying and clingy. I understand her pain.

 Damaged Goods

Laycee and I walk back to the gallery to finish the day. Sara is standing by the bar, still holding the roses. She's singing some crazy tune. I roll my eyes because I know my friend. She is a helpless romantic. She already has the chariot before the horse. That's the reason why her relationships do not last. I am praying that Sara doesn't run Cobby away because I like him. Speaking of Cobby, I have to call him to thank him for getting the gallery ready on time. Sara didn't even notice me walking by the bar to get to the office. She is on cloud nine.

I dial Cobby's number, he answers on the third ring. "Hello pretty lady" Cobby's greeting makes me smile. He continues, "How have you been, my love?"

I want to remain positive. I answer, "I am doing fine."

I think Cobby knows the truth that I'm not okay.

I continue, "Thank you so much for getting the gallery ready so quickly."

He replies, "Are you kidding me? Michael wouldn't let me rest until the gallery was back in operational mode."

A sharp pain hit my rib cage when Cobby mentioned Michael's name.

I hear Cobby's deep breath on the phone. He pauses for a second, then says, "Jazz, I am really sorry for what you are going through. You don't deserve all of the drama."

I reply, "I appreciate you saying that."

He continues, "Michael told me about the incident at your apartment. The same night he managed to pull my ass out of bed, rally up some of our buddies, and go back to the gallery and work all night until this morning. Michael is motivated to make it up to you Jazz."

In a defensive tone, I query, "Why are you always defending Michael?"

Cobby replies, "Jazz, as I told you before, I know Michael. I don't always agree with some of the choices he makes. Unfortunately, his past caught up with him. I am sorry that you are caught up in the middle of it. Believe me Jazz, when I tell you that I have never seen Michael head over heels for anyone. He is different when he is around you. The way his eyes light up when he speaks of you."

Since we're on the subject of Michael, I use the opportunity to ask him a few questions. "Did you know about his ex-girlfriend who committed suicide in his apartment?"

I sense the hesitation in his voice. Cobby continues, "It was a rough time for Michael. He was devastated. Michael blamed himself. He still has nightmares." Cobby continues, "Jazz, Michael is damaged goods. He has abandonment issues. Everyone dear to him ended up abandoning him. His mother died when he was young. He viewed her death as abandonment. He never knew his father. For a long time, he used women to punish his mother for leaving him."

I realize that I'm able to get an honest answer from Cobby, so I let him speak. He continues, "Like I said, Michael is my brother, and I would do anything for him. I even suggested that he gets help for his issues. You know men and our egos; it was out of the question."

Cobby pleads, "Jazzy, you bring out the best of him. Michael is a different person when he is around you. He respects you very much and doesn't want to disappoint you."

I have a better understanding of Michael's behavior toward women. Should I give Michael another chance and try to help him with his mommy issues? I quickly shake that idea out of my head. Besides, Michael has not been upfront with me. I have jeopardized my safety to be with him. Every time I feel that we are making progress, he slaps me with another deception. I look at the clock and realize that it's getting late. I thank Cobby for his time and prepare to end the call.

He offers a recommendation, "Please be patient with Michael."

What does he think I have been doing? I did not want to get into it. I simply reply, "I will try Cobby. I have to go. Thank you for helping with the gallery and your advice."

It's already four-thirty p.m., and I realize I haven't called Theo to let him know where we're meeting for dinner tonight. I do not want to go to this dinner alone, but I have no choice. There is something off about Theo that I can't quite put my hands on. It is not because he is an artist. Although artists are usually eccentric, there's something else about him. I decide to text him instead of calling him. I give him a choice between Thai or Cajun. He texts back, "Cajun of course." I text him the address of the Cajun restaurant that Michael and I went to on our first date, and it has become a regular date venue for us. Theo asks if he can pick me up. I decline and reply that I have somewhere to go after dinner. I lie, because I do not want him to know where I live, and if things get uncomfortable, I want to have the choice to walk out. I also meant it when I told Theo that I wanted us to have a professional relationship. I can hear the disappointment in his voice, but he agrees to meet me at the restaurant at six p.m.

I'm gathering my things to head out when Sara plops herself on the chair in the office.

I look at her, "Oh, you are finally down from cloud nine? How is it up there?" I tease her.

Sara throws a pencil and replies, "Shut up, heifer." We both laugh. She confesses, "Don't know what to wear for my date with Cobby?"

I reply, "Girl, anything that you wear, you'll look beautiful."

I'm not just saying that because she is my girl. Sara's beauty is effortless. She doesn't need too much of anything to make an impression.

She jumps up from the chair, "I know exactly what I am going to wear."

She decided we would close early so that we could both get ready.

I reply, "I agree. I have to go home and get ready for the dinner you ditched me for."

She rolls her eyes and says, "I did not ditch you heifer. You wanted the third wheel because he made you feel uncomfortable. Oh! and don't think I didn't notice how he was drooling over you."

It was my turn to roll my eyes. Sara can be so dramatic at times. I explain, "He asked me out on a date."

She looks annoyed, "AND…"

I look at her that as if she's crazy, "What the hell do you mean AND? First, he is our client. Second, you know that I…"

She stops me mid-sentence and yells, "Jasmine, I know you're not about to tell me that you are in a relationship and you're not able to date."

That's exactly what I was going to tell her. Now that she verbalizes it, it sounds insane. I did not respond to her comment because she was right. She drops her head to the side and gives me a suspicious look. I brace myself because Sara is about to preach.

She starts with my full name, "Jasmine Marie Banks, have you lost your mind? Please don't tell me that you're considering letting Michael back in your life after all he put you through. The hell with you, what he put us through."

In a defensive tone, I explain, "No, I was not thinking of having him back in my life." That was a bald-faced lie. I continue, "I am not ready to date anyone right now." It looks like Sara bought my lie. She gets up and leaves the office without saying anything else. I shake my head at her over-protective but well-meaning behavior as she does.

I pick up my things and close shop. When I arrive home, there's a bouquet by the door. I already know who's it from, so I bring them inside and throw them in the trash. I quickly get ready to meet Theo.

I purposely wear business casual attire to make a statement. When I arrive at the restaurant, Theo is already waiting for me by the host stand. He wears a button-down shirt with leather pants. Not my taste, but whatever floats his boat. I am not sure why I am dreading this dinner. This is supposed to be a celebration. I should be thrilled, but I can't shake that something is off feeling. Anyway, I promise myself that I'm going to make the best of it tonight. He spots me through the door and comes to greet me. Theo takes my hand and brings it to his lips; I pull my hand away from his lips and shake his instead.

He smiles a devilish smile, "I am surprised that you did not cancel."

I give him a puzzled look, "Why did you think that?"

Theo replies, "You were trying to get out of it when your partner stated that she couldn't make it."

No, I was trying to get out of it because I felt uneasy. But I did not say anything.

Theo walks to the host to see if our table is ready. I'm not sure why I chose the restaurant Michael and I frequently visit. As the thought comes to mind, I hear Michael's voice calling my name. I do not turn around because I thought my mind was playing a trick on me.

I hear his voice again saying, "Oh, you're just going to ignore me now."

My heart jumps. He is behind me. Of course, he is here the same time I am here with someone. I turn around, and here is Michael standing in front of me with a sad face. He leans in to greet me with a kiss. I back away and put my hand up to stop him. Just as I was about to tell him to stay away from me, Theo comes back to announce that our table is ready. I guess Theo could feel the tension between Michael and me. He looks at me than Michael and asks, "Is everything okay?"

I assure him that everything is fine. I notice the hurt in Michael's face when he sees Theo. Down deep inside, I'm happy because I want him to know that I've moved on, although this is just a business outing. Michael probably thinks that I'm on a date with Theo.

I look at Theo and say, "Are you ready?"

He is happy to oblige. Theo grabs my hand. "Yes, our table is ready."

As we walk to our table, I quickly glance at Michael. He's standing there stunned.

Theo asks as we are sitting down at our table, "Is everything okay with you and the dude back there?"

I reply, "It's complicated, and I didn't want to get into it."

Theo did not push the issue. Instead, he picks up the menu then asks, "Anything you recommend on this menu?"

Theo's question hit me. I usually order for Michael and me since he is not yet acclimated to Louisianan cuisine. I simply tell Theo that everything on the menu is delicious. Wanting to shift gears, I ask him about his art, expectations, goals, and next project.

With a suspicious look, he says, "Wait, I thought this is a celebration dinner? Let's not talk about work."

I can tell that this is going to be awkward. I need a drink. I wave at the server to come over and ask for a gin and tonic. I'm going to need something strong to help me with the night.

Theo orders the same and comments, "My kind of woman."

I annoyingly ask him to please elaborate.

He replies, "There's no need to get defensive. I take you for a wine person, and here you are ordering gin and tonic."

I apologize to Theo. He is right. I'm annoyed by Michael's presence. I am not sure why I picked this restaurant. I decide that I am not going to let Michael ruin this evening for me. To do that, we have to change the venue.

I abruptly stand up and say, "Let's get out of here."

With a confused look, he asks, "Now?"

I shake my head yes. Without a word, Theo gets up and follows me. As we are exiting, the server comes with our drinks. I apologize and tell her there's been a change of plans, then tip her for her trouble.

I explain to Theo, "I am going to take you to this joint near the eastern bayou. I think you're going to like it. They have great food, great music, a lot of artists hang out there."

The drive was twenty minutes away from the city. It is a place in the hole, tucked in the middle of the bayou, hence Bayou's Spot. The clientele is as eccentric as Theo. He will fit right in. The walls are decorated with tiles designed by the customers, which creates a beautiful mosaic throughout the restaurant. The host greets us and gives us two tiles with paint and brushes. The tables and the chairs are also decorated with tiles. The restaurant looks like a beautiful Van Gogh masterpiece. Theo is grinning from ear to ear as we walk to our table. He looks like he is in a candy store.

As we take our seats, I explain to Theo, "The owner and I met at the grand opening of my gallery. She loves art just as much as I do. We met for coffee a couple of times to brainstorm on how we could partner. We're planning an art show for our local artists. I think that it is important to support one another, especially us women."

The place is jumping already. Theo smiles and says, "Ms. Jasmine you are full of surprises."

I reply, "Why?"

He replies, "Because I would never picture you in a place like this."

With an annoying tone, I reply, "It seems that you have some interesting perceived notions about me."

He apologizes, "I am sorry. I should not have assumed that you're bougie."

The nerve of this man. I will not allow Theo to put a damper on my mood, so I will give him a pass. The band is playing smooth jazz in New Orleans style. I love everything about New Orleans, the food, the music, the arts, and the culture. As soon as we take our seats, the server comes to our table to take our order.

She asks, "What can I get for the beautiful couple?"

Feeling annoyed, I ask, "What makes you think that we are a couple?"

She looks at Theo then me, "Oh, I just assumed."

"Well, it is not good to assume Sherrie," I smirk as I read her name tag. She did not know what to say. She apologizes, then recites the dinner specials. We order our drinks and food. She apologies again before heading to the kitchen.

Theo's comment checks me on the way I handle an innocent mistake, "You did not have to chop the poor girl's head off. She was just buttering us up for her tip."

I feel bad for embarrassing the server. I was already annoyed by Theo's assumption of me, and now the server assumes that we were a couple.

He continues, "You act like being mistaken for my woman is offensive to you."

"I assure you that's not it. Things on my mind. That's all. My apologies for making you feel that way."

Seeing Michael at the restaurant earlier did not make things easier either. She returns with our drinks, and this time in a more serious mood. I wanted to apologize to her, but my ego wouldn't let me, so I let it slide. I take a sip of my drink, close my eyes to take in the music, and let the liquor take its effect, forgetting for a minute that Theo is sitting across from me. My frustration subsides a bit, and I feel a little more relaxed in the spirit of getting to know Theo better.

Remembering our earlier conversation, I ask, "Why didn't you join the military like your father?"

He laughs, "I have never been the type who follows conformity."

"Well, that's one thing we have in common," I reply.

He smiles and says, "I believe you will find that we have more than one thing in common. For instance, our passion for art."

I smile because he is right. The music stops, and the singer makes his way to our table with a big grin. I am confused because he is smiling at me, and I don't believe I know him.

As he approaches, Theo gets up and yells, "Son of a gun, Claude, is that you?"

The gentleman rushes over and gives Theo a big hug and replies, "You're the last person I expected to see here."

As I'm observing the male comradery, Claude stops to address me and apologizes for his rudeness. Theo introduces me to Claude. I extend my hand to him.

Without a beat, Claude takes my hand and says, "It is always a pleasure meeting a beautiful lady." He kisses the back of my hand.

What is it with these dudes kissing lady's hands? He grabs a chair and sits at our table. He continues quizzing Theo. "Man, how long you've been back? The last time we spoke, you were chasing some artifacts in Zambia."

Theo replies, "I have been back for a while now. I am busy working on a new project, which involves this beautiful lady here."

I take a sip of my drink, keeping Claude and Theo from seeing that I am blushing.

Theo turns to address me, "Claude and I used to go on these wild adventures looking for artifacts. We used to get into a lot of trouble with the natives."

Claude exclaims, "Oh! I remember this one time in a ritual ceremony we dressed like one of the tribes and little did we know it was a ritual for castration." We all started laughing.

"Man, I have never seen Theo run so fast! It was like he was running a marathon!" Claude continues. "The Natives chased us thinking that we were scared."

"Those were the good old time," Theo chimes in.

Although the stories were interesting and a chance to look into Theo's world, Claude stops and states, "My break is over. I need to go back on stage." He snaps his finger. He asks, "Theo, come on and do a couple of songs with me."

I give Theo a surprising look, not knowing that he is also a musician.

Claude turns to me and says, "This guy was supposed to be the next Brian McKnight, but he chose painting instead."

Theo looks uneasy as Claude is raving about his talent as a singer. Claude cannot contain himself as he introduces Theo on stage as his guest. Theo reluctantly hops on stage and sits on the piano while adjusting his mic. He looks so natural up there. He whispers something in Claude's ear then announces, "This song is dedicated to the beautiful Jasmine."

Everyone starts clapping. I almost choked on my drink because I did not expect him to do a dedication. He clears his throat and tells the audience to bear with him. Theo begins with a beautiful rendition of *Summertime* by Ella Fitzgerald while playing the piano.

Wow! He sounds great. His voice is smooth like Brian McKnight's. You could hear a pin drop in the room. Everyone is mesmerized, taking in every tune, every note, and every word. When Theo finishes, the room explodes with applaud. A performance like this deserves a standing ovation. Theo looks my way, then blows me a kiss. I pretend to catch it, not sure why I did that. I got caught in the moment. He is more at ease. He performs a couple of more songs with Claude and finally returns to our table.

I look at Theo with awe, "Wow, that was phenomenal. Okay, forget about being your art agent. I am going to be your manager, and we are going to get a record deal."

He laughs then replies, "Well, Ms. Jasmine, I will not give up my day job for a record, and maybe you shouldn't either."

The celebration takes another level. I wave to the server and order a round of shots for us. I toast, "To newfound talents, to health and happiness."

Theo adds, "To a new friendship, new adventures."

I did not protest, so I raise my glass and drink. The evening is going better than expected. I have so much fun with Theo. We dance, eat, do shots. He's surprised as to how well I can hold my liquor. It's been a while since I've gone out without looking over my shoulder.

The evening ends with a good vibe. Theo walks me to my car and asks if I'm okay to drive. I assure him that I am.

As we reach my car, Theo confesses, "Jasmine, I can't remember how long it's been since I went out and had so much fun. I even got on stage and sang with my buddy. Thank you so much for bringing me here. I know that you said you wanted to keep our relationship professional. I want to respect that. I would love to see you again, not on a professional level."

I pause for a minute, thinking of what to say. I can hear Sara saying, go for it. Why are you putting your life on hold because of this asshole Michael? Oh gosh! This is confusing.

I explain, "Theo, I'm in a complicated relationship and don't know what my next step is."

Playfully he replies, "Ms. Jasmine it's just dinner."

I pause for a second, then reply, "Let me think about it, and I will give you an answer soon."

It's getting late. I hold my hand to shake Theo's. Instead, he kisses me on the cheek and whispers, "Good night, my beautiful Jasmine."

I smile and say, "I'll text you to let you know I've reached home safely."

The drive home takes an hour. I use the time to recap how much fun the night was. I still feel a bit uneasy; that's why I am apprehensive about going out with him. Why do I think I am betraying Michael if I agree to go out to dinner with Theo? I need someone to slap some sense into me. Sara will be the one to do it. Hopefully, she is done with her date with Cobby. I call Sara while in the car.

The call goes straight to voicemail. "Damn, girl, I need you, so let go of his thing and call me." I laugh at the end of the message.

Two minutes later, my phone rings, and it is Sara. While laughing, she says, "Girl, you are so stupid? Well, I was not holding his "THANG." I was about to ask him to come up for coffee when you called."

I repeat, "Coffee, huh, that's what we are calling it now?"

Sara is getting annoyed. She yells, "Girl, what the hell do you want? I am still on my date. I told him that it was you. That's why I called back."

I know not to mess with Sara when she is annoyed, so I quickly tell her about my evening and how much fun I had. I also tell her that Theo asked me out, and I'm torn.

She's silent for a minute, then she replies, "Jazz, please don't tell me that you think you owe Michael some type of loyalty after he has been screwing other women."

I know Sara is right. The decision for me to go out with Theo shouldn't be a difficult choice. I instruct her to go back to her date and that I will see her tomorrow at the gallery.

Minutes later, I arrive home. I text Theo and let him know that I got home safely.

He responds, "*I want to thank you again for a great evening. I hope that you go out to dinner with me again. Have a good night, Jasmine.*"

I'm too tired to reply.

CHAPTER 20

A Distinguish Gentleman

The next day I get in the office early to set up appointments with art dealers in Miami. I'm motivated to push Theo's work. I wonder if there's also a hidden motive as to why I am trying so hard. Nevertheless, I am doing my job. I stop overthinking my reasons. Hours later, I hear the front door open and Sara's voice, "Heifer, are you in the office?" I don't bother to answer because I know that she'll be coming to the office anyway.

As predicted, Sara comes with a bit of pep in her step and plops herself on the chair in front of me and asks, "What was so important that it couldn't wait that you had to disturb my groove last night?"

I put down the paper I was working on and reply, "Well, good morning, Sara, how are you this morning? I am fine, thanks for asking."

She rolls her eyes and says, "Don't play with me Jasmine."

I stare at her until she realizes that I won't give in and finally says, "Good morning heifer, how was your night?"

"Now, was that so hard?" I reply

She flips me her middle finger. I laugh and shake my head. "I told you last night the reason why I called."

Sara rolls her eyes again, "I don't understand what the issue is."

I explain, "First, Theo is a client. Second, I don't want to complicate things with this mess with Michael."

With annoyance in her voice, she begs. "Please tell me how you're going to complicate things. From the looks of things, it looks like you're available. Theo is available. Where's the complication?"

The truth is that I don't want to go out on a date with Theo because I will be cheating on Michael. I don't dare voice that to Sara because I know that she would not understand. As pathetic as it sounds, I am reluctant to date anyone.

Sara sighs, "Well, you will be stupid if you put your life on hold waiting for prince charming to get his shit together."

I already know that Sara is talking about Michael.

I comment, "I am not putting my life on hold, I am trying to move on, but it is not that easy."

She gets up, "Well, it sounds like you've made up your mind regarding this issue. Why bother asking for my advice if you're not going to listen?" She walks out of the office. I can tell that she's upset. I do not bother to stop her.

My life has become so complicated ever since Michael crossed paths with me. Sara is right. I cannot put my life on hold while he is whoring around. I am going to call Theo and tell him I'll go out to dinner with him. Besides, I had so much fun with him last night, so I am sure it will be fine. Instead of calling Theo, I send him a text to let him know that I will go out to dinner with him just this once. He replies with an emoji of a man dancing salsa. I burst out laughing. He is so peculiar. I went back to what I was doing, scheduling meetings with art dealers for Theo.

I was engulfed in my work when there was a knock at the door. Here comes Laycee holding a beautiful bouquet of yellow roses.

She hands them to me and says, "These were just delivered for you."

I automatically think they are from Michael. He usually sends me yellow roses because he knows they are my favorite. I take them from Laycee, and as I'm about to throw them in the garbage, I realize the card has different handwriting. I pull out the card and put the flowers on my desk. The flowers were from Theo. The card has number one on it and some type of design. I do not understand the card, so I call Theo for more explanation.

The call goes to his voicemail. The voice message is weird: *Thank you for calling. If you are not Jasmine, I am unable to answer your call at the moment. If this is an emergency, please hang up and dial 911. If this is Jasmine, please continue to listen to this vital message. The card you just received will be one of many cards you will be receiving throughout the day. Each card will have a clue as to what you need to do next. Happy hunting!*

Then nothing. I look at my phone, trying to figure out what just happened? I look at the card again to see if I can guess what the clue is. Nothing comes to mind.

Laycee is still standing in the office. I ask, "Is there anything else?"

She sits down and says, "I wanted to continue the conversation we had across the street."

"Did you have a chance to speak with your son's father?" I inquire.

Her face turns red, "He does not want anything to do with me. He is seeing another woman, and he told me to stay away."

I continue with my question, "What's your next move?"

She does not reply. She's just stares. I don't understand these men. If you're screwing around and you know you do not want children, wrap it up. At the end of the day, the child will pay the consequences of the parent's actions.

I pull a friend's business card from my desk and hand it to Laycee. I say, "She specializes in family law. Call her. She will help you."

She reluctantly takes the card and replies, "I don't want the law involved. I'm not trying to get him in trouble."

I'm annoyed by Laycee's response, so I decide to cut the conversation short. I apologize and explain that I'm in the middle of something and will have to talk to her later.

As she is getting up, she whispers, "You're lucky."

I'm not sure what she meant, but I did not feel like dealing with her. So, I just smile.

By lunchtime, I receive two small boxes from Theo. In there are two more cards and one cut-up lace cloth. Both cards are designed like the first one. I put all three cards side by side, trying to decipher the clues on them. Still have no idea what Theo is trying to tell me with these cards. I like his imagination though. I put the lace cloth on top of each card. I think I am beginning to see the clues. I grab a notepad and a pen to write down what I think is a single letter. Card number one had the letter G underneath the design. I know now that I need the lace cloth to look for the clues. I put it on top of card number two, and it had the letter A. I did the same thing for card number three, and it had the R underneath the design G A R.

I'm not sure what it means, but I know that I'm on to something. I look at the card without the cloth, figuring out how he designed it so that the letters don't pop out when you first look at it. This guy is extremely talented! I make another attempt to call him. Again, my call went to voicemail. I did not leave a message, but as soon as I hung up the phone, I get a text from Theo saying that I could only move to the next phase if I texted him the clues on the cards. I text back with G A R. He texts back, "you're a clever lady," with a smiley face.

Two minutes later, he texts again with this instruction: *It is now lunchtime. I am sure that you're famished. Follow the letters, and you will feed your soul.*

I repeat his text aloud, trying to understand the riddle. "Follow the letters, and you will feed your soul." Okay Jazz, you got this! I step outside with the cards and look in all directions for another clue. I notice a street sign with three letters in it, so I walk closer to see the full name of the street and see if I can find the next clue. The street sign reads Garden Isle Drive. I continue walking on Garden Isle to see if there's anything else I can find in Theo's clue, then I remember there's a soul food restaurant on that street. I walk a little faster with excitement thinking that I'm clever enough to solve the clues.

When I arrive at the restaurant, it looks like it's not open for lunch. As I'm about to leave, a young lady runs after me to ask if my name is Jasmine. I hesitantly say yes. She hands me a card with Theo's handwriting on it.

The note read: *now that you have arrived, prepare to wet your palate. You have earned every bite. Enjoy!*

I walk back to the restaurant, and the young lady ushers me to a table in the back with a beautiful bouquet of jasmine flowers and a bottle of wine on top of it. I'm puzzled because the table is set for one. The young lady asks me to have a seat and advises that my server will be right with me. A few minutes later, my server comes out, and it's no other than Theo himself. He is in a waiter's uniform with a white napkin folded over his right arm. I'm smiling from ear to ear to see him in a uniform.

He comes over to the table and announces, "Welcome to Soul de Soul. I will be your server for this afternoon. May I pour you a glass of wine to begin?"

I reply, "Yes, please."

As he pours the wine, he recites the menu, "Today's special is blackened salmon, served over dirty rice and asparagus."

Oh, I said, "Can I get a menu?"

He replies, "I am afraid that will not be possible. The owner prepared a special lunch for a special guest; therefore, no menu is needed."

I look around and notice that I'm the only person in the restaurant beside the workers. I look at Theo with a puzzled look until I realize that he is talking about me.

Theo goes to the back and returns with a plate of mandarin salad. I wait for him to have a seat before I start. Theo stands in front of me like a soldier on his post. I ask, "Aren't you going to join me for lunch?"

He replies, "I am afraid that will not be possible ma'am. The workers are not allowed to fraternize with the customers."

He is doing too much with this role-playing. I pick up my fork and start eating my salad. Theo waits until I'm done, then takes my plate and heads to the kitchen. He returns with a plate and places it in front of me. Just as he promised, it is salmon with steamed asparagus and dirty rice. The smell makes me hungrier. I devour everything on my plate. Once again, Theo removes the plate from me and walks back to the kitchen. This time, the young lady who greeted me at the door comes out with a silver tray holding a single jasmine flower, a card and lots of chocolate kisses. The young lady repeats, "It was a pleasure serving you, and please have a wonderful day."

Once again, I'm perplexed. I take the card, the flower, and a hand full of chocolates. I do not open the card right away but wait until I exit the restaurant to see the next clue. Theo went out of his way to make sure that I was treated special. I forgot about my troubles with Michael and his baby mama drama. I finally open the card, and it says:

This is a prelude to what is to come. At 2100 hours, the chariot will come. Cinderella is going to a ball without her glass slippers. Don't worry. The wicked stepmother is not invited. You won't need to slip out at midnight.

I put the kisses and the card in my pocket as I enter the gallery.

Sara is at the counter with a sour look on her face. She whispers, "Tweedily dumb is in the office. I told him that you weren't here. He said that he would wait."

Damn! I thought to myself, my day was going so well now this jackass will ruin it. I slowly walk toward the back of the office. Just as Sara said, here's Michael. His shirt is wrinkled, his eyes sunken, he looks awful. I walk around the desk without saying anything to him to have the desk between us. Michael stands and moves to greet me with a hug. He smells of alcohol, and from the looks of it, he needs a shower. I put my hands up to stop him from coming closer.

I ask, "What the hell are you doing here Michael?" I haven't been in contact with Michael nor seen him since the restaurant. I blocked his calls, and social media did not want any contact with this man.

Softly he utters, "I miss you."

I look at him like he's crazy and ask, "Why is that my problem?"

Michael takes a deep breath, "Jazz, I understand why you're upset."

I fling my arms around, "Upset? You're delusional if you think that I am just upset! You put my life and my business in danger all because of your whorish ways, and now you're talking about me being upset?"

Blood rushes to my head. I take a deep breath, trying to calm down. "I still don't know which one of your bitches vandalized my gallery. I can't even press charges or protect myself from any of their scorn. I have a feeling you know who's doing it, and instead of telling me who it is, you'd rather protect them."

Michael breathes deeply, then replies, "It was not that simple."

"That's the problem," I shout, "Noting is simple with you. Listen Michael," I lash out, "I have had a couple of peaceful days since you were not around. I'd like to keep it that way. In fact, please leave because I don't want some crazy bitch to come for me."

Michael protests as he is trying to explain. I'm not interested in his explanation. I shout louder, "LEAVE."

Sara must have heard from the front. She forcibly pushes the door open and asks, "Are you deaf? She said leave! Don't you think you have caused her enough pain?"

He looks at me then at Sara and says, "Mind your goddamn business, Sara. I am sick of your shit. You have been giving me grief ever since we met"

Oh hell, he has done it now. Sara walks up to him, "Bitch, who the hell you're talking to? This here is my business." Sara swirls her arms around. "Nobody wants you here Michael, so it's best for you to get to stepping."

He was about to respond to Sara's attack when I intervene. "You know what Michael, Sara is right. Nobody wants you here, so please leave."

He winces as if he has been stabbed. He replies, "You don't mean that Jazz."

As I'm about to respond, Sara cuts me off and says, "Hell yeah, she means it. Get the hell out of here."

With his wounded pride, Michael exits the office. Sara slams the door as he leaves. I could not hold back my tears. Sara rushes to the desk and puts her arms around me. The tighter she holds me, the more I cry. Why is this so hard? This man, who came into my life, tricked me into loving him. He knew his intentions were to have me in his collections of women. I am more upset at myself for not seeing his games before I fell in love with him.

Sara did her best to calm me down. She finally asks, "Jazz, why are you allowing Michael to get under your skin? Move on. Obviously, he is not going to change. You deserve better. Let him go."

It's not as simple as Sara thinks. Every time I have sex with Michael, he takes part of my soul with him. I feel like a drug addict. I know that this relationship is toxic. I keep going back for more. I'm ashamed to tell Sara how deep that I have fallen for him. She thinks I'm insane for feeling this way for a man who doesn't see anything wrong with toying with people's emotions.

Michael and I have been dating for three years, but it feels like a lifetime. This is the most thrilling and emotionally draining relationship I have ever been in. Sara is right. Why am I allowing Michael to get under my skin? I refuse to shed another tear over him. I walk to the bathroom, wash my face, and retouch my make-up. Sara is still in the office waiting for me. Before she says anything, I deflect by asking her about her dates with Cobby. I can tell things are getting serious between them. Sara and I have not hung out for a while. We've only seen each other in the gallery.

Her eyes light up, "Cobby and I are great."

I am happy for Sara. She deserves a good guy in her life. I lighten the mood and tell her about the adventure I had for lunch with Theo, how much fun I have solving his riddles, and how he served me lunch thru role-playing.

Sara asks, "Wait! Which Theo? Our client Theo."

I reluctantly reply yes because I know where she is going with that. This has been one of our rules not to get involved with our clients personally.

I explain, "Before you start with your speech, I have already expressed to Theo I am only interested in a professional relationship." I continue, "He caught me by surprise with lunch by solving riddles that he sent me."

I show Sara the cards, she examines them, but with no attempt to solve them.

She confesses, "I am impressed that he went through all this trouble for lunch. The brother is creative."

"Oh! That's not all," I continue, "He invited me to dinner, and I already accept it." Sara scolds, "Be very careful, especially with the drama with Michael."

I reply, "Weren't you the one who told me to move on?"

Sara gives me a suspicious look as she walks out, "I want you to find closure with dumb ass before you start new adventures."

I ponder Sara's advice. As far as Michael goes, I must think about how to stay away from him. I no longer have the energy to deal with the stress Michael brings in my life.

Laycee pokes her head through the office door to see if I'm busy. She looks as if she has been crying.

"Is everything okay Laycee?" I ask.

She takes a seat and replies, "I just had a fight with my son's father."

I continue with my inquiries, "If he doesn't want to have anything to do with you, why are you pushing him?"

She replies, "I want my son to know his father. I want them to have a relationship."

I continue, "It's a fair request for him to be in his son's life, but if he doesn't want to have a relationship with you, you must respect that."

Laycee gives me a disturbing stare.

She asks, "Have you ever loved someone who doesn't love you back? You can't understand what it feels like. The hurt and the humiliation I feel when he tells me that he doesn't want me or that he's in love with someone else."

Laycee starts crying. I understand her more than she realizes. I walk over and put my arms around her and tell her that everything will be okay. I recommend that she focus on her son, focus on giving him a good life.

Laycee finally calms down and apologizes for the outburst. I assure her everything will work out. I explain, "I am available anytime you want to talk."

She smiles, "I really appreciate your support. You're the only person I can talk to."

Between my drama with Michael and Laycee's drama with her baby daddy, I am exhausted. A few minutes after Laycee exits the office, Sara brings a bouquet of jasmine and a card. I smile because I already know who it's from. Sara puts the bouquet on the desk and opens the envelope. I snatch the envelope from her and call her a nosy heifer. She laughs and says, "And don't you forget it either."

Sara takes a seat waiting for me to read the card to her. It's the same card that Theo used to send the clues for lunch earlier.

Unlike the card I received in the restaurant, it did not have a design. It simply said: *A masquerade ball fit for a princess, many will come to say that they are the prince, but the true prince will not need a mask.*

In Sara's fashion, she asks, "What the hell is all that gibberish?"

I laugh and reply, "It's clue number two for our outing."

Sara laughs, "Well, I am happy you finally have some sense and are giving that fine creature a chance, even though he is a client."

I have no words for this woman, so I kick her out of the office. I keep telling myself that it's just one date and nothing serious. Aside from the two appointments I scheduled with the art dealers, my day went by fast.

CHAPTER 21

The Ball

I stop at the mall to pick up a new outfit that will be right for the occasion. I brought a mask since it's a masquerade ball. I rush home to do my nails and a quick facial. Three hours later, I'm ready to party. The long-fitted strapless white gown makes me feel like Cinderella. I slick my hair back to show more of my face and my earrings. As I'm gathering my things, there's a knock at the door. I look through my bedroom window and see two white horses with a beautiful chariot made of glass waiting. I open the door expecting Theo; but a gentleman dressed in a tuxedo, top hat, and white gloves greets me at the door.

He extends his hand and introduces himself, "My name is Jermaine. I was instructed to take you to the ball."

Jermaine is an older gentleman with salt and pepper hair and a mustache. He put a small bench down to allow me to step inside the chariot. The aroma of the jasmine flowers hit me as I step inside. Theo is trying hard. Jermaine tells me his life story throughout the ride. He is an entrepreneur. We arrive at this beautiful mansion. There are lots of cars and people are rushing to get inside.

I ask Jermaine, "What is this place?"

He replies, "This is Mr. Caldwell's place. He organizes a charity event every year for the local orphanage and group homes."

I'm more impressed than taken back. Theo has amazed me again. Jermaine stops at the entrance, and two gentlemen are standing and waiting to open the chariot door. They are dressed identically with masks. They both hold out their hands to help me out of the chariot and walk me to the mansion. Wow! Inside, the mansion feels like a fairy tale. Everyone is dressed to impress. I'm so happy that I'm dressed for the occasion. A mysterious man comes over and hands me a card with my name on it. I can tell right away the note is from Theo.

I open the envelope; *"Now that you've entered my castle, it is now time to find your prince. The jasmine bouquet will lead you right to him."*

I roll my eyes, great another riddle. I honestly am not in the mood for a scavenger hunt. I grab a glass of champagne as the server passes by. I quickly scan the room and the balcony to see if I can find Theo. I take a sip of my champagne while I make my way upstairs. I figure that I have a better chance of looking from the second floor. I stand on the balcony for a few minutes, then I see someone who walks like Theo. He has a distinctive walk. I rush downstairs to claim my prize, only to discover that the gentleman is not Theo. Disappointed, I give the gentleman a smile, then walk away. As I'm about to give up, I notice a single jasmine on a small table by the door. I walk over and pick up the flower, thinking it is a clue. Another jasmine was on the patio floor. Clever, he is using the flowers as breadcrumbs. I follow the flowers to the gazebo in the garden. The flower trail ends in the pavilion. Theo is nowhere to be found. Is there another clue? It's a bit chilly. I rub my arms, trying to keep warm. Suddenly, a jacket falls over my shoulder.

Theo's baritone voice compliments, "Ms. Jasmine, you look absolutely stunning."

I turn around and smile, "This old thing." We share a laugh in the night air.

"You have kept me on my toes all day, Sir," I confess.

Without a word, Theo hugs me and holds on more than he should. I desperately need this hug with the day I had with Michael.

I am not going to lie. It feels so good to be held. I can feel Theo's erection, so I back up. I did not want to give Theo the wrong impression.

I quickly change the mood and ask, "Why didn't you tell me about your charity event?"

He flashes those pearly whites, "I told you that NOLA is my first love. The charity event it's my way of giving back to the community."

"And this beautiful mansion?" I inquire.

Theo turns to look at the mansion, "The mansion has a great history. My great grandfather bought the land from the slave master and built the house for his family. It went from generation to generation, and each generation upgrades, and now here it is today."

"What a great legacy to leave to your children," I comment.

Theo agrees and tells me that one day he will give me a private tour of the house. He is so sure that he is going to see me again outside of work.

We both are careful about what to say next, which creates an awkward silence between us. Finally, Theo says, "Jazz, I know what you said about wanting things between us to be professional, but I hope that I've proven that I am interested in more than your being my agent. I know it is a long shot, but I am ready to wait for whatever holds you back. Please don't tell me it is because of work because if that's all it is that you are fired as my agent."

I am speechless. It is time to have a come-to-Jesus conversation with Theo so that he knows where I stand.

In an apologetic tone, I start with, "I am in a very complicated relationship." Without going into too many details, I explain, "My heart belongs to someone else."

It pains me to say it out loud. If Theo only knows the nature of my relationship with Michael, he will never look at me the same.

He takes my hand, "There's nothing to apologize for. You told me from the beginning that you're only interested in a professional relationship."

I can hear Sara's voice in my head telling me that how much of a fool I am. How pathetic to think after all Michael put me through that I still choose him. The thought puts a damper on my mood. I quietly ask, "I'm not really in a festive mood. Can Jermaine take me home?"

With a confused look, Theo pleads, "Please don't go. I am sorry that I pushed the issue."

I can feel the tears rolling down my cheeks. I turn so he won't see me crying. Too late, he wipes my tears and says, "Jazz, please tell me what's making you sad."

I can't tell him how pathetic I feel for falling in love with a man whore. How desperate I must be. How can I tell Theo that Michael is my drug? I rush into Theo's arms and lose it. My action takes Theo by surprise. He holds me without saying anything. He lets me cry on his shoulder.

Finally, he says, "Jazz, why are you torturing yourself?"

He holds my face and kisses me on the forehead. I am not sure why I did not stop him. I allow him to kiss me on my cheeks then he softly kisses me on the lips. Not sure what to do next, I back away from Theo's arms and try to run to the house. He grabs my hand to stop me from leaving.

He apologizes, "Jazz, I am sorry for kissing you."

All kinds of emotions are running through my brain. I am confused about how the kiss makes me feel. Theo is all I want - a caring, sensitive, talented man, not to mention that the brother is fine as a glass of expensive wine. But all I can think about is Michael. Ain't that's some bullshit? This man is sleeping with every Tom, Dick, and Harry, and now I worry about betraying him. Finally, free from Theo's grasp, I ask again, "Can you please have Jermaine take me home?"

With pain in his voice, he replies, "I'll take you home."

"Oh Theo, I don't want to take you away from your party. I can call an Uber or a cab," I protest.

The truth is that I am not sure I trust myself around him right now. Theo insists he will take me home. We walk to the front of the house. He signals one of the gentlemen who helped me out of the chariot earlier to fetch his car.

He tells the other one, "Find Alex and tell him that I am stepping out for a little bit and to please make sure that everything is going well."

Minutes later, his car arrives. He takes my hand and asks, "Are you sure you don't want to stay?"

This is going to be an awkward ride home. Apologetic, I reply, "I'm sorry to have ruined your party, but I think I should go home."

Neither Theo nor I say anything during the drive. A few minutes later, he breaks the silence, "Whoever this man is, is very lucky, and he probably doesn't even know it."

I reply, "I think he knows it." I am lowkey trying to defend Michael.

I stare at the window because I'm too embarrassed to look at him. How can I make Theo understand that whatever it is between Michael and me is beyond my control? It's like he has some type of spell on me. How can an intelligent person like me find herself in this toxic relationship? It's foolish of me to think that a tiger can change his stripes. Theo turns on the radio to fill the awkward silence in the car. "Love Don't Live Here Anymore" was the tune playing.

I smile and tell Theo, "I wish that it did not live in my heart anymore."

He replies, "Don't let your heart be hardened by whatever the circumstances you are going through with a man. Jasmine, I've only known you for a brief time, but what I observed so far is that you are a passionate woman."

He continues, "Everything you do it's from your heart. It's fitting that you love hard even when a person doesn't deserve your love. As for me, I would give anything to have a woman who loves me the way that I perceive you love your man. He is a damn fool for breaking your heart this way."

"Who said that he was breaking my heart?" I ask.

Theo responds, "It doesn't take a rocket scientist to see your conflict with yourself." He continues, "If you were in a solid relationship, you wouldn't be with me right now in this car, beating yourself up because we kissed."

Correcting him, I scoff, "You kissed me."

He smiles, "Correction, I kissed you. The reason you're con-flicted is because of how the kiss made you feel."

"You're my shrink now?" I ask him in a sarcastic tone.

Theo smiles again, "As a matter of fact, I am."

I give him my best you are full of shit look. He insists, "Really, I majored in psychology and many other things."

I didn't believe him but decided not to say anything. As we arrive at my apartment building, I notice that a man is sitting in front of the entrance. The person looks like Michael. Has this man got me so fucked up that I imagine seeing him? Theo was talking, but I did not hear him because I was focusing on the man sitting on the pave-ment in front of the apartment.

I ask, "Did you say something?"

Apologetically, Theo says, "I am sorry that he doesn't love you right."

Not really focusing on what Theo is saying, I say aloud, "I'll be dammed!"

I quickly remove my seatbelt and almost get out of the car while it's still moving. Theo abruptly stops and asks, "What's going on? Are you okay?"

I did not have time to respond. I jump out of the car and slam the door. Michael notices me. He gets up and walks toward the car. Theo quickly gets out of the car in the spirit of protecting me from whoever is coming toward me. Michael stops in his tracks when he notices Theo shielding me.

Michael ignores Theo standing in front of me and says, "Jazz, I need to talk to you."

Theo senses that I'm reluctant to step forward. He turns to ask, "Is everything alright?"

Michael yells, "YES, everything is just fine," as he walks toward me.

Theo stands his ground.

Michael addresses Theo, "Listen man, I don't know who you are, but you better get the hell out of my way, or I'll make you move."

I quickly step between them when I hear Michael's threat before their testosterone gets out of hand.

I turn to Theo, take a deep breath and reassure him, "I am so sorry. I am fine. You can go. I'll call you later."

He replies, still eyeing Michael, "Are you sure?"

Before I can answer, Michael yells, "YES, she is sure!"

I quickly give Michael a warning look. He backs down and walks toward the apartment. I apologize to Theo for Michael's behavior.

He asks, "Are you sure you want to be alone with this man?"

I smile, "I appreciate you trying to protect me, but I will be fine."

He says okay, then kisses me on the cheek. I know that the kiss is just a move in their pissing contest. I did not entertain him. I promise Theo that I'll call him later to ensure him that I'm safe. He reluctantly gets in his car and leaves.

I storm up to Michael and get in his face. "Who the hell do you think you are coming to my house and embarrassing my friend and me?"

Michael rubs his head and asks with an authoritative tone, "Who the hell was that chump?"

I can smell the alcohol on Michael as he speaks. My fists are clenched. I reply, "You don't get to ask me anything? And frankly, that's none of your business."

"Are you fucking him?" Michael yells.

I don't remember when my hand reached Michael's face. The only thing I can feel is the sting from my palm and his reaction. Still in shock, I reply, "Unlike you, I am not a whore. You have the audacity to question who I'm fucking?"

The slap shocked him; he did not expect that I was going to react this way. He rubs his left cheek, "Jazzy, I am so sorry, I did not mean that. Can we please go inside to talk?" He pleads.

I walk into the building without saying anything. He follows me without saying a word either. I leave the door open as I enter my apartment. I go straight to my bedroom to change. Without turning around, I hear Michael making his way through the apartment quietly. I shut my bedroom door while I switch into my sweatpants. I return to the living room to find Michael sitting on my couch, looking like a scared puppy.

I walk into the kitchen to make a cup of tea; I make two cups and walk over and hand Michael one. He reluctantly takes the cup and sets it down on the coffee table.

He looks worried, "Jazzy, I want to tell you how sorry I am for bringing you in my drama."

"Michael, I don't need your sorry. I need honest answers." I say sternly

He rubs his head and replies, "That's the reason I am here, I wanted to be completely honest Jazz, but this is hard."

My heart jumps. What else is this man going to tell me? I honestly cannot take another heartache. He gets up and starts pacing the living room while rubbing his head.

With a worried tone, I put my cup of tea down and say, "Whatever you have to tell me, just spit it out so I can go to bed."

He stops pacing and kneels in front of me, "Jazz, you mean the world to me. I don't' want to lose you. Until I met you, I did not know what I wanted to do with my life. Jazz, you make me want to be a better man. I feel whole when I am with you. It is never my intention to break your heart, but it seems lately, all I can offer you is a broken heart."

This man is dumping me in my living room. The nerve of this man.

He continues, "Jazz, I was seeing a young lady, and I just found out that she's pregnant."

I push his hands away from me and ask him to repeat what he said as if I did not hear him the first time. Still processing the news, I feel numb. I don't know how to respond.

Finally, I muster enough courage to ask, "How many months?"

Reluctantly he replies, "Six months."

Michael and I were seeing each other at that time. I am happy I was already sitting because my knees were shaking. This man has been lying to me all this time. He kept telling me to be patient while he sorted out his life. Nothing could have prepared me for this news. I believed his lies when he said that he wanted to be with me. He was just playing me for a fool. I am lost for words. I walk to my bedroom, close, and lock the door like a zombie, leaving Michael standing in the living room. I sit on the floor in my bedroom, not knowing what to do next. All types of emotions are running through my head. I am angry, hurt, and betrayed. Michael knocks on my bedroom, asking if I'm okay. I did not reply.

He knocks again, "Jazz, we need to talk about this. Please don't shut me out. I can't get through this without you."

Oh, that's it. I swing the door open and yell, "You did not need me when you were fucking the girl. Why the hell do you need me now?" He was taken aback by my reaction.

I walk by him and go straight to the front door. "I want you to leave, Michael!" I yell.

He tries to reason, "Jazz, I know you're angry, but I need you right now. I am prepared to do anything so that you don't shut me out."

I was getting increasingly upset. I scream, "Go to hell and leave my apartment!"

Michael left without saying a word. I slam the door behind him, grab the mug on the living room table, and throw it against the wall.

CHAPTER 22

Betrayal

It has been two weeks since Michael dropped the bomb on me. I isolated myself from everyone, including Sara. The ladies called several times. I lied and told them that I had the flu. They offered to come and bring me soup. I told them that it was not necessary. It was delusional of me to pretend that I was the only woman in his life. I believed Michael when he told me that he wanted to take our relationship to the next level and be patient while sorting things out. I feel like the biggest fool for believing him. Theo called a couple of times and left messages. I did not want to see or talk to him, so I sent all calls to voicemail.

After two weeks of not showing up at the gallery or replying to their messages, the ladies insist on stopping by my apartment. I try to make excuses, but they wouldn't take no for an answer. At around six p.m., Sara, Nadine, and Misha show up with orange juice, chicken noodle soup, and flu medication. I feel bad for lying to them, but I am too embarrassed to tell them the truth.

In Sara's own unique way, she looks at me with disgust, "Girl, you look like a train wreck, and it smells like you haven't taken a shower in months." I ignore her insults. I plop myself on my couch/ bed like I have every day for the past two weeks. Sara asks, "What's going on? Please don't give me this flu bullshit."

I can never fool Sara, but I'm not ready to talk about what's really going on.

Nadine sits on the couch by me and says, "Phew girl, at least you could have taken a shower." She pinches her nose while she frowns.

Misha sits quietly, watching me. I need to catch up with the ladies. Honestly, I don't know where to begin. In the meantime, I change the subject. I ask Sara, "How are you and Cobby doing?"

Her eyes light up. She replies, "Cobby wanted to come to check on you, but I told him that I'd let you know that he's thinking about you."

I wonder how much Cobby knows about Michael's news.

Sara senses something deeper is going on with me. So, she asks, "Jazz, what got you so messed up that you had to put yourself on house arrest?"

Nadine and Misha come and sit on the couch I was lying on.

Finally, I confess, "Michael got another woman pregnant. She's six months."

Nadine blurts out, "See Sara, I told you we should have told Jasmine about this man."

Nadine walks to the kitchen and removes a file from her bag. Before she hands it to me, she replies, "Jazz, Sara thought I needed to look into Michael."

I went from ten to one hundred on the anger scale. I get in Sara's face, then yell, "Why in the hell would you go behind my back and have Nadine investigate Michael?"

Sara fires back, "What the hell do you mean why? Jazz, ever since this man entered your life, it has been one lie after another, one drama after another."

I yell, "This was not your goddam problem."

Sara slams her hand on the coffee table, "News flash Jazz, you made it my problem when you decided to get in bed with a whore. Our business was vandalized because of him. Yes, I asked Nadine to follow Michael, and I'm happy I did."

Sara walks to Nadine and snatches the manilla folder from her. The photos spill out of the folder to the floor. Before Nadine can pick the pictures, I see an image of a couple kissing.

Perplexed, I ask, "What is this?"

Nadine replies, "I followed Michael for a couple of days to learn more about him and maybe find out who's harassing you. I took those pictures a day after the truck incident at your place."

Sara interrupts, "Oh, there's more. He lied about why he was fired from his job in Chicago. He was sleeping with the majority of the women at the firm."

My knees are weak. I sit back down, trying to catch my breath. How is this possible?

I turn to Nadine, then look at Sara, spitting my anger out, "So you guys knew about this for weeks and never thought it was something that I needed to know."

Sara walks back to the living room with her fist clenched by her side. She replies, "Jazz, this man got you so whipped, you can't see what's in front of you. I tried to tell you many times, but you wouldn't listen."

Nadine searched for the words, "I am so sorry Jazz, this man has brought you so much pain. Now, you know the truth."

Sara screams, "How the hell is this man still in your life, Jazz? No matter how many times he tells you things are going to change, you know it's a lie."

Sara calms down. She walks over and sits beside me, "I don't get you Jazz. What happened to you? What did this man have on you to keep you from walking away from him? Is it sex? You are risking your health and life for this man. It's evident he has been having unprotected sex with everyone, including you. Your biggest concern should be getting tested for any sexually transmitted infections or diseases. You're smart, beautiful, successful. Any man would be lucky to have you in his arms. Why this joker?"

I cover my head with my blanket, hoping Sara will stop talking. There's only so much I can take.

Sara yanks the blanket off, yelling. "You're going to go in this bathroom and take a shower, wash your hair, and we're going out."

Sara drags me to the bathroom as she continues her rant, "I'll be damn if I am going to let you sit around here feeling sorry for yourself because of this asshole."

She pushes me into the bathroom and closes the door behind me. She comments, "I better hear the water running, or I am coming in to give you a shower myself."

I look at myself in the mirror. It's not a pretty sight. Sara's right. I need to get my life together. I will not allow Michael to have power over me. He is not worth the energy. I need to move on with my life. I take a long well needed hot shower. I feel so much better. I get dressed and re-join the girls in the living room. Nadine inspects me from my head to my feet to see if my appearance meets her approval. I guess I passed the inspection because she smiles.

Sara continues to scorn me, "I better never see you cry about that piece of shit anymore." I just shake my head and walk out of the apartment.

Sara shoves me into her truck. The ladies jump in the back seat, and we are off to our favorite bistro by the bay. There's something about the water. It always brings peace to my soul. We sit outside by the water, enjoying the Louisiana weather. The cool fall breeze feels terrific. I purposely avoid eye contact with Sara. It's not that she's judging me. I am ashamed that I allowed this man to hurt me over and over. The saddest part of this is that I am so desperate to believe his lies. Thinking about it makes me want to cry. I try to compose myself because I don't want to lose it in front of these people. Sara orders pumpkin lattes for everyone. My stomach feels queasy because I have not eaten anything of substance.

Playing the mom, Misha insists that I order soup. I order the French onion soup, I must admit, the soup feels great going down.

Sara confesses, "I am sorry I snapped earlier. Jazz, I hate seeing you like this." She squeezes my hand, making sure that I'm listening.

Nadine chimes in, "Girl, you're the baddest bitch I know. One day you will meet someone worthy of your love. Stop torturing yourself."

I am not really listening to what the girls are saying. I know they are trying to cheer me up. I keep playing the conversation with Michael over and over in my head. I keep seeing the picture of him and another woman kissing.

Misha realizes that I checked out for a minute. She snaps her fingers to bring me back. She asks, "What can I do?" She hugs me.

I reply, "There's nothing anyone can do. My heart is broken into pieces, and it is my fault."

I see the pity in Sara's eyes, and that's the reason I did not want to be around anybody

I confess, "I feel like a fool."

My head hurts. I don't want to be around anyone. I ask Sara to take me home.

She replies, "Hell no, you are not going to go home to have a pity party."

I protest, "You don't have to take me home. I'll take an Uber."

Nadine chimes in, "Jazz, stop being so dramatic. Of course, she'll take you home."

Sara pays the bill then exits the restaurant without a word. We follow her to the truck. On our way home, Cobby calls. Sara's all smiles. I hear her telling Cobby that I'm in the car and we're driving back to my place. She hands me the phone t tells me that Cobby wants to say hi. I'm not in the mood to speak with anyone, especially Cobby.

I did not want to be rude. Timidly I say, "Hi Cobby, how are you?"

Cobby responds, "Oh Jazz, I am so sorry what you're going through. Michael told me everything. How are you holding up?"

I look at Sara, I whisper to her, "He knew?" I roll my eyes.

I return to the call, "I'm fine."

I am too embarrassed to talk to Cobby about this. I wish I was a turtle so that I could stick my head in my shell.

Sara yells, "NO, SHE'S NOT. She hasn't eaten anything for days. I had to make her take a shower."

I put the phone on mute and tell Sara to shut up. I don't want Cobby to know how pathetic I am, crying over this fool.

Cobby assures me, "Jazz, I am here for you if you ever need me. Michael is fucked up in the head." He sounds angry.

I reply, "I appreciate your concerns, and thank you for thinking of me."

I end the call, then turn to Sara, "Cobby knew about the pregnancy?"

In a concerned tone, she replies, "Yes, Cobby suggested that I check up on you."

In an angry tone, "Why the hell did you let me go through the whole story if you already knew?"

Sara says, "Because I wanted to hear it from your lips."

"How long have you known?" I ask her.

She rolls her eyes, "Before I called this afternoon."

I had a feeling Cobby knew before Michael decided to confess. I did not push the issue with Sara because I know that she means well. For the rest of the ride, we stay quiet, letting the radio feel the space. She pulls up in front of the apartment.

She asks, "Are you going to be okay?"

I reply, "I'll be fine. I will see you tomorrow at work." I give Sara a faint smile to convince her that I'm okay so that she can leave. Misha and Nadine kiss me and promise to check up on me later. Sara waves, and off she goes.

I rush up to my apartment, making my way to the living room. I finally find the energy to go through the messages on my phone. There were ten text messages from Michael and three from Theo. I delete all of Michael's messages without reading them. I read Theo's text. He was concerned that he could not reach me. He said that he called several times, and it went straight to voicemail. My phone was off for a couple of days. I did not want to speak to anyone. I check my voicemail, and everyone and their mama called me; Sara, Michael, Nadine, Misha, Theo, Laycee, and a voice I did not recognize. I listen to the unknown message. It was the art dealer saying that I missed our appointment. I jump up from the couch and listen to the message again.

CRAP! The appointment was yesterday. I was too busy wallowing in my sorrow and completely forgot about the meeting. I saved the message to call first thing tomorrow morning.

I dial Theo's number. He answers it on the first ring, "Jasmine, I am so happy to hear from you. Are you okay? I have been trying to reach you."

Theo was talking one hundred miles a minute. He says, "I wanted to stop by your apartment to make sure that you were okay."

Theo did not let me get a word out as he continued with his concerns. "Why didn't you call me back to let me know that you were okay? What is going on Jazz?"

I let Theo finish with his questions before saying anything. Hopefully, he will not be to upset after I tell him that I missed our appointment.

Attempting to convince him, "I'm dealing with some personal issue. I'll be fine."

Theo says, "Do those issues have to do with the gentleman that was in front of your apartment?"

I explain, "The gentleman's name is Michael, and yes, it has to do with him."

I did not want to talk about Michael with Theo.

I confess, "Theo, I'm sorry, I missed our appointment with the art dealer. I will call tomorrow to reschedule."

To my surprise, he replies," I don't care about that. I just wanted to make sure that you were okay." I am grateful Theo is not upset.

The girls were right. I need to take control of my life and emotions and move on. With that being said, I walk to the kitchen and make myself a sandwich, pour myself a glass of wine, and put on some music. I blast the music in the apartment and start dancing. Music always makes me feel better. It feels so liberating.

At about two a.m. I am awakened by a loud noise. I jump up, trying to listen to where the noise is coming from. I hear footsteps outside my bedroom door. I grab my phone and dial 911. I lock my bedroom door and put a chair behind it to support the lock. I go hide under my bed, waiting for the police to get here. The intruder tries to open my bedroom door. My heart is racing one hundred miles per hour. I can see the intruder's shadow underneath the bedroom door. I can hear the police sirens from my bedroom window. The intruder clearly hears them too because I hear them run out of the apartment. I did not leave the bedroom because I was unsure if the person was still in the apartment. Two minutes later, there's a knock on my door.

The voice announces, "This is the police."

I move from under the bed, remove the chair, and unlock the door. I'm relieved to see the police officers with guns drawn ready to act.

An officer announces, "I am going to look around the perimeter to make sure that the perp is not around."

I'm visibly shaken. A tall officer escorts me to the couch in my living room.

He asks, "Do you live alone?"

Reluctantly I reply, "Yes, I live alone."

The officer continues, "Is there's anyone you need to call?"

I automatically think of Sara, so I let the office know that I have someone. With my hands shaking, I dial Sara's number. I explain, "Someone broke into my apartment while I was sleeping."

She screams, "OMG, Jazz, I'll be right over."

The officer who was checking the perimeter comes back and explains, "There's no one out there."

On the living room floor is a ripped picture of Michael and me. My beautiful vase that was on the kitchen counter is also shattered on the floor. I am beginning to see a pattern here. The vase was a gift from Michael.

The taller officer explains, "It appears that there was no-forced entry. Who else has a key to your apartment?"

I respond, "My best friend Sara is the only person that I gave a key to."

"Where is she now?" asks the officer.

I reply, "I just called her. She's on her way. Wait!" I start laughing. "You don't think Sara is the person who broke in."

The officer looks at me as if I insulted him, "Not at all. We are looking at every possibility and motive. Speaking of motives, would you have any idea who would have done this?" He continues.

I divulge to the officers that my place of business was broken into several months ago, the investigation is still open. The taller officer asked, "Do you think it's the same person?"

I confess, "I am not sure."

That's the God-honest truth. Now that I'm aware that Michael has more women than he led me to believe, it's difficult to identify who's harassing me.

As I'm talking to the officer, Sara bursts through the door, runs right to me and holds me tightly in her drama queen fashion. The officers are looking at us like she needs to go to the psych ward. They are probably wondering if I need protection from her. I give the officers a faint smile to assure them that she is okay.

The taller officer speaks first, "Hello ma'am, I'd like to ask you few questions,"

"I am Sara, and you are?" She turns to face the officers.

I stand between the officer and Sara because I can see which direction this conversation is going. Anyone who comes for Sara sideways, she will read, and she doesn't care who you are.

I explain, "Sara, the officers were asking me who else had the key to my apartment, and I told them that you were the only one I gave a copy to."

The chubby officer asks, "Ma'am, where were you tonight?"

Oh boy, this is not going to end well. I brace myself, waiting on Sara's response.

She replies, "What you mean where was I?"

I say, "Sara, behave."

She turns to me, "No, Jazz they should be out there looking for the person who's harassing you. Did you tell them that they broke into our gallery several months ago, and they still can't tell us who did it?"

Trying to defend the officers, I reply, "Sara, they are just doing their job. Please cooperate."

Sara finally calms down for the officer to ask her some questions.

The officer repeats his first question, "Can you please tell me where you were tonight?"

Oh no, here we go. The wrath of Sara is about to come down and strike the officer for asking the question. To my surprise, she simply answers, "I was home sleeping."

Then he asks the follow-up question while looking at his notepad, "Where you home alone?"

She rolls her eyes, "I was with my boyfriend."

"Can he vouch for you?" The officer continues with his inquiries.

Without saying a word, Sara pulls out her phone and dials a number. All she says with sarcasm dripping in her voice is, "Babe can you come upstairs? The nice officers want to know if you can vouch for me since I told him that I was with you tonight."

Oh, Cobby is here. Why didn't he just come up with Sara? A few minutes later, a faint knock comes from the front door. Sara walks to open it. Cobby dressed in casual clothing is a hint for me that he was spending the night at Sara's. Cobby timidly makes his entrance. He greets me with a hug and asks, "Are you okay Jazz?"

The medium build officer addresses Cobby, "Can you please tell me where you were tonight?"

Cobby flexes his chest and says, "Excuse me!"

I explain, "Cobby, Sara is the only person who has a key to my apartment, and the officer wants to know where she was tonight."

That explanation did not help either. Cobby's voice got loud, "So, you're insinuating that Sara had something to do with the break-in?"

Oh Boy! Once again, trying to defend the officer, I reply, "The officers are just doing their job."

He finally calms down and confirms that Sara was with him all night. The officer noted Cobby's response in his notebook. Then he turns and addresses me, "You should probably change the locks and find a place to stay for a couple of days."

I thanked the officers, received a business card with a case number and contact information then walked them to the door.

I'm pissed that I have to leave my apartment because some crazy bitch decided to stalk me. I know that I don't even have to ask, but since Cobby was spending the night, I ask Sara if I can spend a couple of days at her place until I change the locks.

She smacks me and says, "Did you need to ask?"

Sara follows me to the bedroom to help me gather my things. She gives me a gravely concerned look and asks, "Are you really okay, Jazz?"

I pause because I can feel the lump in my throat, "I don't know. I haven't processed everything that just happened yet. Why is this person targeting me? I have nothing to do with Michael."

Sara walks over and hugs me to assure me that everything will be fine.

"Are you going to tell Michael?" Sara asks.

I respond, "I don't want to deal with him. Besides, I know Cobby may have mentioned it to him. The most frustrating thing is that I don't know who I'm fighting and how to protect myself. I am tired of being the victim. The truth is that I am scared. I don't know what to do. I am not even safe in my own apartment. I didn't ask for this."

The lump in my throat would not stay down. I lost it and started wailing. Cobby must have heard me crying from the living room. He rushes into the bedroom to see if I'm okay. Without a word, he opens his arms, and I run to him.

Sara joins in and says, "We will help you get through this. You're not alone."

CHAPTER 23

Friends

I have spent the last two weeks at Sara's house. Truth be told, I am scared to go back to my apartment. I changed the locks. Misha helped me find and install a quality security system. I'm still traumatized by the burglary. I get jumpy and paranoid around strangers. I changed my phone number. No one has my new number except my immediate family and the ladies. I keep a low profile. The girls come to hang out at Sara's instead of our regular outings.

Misha asks, "How are you holding up?"

With a faint smile, I respond, "I am taking it one day at a time."

She explains, "I've installed a high-tech security system in your apartment with a panic button. If there is a problem, the system will alert all of our phones."

I am so thankful for my girls. They have been my rock.

I hug Misha then comment, "I appreciate you, Mish. Thank you for trying to make me safe."

Nadine was already on her second drink when she sat down beside me. She looks at me, "Girl, I am on a lookout for those bitches, and when I find them, I will put down a beating on them NOLA style."

We all laugh, but Nadine continues, "Y'all laughing; I am dead serious. Jazz, you are too soft. And this Michael would be missing certain body parts by now. You get my drift?"

I'm happy the girls are here to help me through this. I will have to contact Theo to let him know that I can no longer represent him due to the circumstances. I understand that this decision will hurt the business financially, but I cannot dedicate myself to my clients in good conscience. Sara agrees to take some of my clients temporarily until I get my mind right. She will run the day-to-day operation of our business. I'll handle the negotiations and contracts with the artists. Since my relationship with Theo is different from the other artists, Sara thinks I should have the conversation and explain why I cannot work with him. I ignore Sara's comment about Theo being a different client. I know what she's implying. Nevertheless, she's right. I must have that conversation with Theo.

The following morning, I call Theo to schedule a meeting to discuss the changes. He picks up after the fourth ring. He did not realize it was me when he answered the phone. "Oh, Jasmine, you changed your number?" He asks.

I did not really go to any details as to why I changed my number. I reply, "I lost my phone."

"How have you been?" I ask timidly.

He comments, "Well, you ghosted me."

Oh boy! The melodramatic artist. If he knew what I was going through, he would cut me some slack.

Instead, I say, "I have so much on my plate, I had to take a time-out."

He laughs and says, "Wait, you put yourself on a time-out."

I laugh and reply, "I almost forgot why I called. I wanted us to meet to discuss some temporary changes with the gallery."

He sounds worried, "What's going on? Are you closing the gallery?"

Why is this man so dramatic suddenly? I explain to him that the gallery is not closing, but some temporary changes are taking place. Shifting from my chair, I realize the conversation wasn't going anywhere. I ask, "I think we should discuss this face-to-face. Are you available this morning?"

He replies, "I would rather that we meet for lunch."

"Sure, where do you want to meet?" I inquire, hoping he won't try any new tricks.

We agree on meeting at the restaurant he lured me to with his scavenger hunt ruse at twelve-thirty p.m.

Sara and I usually carpool to the gallery, but I wanted to take my car this morning in case I need to do something after work. The drive was a quiet one. I did not turn on the radio, nor did I have to deal with Sara's road rage. I arrive at the gallery, open the doors, turn on the lights, and turn off the alarm. I notice two new pieces of art that I have not seen before. Not that I would because I have been like the walking dead for the last couple of weeks. I make up my mind that I will stop being a victim and regain my life. I put my stuff down on the counter then toured the gallery to get reacquainted. The gallery used to be my happy place, my pride and joy. Sara and I put a lot of sweat into this place. I walk back to my office to start working on projects that I have neglected due to my drama. I know that the business suffered because of me, but Sara held it down. I look at our accounting books, and they're not pretty. I'm usually on top of things. It's time for me to go to work. I fire up my computer and start balancing our books. I must have been engulfed in what I was doing because I didn't hear any of the doors or door chimes connected to the security system. I look up to find Laycee standing over me, staring. My heart shoots up to my throat. She smiles with satisfaction when she realizes she scared the crap out of me. Laycee has been acting peculiarly ever since the incident in my apartment. I told Sara about Laycee's strange behavior recently, but she said that I was being paranoid.

With a smirk, Laycee comments, "I didn't realize you would be in so early."

Feeling uncomfortable, I reply, "I wanted to start my day early because I have to catch up."

She's still standing over me with this strange stare. I finally ask, "Do you need something?"

She cocks her head to the side and replies, "No, I don't need anything."

I want her to leave the office, so I offer, "I brought coffee and muffins. They are on the counter outside. Please help yourself."

She thanks me and walks out without explaining why she was staring at me or offering how long she was standing there before I looked up.

Minutes later, Sara enters the office. I'm relieved to see her. I did not want to be in the gallery alone with Laycee. Ever since her little tantrum at my apartment when she saw Michael's picture on my nightstand, our relationship has not been the same. She never met Michael. I am curious to know what her issue with his picture in my house was. Could she be...nah, she could not be. Maybe Sara was right. I am paranoid.

Sara plops herself on her regular chair in the office and says, "Where did you have to run off to so early this morning you could not wait to carpool?"

I perk up my lips and flare my nostrils, then reply, "I wanted to get an early start this morning, and I did not want to wake you up."

She sighs, "Well, what are you working on?"

I respond, "I'm looking at the accounting, and it is a mess. I have to take the time to get things in order."

She replies, "Well, you know numbers were never my strong suit. I gave Laycee that responsibility while you were away."

An alarm went off. Now, I must triple-check the numbers to see what's going on.

"Have you noticed that Laycee has been acting strange lately?" I ask.

She replies, "Yeah, I noticed that she has been acting different ever since the break-in."

I confess, "The last time she dropped me off at my apartment. She followed me in my bedroom when she noticed a picture of Michael and me on the nightstand, she threw a fit. I caught her hovering over me in the office this morning."

"Humm, that is strange. Does she know Michael?" She asks.

"Funny you say that," I comment. "I was wondering if it is possible that she's the one who has been harassing me."

Sara pauses for a minute then asks, "What do you know about her? Where is she from?"

I did not think that Laycee could have a connection to Michael. I respond, "Laycee is from Huston, Texas." I dismiss the crazy thought.

Sara put both her elbows on the desk, "I think we should have Nadine investigate her."

I roll my eyes and reply, "No, that won't be necessary. She has not crossed paths with Michael. So, drop it."

I tell Sara that I miss my home and I've decided to go back. I refuse to be a victim. My life has turned upside down, and it's time for me to take control.

Having said all that, I announce, "I am buying a gun."

Sara's eyes widen as she gasps for air. Her reaction is what I thought it bed, especially since we share the same sentiment on guns.

I confess, "When the intruder entered my apartment, I was scared and powerless. I will never allow someone to take my power away from me again. I may not know who is stalking me, but I am not going to let them win."

Sara yells, "That's the Jasmine I know and love! Well, you know Cobby is military, so he can help you with the gun and teach you how to shoot."

Sara has always been my rock, my confidante, my protector. She is more than blood to me. I assure her that I'll be fine and not to worry. Sara hugs me and reminds me that I am stronger than I think. Her hug gives me the strength I need. Sara makes her grand exit from the office. I just laugh and go back to continue looking into the business account and the expense ledger. I notice some big discrepancies, so I pull the vendors' list to look at invoices and pay-ables. I make a note to ask Sara about those invoices and withdrawals on the account. Sara and I are cautious about business expenses. The goal was to hire a professional accountant, but we decided to hold off until more revenue was generated. I print the expense reports, invoices, and bank statements, trying to make sense of this mess. Before I realize it, the noon hour hit. Crap, I'm going to be late.

I grab my purse, rushing out of the door. I can hear Sara yell, "Where are you going in such a hurry."

I reply, "I'm meeting a client for lunch, and I'm running late."

Technically, Theo is a client. I did not feel that I had to tell her that it was him. As I walk into the restaurant, I rehearse what I am going to tell Theo. Although I decided to regain my clients, Theo is one of the clients I wish not to work with personally. I will let him know that Sara will be taking over his account and that if he decides to go with someone else, I would understand.

Theo was already waiting for me when I arrived. Wow! Full house. A significant difference from when I was here last. He waves to get my attention from the back of the restaurant. Thank goodness we're sitting in a private booth. Like a gentleman, he stands when I reach the booth and hugs me.

Theo could not hold his excitement. He says, "I have some exciting news, but let's order first because I am starving."

I did not protest because of my stomach's growling. We order lunch with a bottle of wine. Theo tries to pry why I change my number and simultaneously scolds me about why he has not heard from me. I decide not to answer his questions. Instead, I put on a fake smile and say things are good.

Theo senses that I am blowing him off. He complains, "Jazz, why can't you let me in?"

I take a deep breath, "Theo, we've gone over this. I do not wish to discuss my personal matters with you." I continue, "Which leads me to the reason I asked you for this meeting. You will be working with Sara effective immediately. I'm not able to devote the time the clients rightfully need and deserve right now."

. He smiles, "Funny, that's what I wanted to talk to you about."

I reply, "What! You were going to fire me? I am offended."

We both laugh. In a serious tone, he continues, "I am no longer interested in a professional relationship with you Jazz." He reaches for my hand. With a piercing look into my eyes, he presses, "Jazz, I am not going to change my mind."

I wish the conversation would have stayed professional.

Theo asks, "Why are you so scared of being happy? This guy you gave your heart to brings you nothing but pain and misery." I did not realize that I was crying until a tear rolls down my cheek. Theo realizes that he struck a nerve. He comes to sit beside me, "Jazz, stop torturing yourself. You're beautiful, intelligent, and independent. A man that hurts you is a fool. I am offering my shoulder for you to lean on, nothing else. Please allow me to be a friend."

I am uncomfortable talking about my issue with Theo. I confess, "It is more complicated than that."

He replies, "Then uncomplicate things. Why are you choosing to stay with someone who makes you unhappy?"

I did not have an explanation for Theo. He is right. Ever since I got into a relationship with Michael, it only brought me heartbreaks and misery. Now my life is in danger because of his lies. I don't know how much more of Michael's deception and dangerous baggage I can endure. Theo is giving me a way out. Any sane person would jump at the opportunity to get away from Michael. This is too much; I did not come to meet with Theo to discuss my personal life. With tears rolling down my cheeks, I explain to him that the meeting is over and stand to leave.

Theo pleads, "I did not mean to upset you. Please stay."

Theo wraps his arms around me. This gesture makes me cry harder. Thank goodness we're sitting in a private section. He gently rubs my back, trying to calm me down. Why am I so emotional? Just this morning, I told Sara that I would take control of my life and not be a victim. After a few minutes of crying, I free myself from Theo's arms. He was about to move back to his chair. I hold his hand to let him know that he can stay.

He relaxes a little and asks, "Are you okay?"

I take the opportunity to let Theo in a little. I explain, "Someone broke into my apartment while I was sleeping."

Theo acts as if the break-in just happened and starts checking me over like a worried parent whose child had fallen out of a tree. "Are you okay? Did they hurt you?"

I appreciate his concerns. I assured him that I was fine, and they did not hurt me.

He continues his interrogation, "Did you call the police?"

I explain, "I did call the police, and they did not find anything. I had to move to stay with Sara for a couple of weeks."

He pulls me closer, "I'm so sorry you had to go through this."

He kisses me on my forehead and holds me for a while. Our embrace got interrupted when the server approached to ask if we needed anything else. I compose myself and move away from him.

His demeanor changes. His face hardens. He replies, "No, we don't need anything."

He quickly changes from the soft, caring Theo to harden jackass. The servant got the hint, nodded his headed and walked away. I feel better after I talked to Theo about the break-in.

I look at the time and realize I've been in this restaurant for more than two hours. I explain, "I have a lot of work to do. I must head back to the gallery."

He flags the server for the check. As I'm about to leave, he says, "Can I walk with you to the gallery to make sure you're safe?"

As we make our way to the street, Theo reaches to hold my hand. I cross my arms so that he doesn't have access.

He laughs, "Jazz, I know you feel the connection between us. Why are you struggling with it?"

Defensively I reply, "I am not fighting anything because there's nothing there."

I know that's a lie. To be honest, Theo is growing on me. We walk through the park where the children were playing, which prompts me to ask if he has children. He replies, "Children are extraordinary gifts from God. I have to find a special person to have my children. What about you?"

I pause for a second, then reply, "Children have not crossed my mind. Mentally I'm not in a position to bring a child into the world."

He comments, "That's a shame. You would make an exceptional mother."

I smile at the thought of having a baby. That idea quickly fades. Like Theo, I too, have to find an exceptional person to have a child with.

We arrive at the gallery and say our goodbyes outside. I make an excuse that I am late for my next meeting to keep those goodbyes brief. Surely Sara will have something to say if she sees Theo.

He smiles as he asks, "Can I call you later?"

I can use a friend right now, so I entertain the idea of staying in touch with him. He kisses me again on the cheek and whispers, "Later Jazz."

I smile and say later.

Sara is peering through the door as I enter. "Who were you having lunch with?" She asks as if she did not see Theo through the glass door. I roll my eyes as I walk to the office.

She shouts, "Oh, you can act stink if you want to, but I am not going to tell you that lover boy is in the office waiting for you." Her statement stops me in my tracks. I turn around and ask, "Why didn't you tell him to leave?"

Sara replies, "Jazz, I tried to tell the man that you're not here and probably don't want to see him. He waltzed on by without saying a word. I even threatened to call the police. He said he did not give a shit."

I am not in the mood for his bullshit today. I brace myself because I know that a fight is coming. I slowly open the door, and Michael standing facing the door, waiting for me. He looks unrecognizable. This is not the overconfident man I am used to. He looks as if he hasn't shaved for weeks. His eyes are puffy, as if he hasn't slept for weeks. We both stand in silence, waiting for the other one to speak first.

Finally, the silence was too much. I ask, "What the hell are you doing here Michael?"

He looks at me like a wounded puppy and replies, "You blocked me from all forms of communication. Cobby told me that you had a break-in while you were home. Are you okay?"

I shout, "Don't I look like I am okay?" My blood is boiling, knowing that it was Michael who put me in that predicament.

He ignores my question and asks, "Have the police identified the person?"

I no longer have the patience to be interrogated by Michael, so I say, "Yes, one of your obsessed bimbos broke into my apartment and guess what they didn't take anything; but they managed to break a vase you gave me and a picture frame holding our picture."

I can see the arrogant smirk on his face when I tell him about the picture frame. At that moment, I wonder why I still have his picture in my apartment.

I continue, "The police said that there was no forced entry to my apartment. Which means someone had a key. You and Sara were the only two people that had a key." I lied to the cops and told them that Sara was the only one with a copy. I refocus on our conversation, "Michael, let me ask you this, which one of your bimbos might have taken your key to break into my apartment?"

He was taken aback by the new revelation, and he realizes finally that he was the root of the cause of my problems.

"Jazz…"

I abruptly cut him off. "DON'T CALL ME THAT! You don't have the privilege to call me what my friends call me."

He paused for a moment, swallowed that bitter pill, and said, "Jasmine, I am so sorry for what you're going through."

"I don't give a damn about your sorry Michael," I shout.

"Your sorry doesn't stop your bad decisions from coming after me. Your sorry doesn't make me safe in my own home. So, Michael I have had enough of your sorry." Without missing a beat, I continue, "You and I have nothing to talk about. Leave me the hell alone and let me move on with my life. You no longer exist to me. You're the mistake I wish that I did not make. Don't come around the gallery nor my apartment. Just in case it was not clear, whatever you thought we had, IT'S OVER. You can go to hell Michael! Now, leave my office before I have the police come and throw you out of here." He stands there like I had not said a word. I yell, "Get the hell out!"

He walks out of the office without a word. I slam the door behind him. I collapse in my chair. To my surprise, I did not cry. I'm too angry to cry this time. I have made up my mind that I will no longer shed another tear for him. He is no longer that important to me. I will no longer play the victim. A few minutes later, Sara comes to check on me. I assure her that I am fine. And realize that honestly, I am better than okay for the first time in months. My newfound strength will help me through it. I remind Sara to please ask Cobby if he can teach me how to shoot. She opposes the idea of me having a gun because she doesn't like them. But Sara understands that I must protect myself, so she promises to speak with him.

As she's exiting the office, Sara says, "I am so proud of you Jazz. You will get through this and get over that asshole."

I smile and thank her for being so supportive. I turn my attention back to the business account I was working on. The discrepancies were all over the place. When did we buy all of these items? Where are the invoices? Our poetry nights have not been in high demand lately for us to buy so much alcohol. I need to discuss these transactions with Sara and Laycee. It will have to wait. I am drained, so I decide to call it quits.

I gather my things and make my way to the front door when Laycee approaches me, with excitement in her voice, "My son's father decided to give the relationship another chance."

I can use some good news, although it's not my news. I reply, "I am so happy for you. I am sure your son is going to be very happy to have his father with him."

Laycee claps her hand and says, "I think he's thinking of proposing."

"That's great! See, things are looking up for you," I exclaim.

Laycee looks like she's on cloud nine.

"Oh, which reminds me, I have a couple of questions regarding recent transactions I'd like to discuss with you tomorrow," I explain.

Laycee's demeanor changes. She simply says sure.

I leave the gallery and go straight to the gun shop. I decide not to go to my apartment without some sort of protection. A permit is not needed to buy a gun in Louisiana, so I will be able to take the gun right away. Walking in a gun shop for the first time is a bit intimidating. The glass counter is packed with various firearms, knives, and other weapons. The gray wall has posters of girls in bikinis with machine guns. I can never see the logic of having a half-naked girl holding a gun.

The clerk senses my apprehension. He asks, "How can I help you?"

I explain, "I need a handgun, easy to shoot."

He continues, "Have you used a gun before?"

Although my father was in the military, I have never held a gun, let alone shot one. Daddy carefully secured the guns around our house.

He says, "I have the perfect one for you."

He put two nine-millimeter guns on the counter and suggested I hold each to see how they fit in my hand. I like the way the first one feels. I buy the gun, put it in my purse, and head home.

The apartment feels strange after not being in it for the past couple of weeks. I take the gun out of my purse and place it in the drawer of the nightstand. I promise to call Cobby to set up an appointment to teach me how to shoot. No one is going to make me feel like a victim ever again. As I walk to the kitchen to make something to eat, my phone rings. It's Theo. He asks, "What are you doing?"

I reply, "I just got home, and I was about to make something to eat."

In a serious yet light tone, Theo says, "Don't you know it is against the law for a beautiful lady to eat alone."

I reply, "Oh really? Whose law is that Sir?"

He laughs and replies, "The New Orleans Gentlemen's Law."

I start laughing too. I have been depressed for a long time; it feels good to laugh again.

He continues, "Now, I know you're a law-abiding citizen and wouldn't want to break any laws; therefore, I think you should have dinner with me."

I have not been in the apartment for more than two weeks. I want to stay home. I reply, "I'm not in the mood to go anywhere."

He replies, "Even better, I will bring dinner to you."

I really can use the company, so I agree that he can come over.

Sounding excited, "Give me an hour, and I will be at your doorstep with nourishments."

I scan the apartment to make sure that it is up to par to receive a visitor. I light a couple of candles and activate the scented lamp. I take a shower and change into jeans and a t-shirt. I use the time waiting for Theo to check in with Sara. Her phone rings twice before she picks up. Sara sounds concerned, "You did not have to stay in the apartment alone Jazz."

I assure her that I am fine. Besides, I wanted to give her and Cobby their privacy. I let her know that I've purchased the gun.

I confess, "I want to feel safe in my own home."

I remind her to please confirm with Cobby when we can go to the shooting range.

She replies, "He thinks it's great that you have a gun and is happy to teach you how to use it."

There's a knock on the door while speaking with Sara. I tell her that I have to go because someone is at the door. She sounds panicky on the phone. I urge her to relax. "I know who it is to please stop worrying." I love Sara. Honestly, I do, but she could be such a drama queen. I know she means well, but she needs to relax. I hang up with Sara and make my way to open the door.

I was happy to see Theo had jeans and a t-shirt on too. We've never seen each other in casual clothes before, so it was a little weird. He looks good in jeans. Theo has two bags in his hands. He kisses me on the cheek and walks past me.

I follow him to the kitchen as he unpacks the food. I ask, "Are you planning to feed an army."

He stops and looks at me, "Now, Jazz, I don't know why you're fronting. You know you can eat."

I pick up a dinner roll and throw it at him, and we both laugh. I make my way around him to get plates and wine glasses. He purposely brushes against me. He kisses me on my neck, and my body alerts me that I'm in danger if I don't stop him. I hand the plates to him. He chuckles, "I know what you're up to."

I walk to the other side of the counter to grab the glasses. I hand Theo the glasses from the other side of the counter to have no physical contact. He looks at me, "Oh, that's how it's going to be?"

I nod my head to say yes. He takes the bottle of wine then pours two glasses. He purposely touches my fingers as he hands me the wine. I grab my drink and walk to the living room leaving Theo in the kitchen by himself.

I sip on my wine, trying to calm my body down. This is not the time for my body to start acting on its own. I cannot allow myself to be in a position where I do something I regret. Although I told

Michael that it was over between us, it was not that easy. I don't wish to sleep with Theo as a rebound. My body is saying something else. I yearn to be held and loved, but unfortunately, this is not the right time. I don't want to complicate things with Theo. The more I spend time with him, the stronger my attraction is for him. I am mad now for inviting Theo to my house. More upset because he doesn't respect my boundaries. I walk back to the kitchen to get the bottle of wine because I feel that I will need it.

Theo makes a beautiful presentation with the red coconut curry and brown rice. He is a true artist. He hands me my plate and says, "A beautiful plate for a beautiful lady."

I pick at my food, not really eating.

He notices that I'm not eating, "I thought Thai food was your favorite?"

I answer, "Yes, it is."

"Then what's the problem?" he asks.

I lie, "I'm tired."

He put his fork down and says, "Jazz, come on, I am not stupid. Something is wrong. Please tell me what's wrong."

I put my napkin down and ask, "Why do you think that something is wrong?"

He replies, "Well, first, you left me alone in your kitchen for a minute after I kissed your neck."

I stop him and ask, "And why did you think that it was a promising idea for you to kiss my neck after I expressed to you that I am not interested?"

In a deep breath, he says, "Jazz, you're a beautiful, sensual woman. It's hard to behave around you. I promise myself to respect your wishes, but any man would be a fool for not trying to get close to you."

Theo put his wine down and confesses, "Look Jazz, the first time I saw you at your opening, I said to myself, now this is a woman I want to be with. If it is a friendship you can offer right now, I'll take it." Theo continues, "I would rather be your friend than not be in your life at all. But Jazz, you cannot put your life on pause because a dude does not know or value when he has a good woman. This is not on you. It's on him."

If only Theo knew half of the drama I am in, he would say I'm desperately insane. I hear what Theo is saying and I agree with him. But only if it was that simple to move on from Michael. My heart is continually playing tug-of-war with my mind. I understand the logical thing to do is to stay far, far away from Michael. But my heart starves whenever he is not in my life.

I explain, "I appreciate your concerns, but you don't understand how difficult things are."

He put his napkin down and says, "Make me understand Jazz. I don't understand why women allow men to get away with treating them like shit. I watched my mother suffer in silence while my father ran around with other women."

Theo continued, "My mother was a beautiful, vibrant woman. My father's indiscretions finally broke her. He left my mother for his younger lover after thirty-six years of marriage. My mother died of a broken heart."

Now I understand why Theo is so protective.

I assure him, "It's not the case with Michael and me."

I lied. I'm too embarrassed to tell him that Michael has a child on the way as we speak. I walk on the other side of the kitchen counter to pour myself another glass of wine, then pour Theo another glass too. The mood is too heavy. To lighten the mood, I tell him to follow me to the living room. I put on *No Woman No Cry* by Bob Marley and started dancing.

Theo follows suit and starts dancing too. I ask, "What do you know about this music here?"

In a phony Jamaican accent, he replies, "*Ya Mon, mi know lot about Bob Marley and mi feel irie.*"

I laugh so hard I spill my wine on Theo's shirt. "Oh, crap!" I yell. I tell Theo to take the shirt off so I can clean it before it is stained.

He tells me not to worry about it, but I insist.

He reluctantly removes his shirt. I run to the kitchen and grab the seltzer water, pour it over the wine spill.

Theo comments, "Jazz, I don't know why you're making such a fuss about the shirt."

I feel bad for ruining his shirt. After letting the shirt soak for a minute, I drop it in the washing machine. When I return, Theo is standing in the middle of the living room shirtless. The sight catches me by surprise. I nearly trip on the couch. Damn! I never realized how good Theo looks. His perfectly sculptured body is screaming, "touch me." I did not know what to do. My eyes were scanning every fiber of his chest and abdomen.

He notices that I'm staring. He playfully put his hands over his nipples and says, "Now, I know what it feels like when women get undressed by guys on the streets."

I laugh and reply, "Well, you are getting some of your own medicine."

He shakes his head, "Miss Jasmine, please don't put me in the same category with those men who see women as sex objects."

I playfully cross my arms and say, "Oh really, Mr. Theo, just an hour ago, I was afraid to stand near you because you couldn't keep your hands to yourself."

He comments, "That's different."

I look at him, "How so? Please enlighten me."

He responds, "Well, first of all, I was not lusting over you or undressing you with my eyes."

I reply, "Lusting, I beg the differ. I'm not lusting over you nor undressing you. I'm just surprised."

"Okay!" he continues, "So, if I walk toward you right now, you will not try to grab me and take advantage of me?"

I know that I'm playing with fire by accepting Theo's challenge. I don't care. I tell him that he is grown, he can do whatever he wants. He smiles then starts to unbuckle his belt. I panic. What is he doing? How am I going to get out of this? I want to call his bluff, so I pretend that his little stunt is not affecting me. Theo continues to unbutton his pants; With my hands in front of me, I yell, "Stop!"

He smiles and says, "I win."

He knows that I wouldn't let him undress in my living room. Standing here, I am hot and bothered. My head is pounding with lust, and I don't know what to do. Damn! Why does he have to be so sexy? I take one small step toward him, then another. I come closer to him. He stands still, not sure what to do. I touch his chest softly.

He flexes his muscle, then grabs my hand. He says, "Jazz, are you sure you want to go this route?"

His question stops me. I do not want to open that Pandora's box. I need to be clear that Michael and I are over. Things are complicated for me, and I don't want to make it more complex by sleeping with Theo. I was too ashamed to face him, so I turned away.

Theo comes behind me, "I am so sorry Jazz, I didn't mean to make you feel bad." Tears are rolling down my cheeks. He continues, "Don't get me wrong Jazz, any man would jump at the chance to sleep with you. But you mean more to me than just sex. I want all of you, mind, body, and soul. I know that you are not in a position to give me that right now."

He turns me around to face him. He wipes my tears, "Oh Jazz, I can see you're in pain. What can I do?" His concerns made me cry harder. He holds me, "Please talk to me. I promise I will not judge." He rubs my back and asks, "How can I make you feel better?"

I decide to take Theo to his word. I take his hand and walk to the couch; we both sit down. With a sad tone, I explain, "Besides the break-ins, someone is stalking me. The police are not able to identify who it is." I continue, "I decided to buy a gun to protect myself."

His eyes widen as he asks, "You own a gun?"

I muster enough courage to tell him about Michael's extracurricular activities and that he is expecting a child with one of his concubines. I also explain to Theo that I love Michael. It is a hard pill to swallow.

He sits with his mouth wide open, processing. Finally, he says, "I am sorry that you're caught in this dangerous web." As promised, he did not judge. He simply says, "Jazz, I am here for you whenever you need a shoulder to cry on."

I appreciate Theo's offer, but given the circumstances, I think it is wise to stay clear of him for now.

There's a knock at my door. I instruct Theo to see who it is while I go and put his shirt in the dryer. I wasn't expecting anyone, so I did not think twice about having Theo open the door. I'm in the back starting the dryer when I hear someone screaming my name, and Theo is screaming too. I run to the living room to see what the fuss is about. When I get to the living room, Michael and Theo are standing nose to nose arguing. I quickly get in the middle of them and turn to Michael to ask him what the hell was he doing in my apartment.

He is clearly drunk when he looks at me, "So, this is your new boy toy?" Michael yells, "You did not waste any time before you start fucking someone else. You're nothing but a whore."

Theo grabs him by his collar and says, "You will not talk to her like that."

Michael throws a jab at Theo but misses. Theo counters with a punch, knocking Michael to my couch. Michael launches at Theo; they both fall on the floor. I had to do something before they ended up killing each other. I grab the vase on my dining room table and slam it on the floor, and scream, "Stop it!"

They stop and look in my direction. I go straight to Michael, "Who the hell do you think you are coming to my house with this kind of shit? Have you lost your goddam mind?"

Michael attempts to walk toward me. Theo runs past him to get between us. I'm thinking, not this again. I ask Theo to please give me a minute.

He looks at Michael, then at me. "Are you sure?"

I reply, "I got this. I'll be fine."

Theo goes to retrieve his shirt from the dryer. I wait until he leaves the room to unleash my wrath on Michael. "I don't know about your other bitches and how you treat them but don't you best NEVER, and I mean NEVER, call me a whore." Michael was about to speak. I shut him up, "I am not finished. Who I am sleeping with or not sleeping with is none of your business. If I am a whore, what does that makes you Michael? You have balls showing up at my house disrespecting me and my guest."

Michael pleads, "I am so sorry, Jazz. Baby, I am going out of my mind. Losing you is the worst thing that can happen to me. Jazz, I can't deal with not having you in my life. I know I messed up, but please, we have something good."

"Correction. HAD!" I shout.

He stops, takes a deep breath, and begs some more, "Jazz, the other women are not like you. It's just sex with them, but with you, you stimulate my mind, you make me want to be a better person. I need you in my life Jazz."

"You believe your own bullshit, don't you?" I walk toward Michael thinking I may knock the hell out of him. "Please do not insult me by saying that it is just sex with these women. You're a narcissistic, sex-craved asshole who would sleep with anything that has a pulse. I am mad at myself for buying into your bullshit for this long,"

Michael kneels and says, "Please, Jazz give me another chance, give us another chance. I promise you…"

I stop him, "I don't need your promises. You and your bitches deserve each other. So, please, don't you ever come to my house, especially with this bullshit stunt you just pulled."

He was about to protest. I yell, "Get the hell out of my house and out of my life!"

I guess that is the queue Theo needed. He walks toward Michael and flexes, "You heard the lady."

Michael lunges at Theo again. I stop him and say, "Michael, don't make me call the police. I need you to leave my apartment and don't ever come back."

Michael turns and heads to the door. He stops by the door, stares at Theo, and confesses, "No man will ever love you like I do."

I reply, "That's exactly what I am counting on," I slam the door in his face. Theo rushes by my side to see if I'm okay. "I am fine. I just need to be alone right now."

"Jazz, I don't think you should be alone right now," he pleads.

"DAMN IT! I'm sick and tired of men telling me what's good for me." Theo is stunned. I realize that I'm lashing out at him for no reason. I explain, "I apologize. I'm just lashing out."

He replies, "Jazz, I understand."

He grabs his things, kisses me on my cheek, "I will call you to check on you later. I am sorry too for all of this. I couldn't stand by and let him disrespect you like that."

I thank him for defending me as he heads out. I lock the door then collapse on the floor, crying.

CHAPTER 24

Treason

It was weeks since Michael came to my apartment, causing a scene. Although I haven't seen Michael, he occupies my mind day and night. Wonder what he is doing, who is he doing it with, does he sleep or eat. Reminiscing on the memories we had together. He was my drug. Before my world came crashing down, Michael and I were good together. He made me laugh, challenged me, and had great conversations, not to mention that he was great in bed. I guess he had to be an experienced lover with all of these women he was sleeping with. I fought so hard to push Michael out of my mind. The more I tried, the harder it became to forget about him. Everything reminded me of him. My computer screen savers are pictures of trips we've taken together. The souvenirs he bought for me during our trips are all around the apartment. I miss his goofy laugh when he is excited and how he rubs his head when he is thinking about something or nervous. I miss the way he calls out my name. Truth be told, I miss him, but what price was I willing to pay to bring him back into my life.

Theo and I have gone on a couple of dates, but nothing serious. He is trying hard to keep my mind off Michael. Little does he know that there's nothing he can do to take my mind off Michael.

At the gallery, I dive into the books trying to make sense of the discrepancy in the accounts. I contact three vendors, and they all state that they have not delivered any products to the gallery. I check online to look at the signatures on the checks that were written for the vendors. "How could that be?" I ask. The signatures are all similar. I print out several checks, call Sara to verify the signatures. She jumps off her seat and screams, "Someone has been embezzling money from our business."

I whisper, "Keep your voice down." Fearing Laycee can hear her.

She continues, "I gave Laycee access to the business account while you were out."

I pull Laycee's employment file, and her signature matches the signatures on the checks. In a lower tone, I explain, "Sara, we cannot let Laycee know we are on to her until we have all of the information."

Sara's face turns red. She yells, "The hell with keeping this under rap. I'm calling the police."

I beg for empathy, "There has to be an explanation, Sara. Besides, she has a son. I don't want to get her in trouble."

Sara replies, "That's your problem Jazz; you're too soft."

It took some convincing for Sara to agree not to call the police. I call our lawyer for advice. Jacques is a friend as well, so I knew his advice would be in my best interest.

Jacques explains, "If it is $10,000 or more, it is considered embezzlement. You can press charges if you choose to."

I side-eye Sara, then reply to Jacques, "I'm just going to let her go. Having her arrested is not going to bring back the money."

I turn to Sara, "Can you please give me a couple of days before we fire Laycee."

Sara replies, "Jazz, it's either now, or I'm calling the police."

I don't want Laycee to be arrested, so I plead, "Sara, can we do it this afternoon when her shift is over?"

Once Laycee's shift is over, Sara calls her to the office. Laycee enters, and Sara is standing beside me with her hands on her hips.

Laycee cocked her head to the side, "Something wrong?"

With a blank stare, I respond, "Yes, something is wrong. Please have a seat."

She looks nervous. I walk around the desk to be directly in front of Laycee. Without a word, I place the forged checks in front of her. I ask, "Can you please explain these forged checks?"

She shifts to the left of her chair, creating a gap between us. She looks at the documents and replies, "I don't know anything about that."

Sara jumps up in front of Laycee, "You better stop lying, or your ass is going to jail."

Laycee jumps up, enraged, "Bitch, who do you think you're talking to?"

I have never seen this side of Laycee before. She looks like a different person. I get in the middle of the ladies trying to deescalate the situation. Finally, I had enough with one pulling my arm and the other pushing me. I yell, "Stop!"

I turn to Sara, I say, "I got it. You can leave." She was about to protest. I shoot her a look. She leaves but not before she tells Laycee, "You're nothing but a petty thief."

I walk back to sit down in my desk chair, holding my head with both hands, trying to catch my breath, and giving Laycee time to calm down. I continue with my inquiry before Sara's blowout. I say, "Your signature matches the checks."

She gives a defiant look, still not a word of explanation.

Losing my patience, I ask Laycee why?

She replies with such anger, "You think this salary you pay me can feed my son and me? You have no idea what it's like not having money to give your child what he needs."

Disappointed, I reply, "You could have come and talked to us instead of deciding to steal."

She laughs, "You don't give a damn about me." She points at me and continues, "You walk around here with your head dug up your ass with your man drama. When would I have time to talk to you?"

"Don't play the victim, Laycee. You know you could have always come to me." I reply. With a calmer voice, I say, "I need you to gather your things and leave the gallery. You're fired."

Laycee bounces off her chair and stands over me. With hatred in her eyes, she growls, "You think your life is a mess now? Wait! You haven't seen anything yet."

Sara, who was pacing outside the office, barges in when she sees Laycee get too close to me. "Bitch, I wish you would." She sizes Laycee up.

Still shaken from Laycee's threat, I say, "Laycee leave before I press charges."

Laycee grabs her purse. As she exits the office, she stops and says, "You'll regret this. You haven't seen the last of me."

Sara launches toward Laycee, "Bitch, are you threatening us? You have balls." Sara turns to me and says, "See Jazz, this is what I mean. We should have called the cops you're lucky Jasmine is too soft because your ass would have spent years in jail."

Oh great! I thought to myself, not only do I have Michael's crazy girlfriends to worry about, now I must worry about a disgruntled employee. I remind Laycee she's lucky that I am not going to press charges. She storms out of the office without looking back. Sara follows her out.

Something Laycee said haunts me. What did she mean if I thought that my life was a mess now, just wait? My first instinct is to call Michael to talk to him about what happened today. I decided to call Theo instead. He says that he'll meet me across the street at the coffee shop for lunch. As I enter the café, Theo is sitting in my regular booth. He flashes a smile when he sees me. Like a perfect gentleman, he stands as I approach and greets me with a big hug. Theo has already ordered my drink.

I take a sip then ask, "How do you know what to order for me?"

He looks at me with a crooked smile, "I know more about you than you think."

Suspiciously, I reply, "Okay, do I need to do something about your stalkerish tendencies?"

Theo laughs, which makes me laugh too.

I ask Theo about his day.

He replies, "I've been busy working on a special art piece."

"I had to fire the only employee we had. She was stealing from us," I tell Theo.

With a concerned look, he says, "Wow, Jazz, you need a break from all of this."

He is right. I need a break.

Theo asks, "What can I do?"

I smile and say, "You're already doing it. You're lending me your ears."

He smiles, "I am happy that I can at least lend my ears. I am here for you Jazz, always."

Theo says that he must go back to work, and so do I.

Sara is at the counter when I enter the gallery. She ushers me over, signaling that she's on the phone with Cobby. I hear her telling him about Laycee's threat. I roll my eyes at Sara because she's making too much out of what Laycee said. She was angry and embarrassed that she got caught.

She finishes her conversation with Cobby and turns her attention to me. "I told Cobby to hurry up and teach us how to shoot because I will not be one of the missing women in the news."

Leave it to her to always take it to the extreme. I look at her and say, "Girl, why are you always so extra? Don't worry so much."

Sara shoots back. "And you always take things too lightly. You did not see how she was looking at you. Anyway, Cobby agreed to teach us how to shoot this afternoon. So, heifer, we are going!"

I reply, just to shut her up, "It's fine. I am free for the afternoon." I walk back to the office to finish filing paperwork and clean up the mess Laycee left on the account. I am not sure how we can make up for a $10,000 loss. I will have to hit the pavement and sign more artists and continue with our weekend events.

I run the idea by Sara; she agrees that we must do something.

I call Theo and ask, "Hey, do you think your friend Claude can play one weekend out of the month for us?"

Theo replies, "I think Claude will be happy to do me a favor. I'll ask." I also take the opportunity to beg Theo to perform as well. He reluctantly says yes, "Jazz, I have not played for the public."

I make several calls to other local artists I worked with in the past. They were happy to take part. I did not realize the time until Sara screams, "Heifer! Cobby is here." I roll my eyes and thinking this lady does not know when to quit.

Cobby is standing by the door, waiting patiently. It's nice seeing him. I decided to take my car instead of driving with the lovebirds.

Sara protests, "Jazz, leave your car here and drive with us. I don't want you to drive alone after Laycee's threat."

I refuse to let Laycee scare me, so I insist on taking my car. When we arrive, Cobby takes out a duffle bag which I assume has his guns. This is my first time at a shooting range, so I don't know what to expect. Sara looks like a child in a candy store. I'm confused because Sara doesn't like guns, and she did not even want me to get one. Cobby walks up to the counter and asks for a booth. He shows the clerk his weapons and asks for ammo, earplugs, and protective gear.

Cobby asks, "Jazz did you bring your gun?"

I take it out of my purse and hand it to Cobby. He looks at the gun, rolls his eyes, "Women,"

Sara walks up to him, "And what's that supposed to mean?"

He smiles." Oh, women are beautiful, wonderful creatures." We all erupt in laughter.

Once we reach the booth, Cobby explains, "Using a gun is serious. Your decision to shoot at a person cannot be emotional. You cannot have second thoughts when pulling a gun on someone."

He loads the clips with bullets and adjusts the shooting target to make it easier for me. He instructs, "Put your earplugs on. Hold the gun firm."

Cobby continues, "Take a couple of deep breaths to sync with the gun. Once you feel that you've become one with the weapon, then squeeze the trigger." I follow his instruction, take a couple of deep breaths, squeeze the trigger, and boom. There's a kick once the bullet shoots out of the gun. My hand jerks up automatically. The reaction feels so empowering. I practice the entire magazine to be sure that I'm comfortable with the weapon.

Cobby smiles, "I am impressed. You're a fast learner."

He lectures us on how to properly care for the gun. He explains that it's important for me to clean the gun periodically to keep it running smoothly. Cobby reiterates that if I pull a gun on someone, I have to be ready to use it and live with the consequences. I ponder what Cobby is saying. Do I want to know the consequences of killing someone?

Feeling empowered, I stop at Jack's place to get dinner. I have an eerie feeling that someone is following me. I dismiss the thought then head to my car. As soon as I pull out of the restaurant's parking lot, a bright light comes from my car's rear, blinding my view. In panic mode, I drive faster, giving space between the car behind me. I notice the black truck is speeding up to catch up with me. I switch lanes to allow the truck to pass. The truck moves to my lane with its beams blinding me. I make a left turn to see if I am not paranoid. The truck turns left and right on my tail.

Scared out of my mind, unsure what to do next. I call Sara, "Sara, someone is following me in a black truck, and I am afraid they are going to run me off the road."

She replies, "What! Where are you?"

I explain, "I was on St. Anne heading home, but when I realized that I was being followed, I made left on Bourbon. The truck is still on my tail. What do I do?"

Sara must have had me on speaker, Cobby replies. "Whatever you do Jazz, don't stop. Drive to the nearest police station."

Sara screams, "Go to the one on Royal Street. We'll meet you there."

I did just as Cobby suggested. I did not stop. With the truck still on my tail, I zip through the police parking lot. With my heart pushing up to my throat, I look back as the truck speeds off. She replies, "Don't get out of the car. We will be there in two minutes."

Sitting in the car, I remember what Laycee said this morning. Could she be the one who was following me? How long has this person been following me? I have a million questions running through my head. I lost my shit when someone banged on the driver-side window. I'm relieved to see it's Sara. I open the door and jump in her arms like a scared puppy. Through my tears, I say, "Oh Sara, Thank God it's you."

She replies, "Are you okay? Did you get a chance to see who it was?"

Catching my breath, I reply, "No, I could not see who was driving. It was a black truck."

Cobby chimes in, "Jazz, since we're here, we might as well go inside and file a police report."

"I just want to go home Cob. Besides, the police are not going to do shit. We still don't know who broke in the gallery."

Cobby was lost for words. He just hugs me, trying to reassure me that everything is going to be all right. He replies, "Okay, let's get you home."

Sara chimes in, "I'll drive your car while Cobby follows us."

I jump in the passenger seat as Sara hops in the driver's seat. Cobby returns to his truck. During the short drive home, Sara did not say a word, which is great because I'm not in the mood to hear her rant. Fifteen minutes later, we arrived home. Cobby parks beside us. He signals us to remain in the car while he scans the parking lot. Sara holds my shaking hand. The warmth of her touch serves as a security blanket, assuring me that I am not alone in this nightmare. Cobby opens my door and says, "All is clear." He holds out his hand to help me out of the car.

My legs feel like Jell-O trying to get out of the car. I stumble into Cobby's arms. Sara rushes to the passenger's side and screams, "Oh My God, Jazz, are you okay?"

She did not give me time to answer. She orders Cobby to help me in the apartment. Sara is mumbling something under her breath as she is trailing behind Cobby and me. In the apartment, Cobby sits me on the couch while Sara walks to the kitchen. Cobby asks, "Are you okay Jazz?"

I nod my head that I am okay. Sara comes back with a glass of water, puts it in my hands, then says, "Jazz, I don't' think you should be alone tonight."

I want to be alone, so I reply, "I'll be okay, Sisi. Go home. I'll call you in the morning."

Sara protests, "Jazz, you don't have to do this alone."

I take a sip of the water then get out of my seat. I reply, "Girl, I'll be fine. Besides, I have my gun remember."

Sara eases up a bit, then comments, "If you need anything in the middle of the night, ANYTHING, call me." I hug Sara then assure her, "I will. I love you."

Sara chokes up for a minute then replies, "I love you too, Jazz."

Cobby hugs me as they leave. I walk back to the kitchen to put my dinner in the refrigerator since I have lost my appetite. I make chamomile tea then make my way to the bedroom.

Two hours later, there was a knock at the door. I assume that Sara changed her mind and decided to spend the night. I open the door, prepared to give her a make up your mind speech. "Sara, I am…"

It's not her, though. It's Michael, this time, he is not drunk. He cleaned up well. I push the door to close it, he stops it with his foot.

"Jazz, Cobby called me and said someone was following you. Since I can't call you, I just wanted to make sure that you're safe."

Still not letting him in, I waved my hands and spit my words at him. "As you can see, I am doing fine. Now, leave."

Michael pleads, "Jazz, I don't think it's safe for you to be alone right now."

I don't have the energy to cuss him out. I left the door open and walked back to the kitchen to open a bottle of wine. He stands at the doorway, not sure what to do next. After a few minutes of uncertainty, Michael comes in and shuts the door. I can see him pacing and rubbing his head in the living room through my peripheral vision like he usually does when stressed or angry. It's those minute details I notice about him. Without a word, I take my wine bottle and walk back into my room, leaving Michael by himself in the living room. I hear him on the phone. He must have been talking to Cobby because I hear him say, "Yeah! She's fine. She's in her room." He mumbles something else then hangs up.

A few seconds later, there is a light tap on my bedroom door. I ignore the knock. He taps on the door a second time, "Jazz, you have to talk to me, please. We have to talk. Ignoring me is not going to make the problems go away." He pleads.

He taps for the third time. This time I make my way to the door and swing it open, startling him. I walk back to my bed, sipping my wine, pretending that he is not here.

It's not that I don't want to talk to Michael. I'm in too much pain. I don't know where to start. I pour myself the last glass of wine. Michael grabs the glass, "Don't you think you had enough?"

His words anger me, "Who the hell do you think you are?" As I try to grab the glass from him, I accidentally spill wine on his shirt. I start laughing.

He looks at his shirt, "Oh, you think that's funny?" He removes his shirt, his face frowned up.

I reply, "No, that's not funny at all." Still laughing, I continue, "It seems spilling wine on guy's shirt is my specialty."

He looks confused, "You're drunk, Jazz."

Seeing Michael brings all kinds of emotions out of me. But for now, all I want to do is cry. As the tears roll down my cheeks, Michael rushes over and holds me. I try to fight him off, but he overpowers me. I feel helpless.

Michael whispers, "Jazz, it breaks my heart that I am the cause of your pain."

I break free from Michael, lay on my bed, and let the tears soak the sheets. He lays next to me then pulls me closer to him. Once again, my body betrays me. It feels good being in his arms. My body misses his touch, his kisses, his way of making love to me. I hate the fact that I am in the same bed with this huge source of pain. Still, I scoot closer to him. Michael responds by kissing my neck, which sends chills down my spine. Why can't my body be as faithful as my mind? Every time my body and my mind are in a battle over Michael, my body wins. He pulls me closer to him. I can already feel his erection.

I am drunk, lonely, and horny, so it might as well be Michael. I allow him to make my body feel good. He gets up, goes to the closet, and undresses. Damn! I forgot how good he looks naked. Some look good in clothes, but I can look at Michael naked all day. His body is perfectly sculptured. He pulls me to the edge of the bed and starts to undress me. I surrender and allow him to do as he pleases.

Michael looks at me, "God, I missed you." His words don't phase me at all because I know it's all lies. He pulls me closer to the edge of the bed as he kneels. My body excitedly welcomes his touch. Michael knows all my hot spots. He kisses my big toe, and the sensation shoots to my head. I thank God I just had a pedicure. I give a low moan as he sucks my toe. He moves up, kissing my leg, moves up to my inner thigh. I am now trembling with desire.

He stops abruptly, "I'll be back."

Wait! What! Where is he going? How is he going to stop in the middle of the most critical act? My body is too weak to move, so instead, I stay in the same position. Minutes later, he comes back with a can of whipped cream and honey from my refrigerator. He grabs a towel in the bathroom and instructs me to lift my butt. I follow his direction. He pours a little honey on my naval. I jump. I did not expect the honey to be so cold. He licks the honey off my naval. He sprays the whipped cream on my nipples and devours them. My body's now on fire. Without a word, Michael turns me around with my butt in the air and allows the honey to drip slowly. It runs through my rear and drips down to my sex. Michael has his head under me so that the honey will drip in his mouth as he pours more. He uses his tongue to clean the honey off. He repeats the ritual three times, then the third time I cum in his mouth. He whispers, "Sweet nectar." He gets up, "Let's go wash you off in the shower." I follow Michael in the shower, open and excitedly awaiting whatever.

I did not utter a word to Michael throughout his acts. He turns on the water and ushers me into the shower. He grabs my washcloth pours soap on it and begins to wash my back, running the washcloth between my buttocks. Michael turns me around and lets the warm water run on my back while he rubs the washcloth over my breast, my stomach. I take a deep breath as he lowers the velvet washcloth between my thighs. The silky touch of the washcloth makes my legs quiver. Michael attempts to move up. I stop him and say, "Stay there."

He drops the washcloth and uses his fingers instead. Michael's finger moves in a circular motion. The motion drives me crazy. That is all I need; I grab him by his shoulder as I was close to climax. Michael has a stupid grin on his face as I cum again. He whispers, "Missed me."

I look straight at him, "No, I did not miss you; my body is the traitor."

He became serious, "What do you mean that your body is a traitor?"

I choose not to fight with Michael while we were in the shower. But I use the opportunity to let him know how I feel. "I am at war between my mind and my heart. Torn between the pleasure of my flesh and the reality of our situation."

Well, my response ruins the moment. Michael replies, "I am so sorry that you are at war with yourself. As for me, I am clear that I want to be with you, mind, body, and soul."

I rinse my body, leaving him in the shower alone. By now, I'm hungry, so I go to the kitchen to warm up my dinner and make tea. A few minutes later, Michael joins me in the kitchen. He is fully dressed. I'm perplexed as to why Michael looks like his dog just died when I'm the one who's going through the drama.

I ask, "What's your issue?"

He responds, "It hurts knowing that I am the cause of your pain."

I soften my tone a bit because I can see that he is sincere. "I was the stupid one for ever getting involved with you. I am mad at myself for allowing it to get this far."

He asks, "What do you mean to get this far?"

I reply, "You and I should have never happened. I was bamboozled by your charm and promises. I let my ego get in the way, thinking that I was special."

Michael commands, "You make it sound like I was the worst thing that happened to you."

I put my cup down because I need him to pay attention to what I am about to say. "Listen, Michael, after my breakup with my ex I promised myself that I would not let another man get close enough to break my heart. It took me a long time to open up to you."

He rolls his eyes, "Yes, I remember."

"It felt great to finally take down the protective wall I built. When you told me that you wanted to be with me, I believed you. I never wanted to be here, you asked me, no, you begged me to be patient as you try to fix your life. But all you managed to do is impregnate another woman, protect the person who has been harassing me, and lie about your ex-fiancé. The list of your deceptions keeps growing."

Michael interrupts, "Jazz, you have every right to be skeptical. I know I messed up."

"What kind of women are you involved with? Don't answer that, I am no different from the others."

Michael replies, "Don't say that. You are so different from any other woman…."

I look at him, "Cobby often tells me that I made you want to be a better man. His statement could not be further from the truth. You don't want to change."

Michael walks around the kitchen counter and holds my hands, "You have no idea how you've changed my life." He continues, "I was telling Cobby that whenever I am with you, I feel like I am on top of the world. I love your strength, the way you care for people. I love the way you up your game to the next level. I love your passion for life."

"I am over your lies, and flattery won't get you on my good side," I explain.

With a serious tone, he asks, "Would you still be conflicted if I didn't have all of this drama?"

I reply, "We all come with baggage, but your baggage is dangerous, to be honest."

My gut is telling me that he still has not been fully honest with me. I am drained. I did not want to talk anymore because I was afraid of what else he would divulge.

I walk back to the room without saying a word and come back with sheets and a pillow for Michael. With a surprising look, he asks, "Am I in the doghouse?"

I reply, "You're always in the doghouse, sir. Make yourself comfortable on the couch if you want to spend the night."

I hand him the linens and say good night. In Michael's fashion, he jokes, "Can you at least tuck me in?" I did not entertain his request. I walk back to my room.

I change to my pajamas and get ready to hop on my bed when there is a knock on my door. I roll my eyes and proceed to tell him off as I open the door, "Michael, I am tired, and I don't have time to for your crap."

Michael is standing at the door with a woe-is-me look. He pleads, "I am a big guy. Your couch is not the most comfortable couch to sleep on."

It's true. My couch is not the best couch to sleep on. I open the door wider to let him in. In a frustrated tone, I mutter, "Come on, and no funny business."

He looks at me and crosses his heart with his finger, "I will be good, I promise."

I know that he's lying, but I let him in any way. He goes to the opposite side of the bed, and I stay on my side. I must have slept through the night because I was awakened by the smell of eggs cooking in the kitchen. I go to the bathroom to brush my teeth and wash my face. I go to the kitchen, and Michael wearing my apron and nothing. I did not expect that. I give a belly laugh. He turns around with a wicked smile, "Is this how you greet your chef?" He kisses me on the cheek.

I say, "Boy, please go and put your clothes on. I do not want to see your ass while I am eating."

He holds his heart as if he has a heart attack, "I am hurt. Once upon a time, you loved my ass."

I reply, "Yes, once upon a time."

He fixes me a plate of veggie omelets with fresh fruits. Michael has always been good in the kitchen. As for me, cooking was never my strongest suit. The omelet is delicious.

With a devilish look, Michael says," I'm going to take a shower. You're welcome to join me when you're done with breakfast." I give him a dirty look.

He replies, "Your loss." He laughs and goes into the bedroom.

I think about Michael's proposal. I quickly eat my breakfast and strip off my pajama and tiptoe in the shower. I hug him from the back. He did not expect me to take him up on his offer. He grabs my hands to hold him tighter. It feels good holding him. We stay under the shower without saying a word. He turns to face me. He kisses me then holds me tighter. I am not sure if it's him holding me or just the atmosphere. I started crying but did not know why. There's no secret that I love him, but my head cannot comprehend why my heart wants to be with this messed-up man. This is too much. I leave him in the shower. While getting dressed, Michael's phone keeps ringing, I glance at the phone and the caller ID says, Mona. She was persistent because she called three more times. On the fourth ring, I pick the phone up and take it to Michael. I thought about answering, but I refuse to play the jealous side chick. Instead, I hand the phone to him and let him know that someone was ringing his phone off the hook, and from the looks of it, it must be important.

He looks at the phone screen then looks at me, "Jazz, can you please excuse me for a minute?"

I look at him as if he had lost his mind, "You better not open your mouth and ask me to step out of my OWN bathroom so that you can speak with your trick."

Michael smiles, "No, I was going to tell you that you're amazing and you did not have to bring me the phone. I will call her when I am ready." He did not hide the fact that it was a woman calling him.

Michael finishes and goes out to the living room to make his call. I stay in my room and get dressed. I hear him on the phone arguing. It wasn't necessary for me to eavesdrop because he was screaming on the phone. I assumed that he returned Mona's call.

In the conversation with whoever was on the other line, he yells, "I don't have to run to the phone every time you call. I am sick of your threats, Mona; you can go to hell." Then silence.

I waited about ten minutes before I step out of my room. I find Michael pacing in the living room while rubbing his head. He stops pacing once he notices that I'm looking at him. "I am sure you heard me from your room."

I reply, "Yes, and I'm not interested." He did not know what to say.

I look at him without responding. Michael states, "I'm still concerned about your safety. Can I drive you to work?"

I decline his proposal. I simply say that I will be fine.

He asks, "Can I come by tonight?"

I reply, "It was a mistake letting you in my house and probably thinking that it's that easy for you to come back into my life."

After his phone call, I realize he'd never be free from his drama. I tell Michael that he has to leave because I must go to work. He reluctantly does so. I sit at the kitchen table, contemplating what my life has become.

CHAPTER 25

The Set-up

I am on edge driving to work this morning. I look at the rearview mirror constantly. I look to see if any cars are driving too close behind or beside me. I make it to the gallery and park in the front to watch my car during the day. Sara is already waiting for me at the door when I arrive. She greets me with a warm embrace and asks, "Are you okay Jazz?"

Oh! It's too early for her interrogations. I just say, "Fine," and continue walking to the office.

She continues, "Did Rico Suave shows his face at the apartment?"

I respond with a faint yes. I don't have the energy to go into the details of my encounter with Michael to Sara.

She asks again, "Are you truly, okay?"

I give her a fake smile, "Sara, you worry too much."

Thinking that she would let it go. She comes at me in full force, "Well, somebody has to do the worrying. You have crazy heifers breaking in your home, following you, breaking into the gallery, and you don't think it is normal to worry."

"Sara!" I scream. "Not now. I can't do this right now. I said that I was fine, now leave it the hell alone!"

In all the years Sara and I have been friends, I don't recall having to raise my voice at her. I'm overwhelmed. It's not fair that I'm taking it out on her. She just wants to be sure I am safe. Truth to be told, I am numb, I don't know how to feel. I am scared that one of his crazy girlfriends may put a bullet in me.

I pause for a second, "I am so sorry." I explain, "I did not mean to yell. I appreciate your love and support. I just need to breathe."

Sara walks over and gives me another hug. That hug was what I needed, especially after this morning's fiasco in my apartment.

I keep myself busy at work to keep my mind off my troubles. There are two fresh artists I was targeting. I met them at the New Orleans art festival. I was impressed with their work and wanted to meet them. One specializes in contemporary art and the other in modern art. They merge their talents and create beautiful master-pieces. Their work is like Van Gogh meets a graffiti artist. It was a fresh new idea and I wanted to represent them. I set up an appoint-ment to discuss the possibilities of working together. After I hang up the phone, I shout a big YES! Sara comes running into the office, ready to fight. I laugh at this petite firecracker. She's always ready for a battle. That's one of the reasons why I love this woman. She is annoying at times, but her heart is in a good place.

Still laughing, I tell Sara to please put her weapon away and quickly explain I'm excited about the two artists I want to work with. Her look of disappointment made me laugh harder. I come around the desk and give her a kiss and a big hug. She tries to push me away. I know that she's faking, so I hold her tighter.

Sara's mood changes, and she's back to her jovial self again. She exclaims, "Let's go out to lunch and celebrate."

I reply, "We can't afford to close the gallery. Why don't you call the restaurant around the corner and have them deliver instead?"

A few minutes later, I hear her fussing with someone on the line. She states, "The last time I ordered lunch from over there, you messed up my order. Please be sure that it's not the case today." As Sara is placing our lunch order. I shake my head, looking at this little tyrant bullying some poor order taker. She comes back with a bottle of wine from our inventory.

Jokingly I ask, "Did you pay for that?" She gives me the middle finger. Thirty-five minutes later, the delivery guy shows up with our food. Sara is giving the poor delivery guy a tough time.

She hollers, "I already told the person who took my order that I was not going to pay for the food if it wasn't delivered in thirty minutes. You are five minutes late, so you better call your supervisor and let them know that I ain't paying."

I grab my wallet, pay for the food, and tip the poor guy a big tip for his trouble. Sara says to me, "You're such a softy."

Sara did all the talking while we were eating. I replay what happened in my apartment this morning. I'm too embarrassed to tell Sara that this man asked for privacy so that he could call his female. When did I lose my self-respect to allow a man to disrespect me in my own home? How desperate am I to allow this man to touch me, knowing someone else is getting ready to have his child?

The day ended, I decided to take a different route going home just in case someone was following me. I look at every car passing to see if I recognize the car that was following last night. I try to memorize every license plate that passes me. My paranoia is at an all-time high.

I arrive home safely. I pour a glass of wine while taking off my shoes when there's a knock at the door. It better not be Michael; I don't have the energy to deal with his ass. I look through the peephole, and two officers are standing in front of my door. I am hoping they have news on the person who broke into my apartment.

I open the door, and a tall officer asks with a stern voice, "Are you, Ms. Jasmine Banks?"

With a puzzled look, I reply, "Yes, I am Jasmine. Can I help you?"

His partner, who looks like a retired wrestler, asks, "Can we come in?"

"Not until you tell me what it is about," I reply.

The smaller-built officer seems to be the dominant one. He replies, "We received complaints that this apartment had illegal activities going on."

I laugh, thinking someone is playing a prank. I reply, "That's funny. This must be a prank. Please let whoever it is know that I don't have time for jokes." With that, I shut the door.

The cocky officer stuck his foot out, preventing it from closing. Clearly pissed off by my action, he scolded me, "I can assure you, Ms. Banks, this is not a joke."

I noticed two other officers standing just outside of the doorway, ready for action. I realize that he is serious, so I change my tone, "Who complained? What illegal activity?"

The bulky officer seems nicer. He instructs, "Ma'am, I'll need you to step outside while we search your apartment."

Defiantly I ask, "Do you have a warrant?" He pulls a paper from his back pocket and hands it to me.

I can't believe my eyes as I am looking at a legal warrant for a search with my name on it. "This must be a mistake." I plead with the officer.

He gives me a crazy look, "Step aside, ma'am."

I comply and step aside as the officers walk into the apartment. I quickly dial Sara's number, letting her know what's happening. She thought I was joking. I tell her that the officers are searching my apartment as we speak.

In a panic, Sara asks," Have you called Jacques?"

I explain, "There has to be a mistake. I don't think I need to call him."

Sara screams, "Jazz, why are you so naïve? Call Jacques and let him know what's going on."

I hang up with Sara and immediately call Jacques. Jacques and I have been friends since college. I was so excited when he passed the bar, and I became his first client. He works for a non-profit organization defending the underserved. I was happy when Jacques picked up the phone.

With fear in my voice, I say, "Jacques, thank God you picked up."

Sounding concerned, he replies, "Is everything okay, Jazz?"

"The police showed up to my apartment with a search warrant, saying that they received complaints of illegal activities," I explain in one breath.

"What? Wait! You're joking." He comments incredulously.

I reply, "I wish it was a joke. The police are inside searching as we speak."

"Okay, I am on my way. Please don't say anything until I get there. Send me a copy of the warrant," he comments.

I started pacing up and down the hallway, hoping this was a dream. I am going to wake up any minute. Twenty minutes later, Sara and Cobby show up to find me pacing. Sara asks, "Why are you in the hallway, Jazz?"

Cobby hugs me and asks, "What can I do?"

"Can you make this nightmare go away?" I ask while holding on to Cobby.

As Sara tries to go inside my apartment, the first officer that spoke to me steps outside with three Ziplock bags full of pills and other unidentified substances.

He walks up to me and says, "Ms. Banks, you're under arrest for possession and intent to distribute narcotics. You have the right to remain silent. Anything you say can and will be used against you in a court of law. You have the right to an attorney, and if you can't afford an attorney, one will be provided to you."

"Surely, it has to be a mistake!" I protest. "I have never seen these things before. Officer, I don't even smoke."

Sara jumps in, "This is some bullshit. You got the wrong person. There was a break-in, and nothing was missing. If you all did your job, she wouldn't be in this predicament."

The officer ignores Sara's rant and asks that I put my hands behind my back.

This is not happening. I am being arrested for something I did not do. My legs start to shake. I did not know what to do.

Sara yells, "This is bullshit!"

The officer snaps back, "Stay back, or you're going with her."

Cobby tries his best to calm Sara down so that she wouldn't get arrested too.

Sara continues with her rant, "Cobby, can't you see Jazz in being set up, and these officers don't give a shit about the truth."

Cobby trying to reason with her, begs, "Sara, you're not going to do Jazz any good if you're arrested with her."

"I don't give a shit," she continues screaming. "Let them come for me. I am not Jazz."

Sara pulls out her phone as she's yelling at the police. She puts the phone to her left ear and freaks out, "Get your ass over here. They found drugs in Jazz's apartment, and now they're arresting her."

I assume that she's talking to Jacques. I can hear Sara's voice from a distance because I'm no longer in my body. I can only feel the officer's cold metal bracelets fastening on my wrists as he mumbles something. I have never been in trouble with the law. I don't even have a ticket, now here I am being handcuffed for possession of narcotics. I don't smoke. I drink wine occasionally. I don't do drugs. There must be a mistake. Someone has gone to great lengths to set me up.

I can't put one foot in front of the other as the officers usher me to the car. They carried me to the back of the patrol car. The back seat is cold and hard. My wrists are throbbing, the handcuffs are too tight. Sara is still fussing with the officers. Sara better not get herself arrested because I need her to get me out of this mess. My life is out of control, and there's nothing I can do about it. Someone hates me enough to go to such drastic lengths to set me up for drug trafficking.

The patrol car starts to move then I realize that this is real. I look back to see if Cobby and Sara are following the patrol car and thank goodness they were. I keep my eyes on them instead of facing forward to look at the back of the officers. It's a twenty-minute ride, but it feels like an eternity. I'm going through the list of people who've entered my apartment invited or uninvited. Laycee, Theo, Michael, the intruder, Sara, and Cobby, Misha and Nadine. I start a process of elimination. Well, I know that it's not Sara or Cobby. Michael wouldn't do that to me. The intruder is my first thought. Laycee interestingly is the second person who comes to mind. What motive would Laycee have to try to destroy my life though? I had not done anything but be nice to her and tried to help her when she needed help. Although she stole from us, I did not press charges or call the police. Why would she want to destroy me?

The arresting officer ushers me to a desk where a female officer is sitting. She introduces herself as Detective Dubois. She seems polite, even asks if I want anything to drink. I decline because, frankly, I don't trust anyone. She moves a family photo near her computer to make space on the already cluttered desk. She begins asking me basic questions, my name, date of birth, my address. Thirty minutes later, she finishes her interrogation and takes me to another room to be fingerprinted and photographed. I want to scream that I'm innocent, but I am sure they have heard that from everyone they arrest. Instead, I hold the photo sign and pretend that I'm doing a photo shoot. The camera flash startles me.

The officer barks, "Turn to your left." FLASH. "Turn right." FLASH. He barks again, "Stand by the fingerprinting station and wait your turn."

He makes it sound like there's a reward at the end of the line. I patiently waited for my turn as the officer demanded. Then I'm put in a holding cell with two drunk women. The cell is smaller than what I've seen in the movies. It has two metal benches against the wall. The cell smells like feces and urine. My germ phobia kicks in. How did I get here? How did I go from an upstanding citizen to an accused felon? I got involved with the wrong man. It is now two in the morning, and no judge is available. I sit in the corner on the cold floor, away from the two drunk ladies who seemed to be having an explicit conversation.

Later that morning, a female officer who seems to have had a bad night, shouts, "You ladies are going to see the judge make yourself look pretty."

She handcuffs us and directs us outside to a bus. There are other prisoners on the bus waiting. I take the first seat upfront, trying not to make eye contact with anyone. A young lady comes and sits beside me. She looks as if she's a frequent flyer in this arena. She has dirty blonde hair and is covered with tattoos.

She asks, "What's your name?" I was not in a talking mood, so I did not entertain her interrogation. She comments, "Oh, a silent type."

I give her a dirty look. I hope it warns the heifer to leave me alone. She gets the message and does just that. The ride to the courthouse is a short one. Once the bus stops, the officer riding with us announces, "Please make a single line and follow the yellow line entering the court."

I've always wondered how prisoners get in the courthouse without being seen by the public. The officer places us in a waiting room and then calls for those who have lawyers arriving to discuss their cases. That's the best news. I need to speak with someone I trust.

Ten minutes later, I see people in suits entering the waiting room where we were. I assume that they are lawyers. I spot Jacques as he enters the room. He is six feet three inches tall and as fine as he can be. A native of New Orleans, Jacques could have worked for any major law firm in the city. Instead, he opted out to work as a defense attorney in a small firm. He notices me from the entrance. He flashes his beautiful smile to say that he is here. The young lady who was harassing me on the bus walks over, "Damn! Is this your man or your lawyer?" Once again, I ignore her and walk over to meet Jacques.

He looks around to see if there's a secluded area where we can talk. Luckily, there's a small room with a chair and a table that's unoccupied.

Once we were away from everyone, he hugs me and asks, "How are you holding up?"

I respond, "I am scared."

He pulls out his notepad and comments, "Start from the beginning, tell me everything."

I start from the time that I met Michael, my history with him. How I have been harassed and threatened by his girlfriends. I let him know that someone broke into my apartment while I was sleeping, but nothing was taken.

He asks, "Do you think that the person who broke into your apartment might have planted the drugs in there to make it look like they were yours?"

"I've been thinking about who has access to my apartment, and the only person I can think of is Laycee, an employee that I fired for stealing," I answer.

Jacques jots down some notes and explains, "You will be charged with possession with intent to sell. Since you don't have any priors, I'm going to request bail."

He cautions me that the judge we are going to see is tough on drug traffickers. I did not want to hear that. I started crying, thinking I had to spend another night in jail for something I did not do. He assures me that he will do everything in his power to get me out of here. I trust him, but the idea of spending another night in jail scares me.

It's our turn to appear in front of the judge. I shiver as I enter the room. The judge has her hair in a tight bun which makes her look like an angry librarian. Her thick glasses make her look old. Her lips twist to one side as the bailiff makes his announcement.

The bailiff yells, "People versus. Jasmine Banks." My heart shoots up to my throat, hearing my name in this place. The room suddenly got colder. My hands are shaking. Jacques notices and encourages me, "Don't worry, you don't have to speak. I will do all the talking."

The lawyer for the State Attorney's office looks like he just passed his bar exam. He is tall and slender with an overconfident stance. The young lawyer addresses the judge, "Your honor, Ms. Banks is charged with possession with intent to sell. Her residence was searched after the police received a tip that illegal activities were taken place in her residence. Officers found one hundred and fifty oxycodone and two hundred methadone pills. Due to the number of drugs found in Ms. Banks' home, we ask that bail be denied until the trial."

I wanted to scream. I don't even know how to sell drugs. How in the hell would I know where to buy them? When it's Jacques's turn to speak, he opens a folder and addresses the court. He commences, "Your honor, Ms. Banks had her house broken into three months ago, ironically nothing was missing. Ms. Banks has also been the victim of a stalker since entering a relationship with her current boy-friend. Her business was vandalized, her apartment was broken into, her car tires were slashed, and she was followed by an unidentified individual. The police reports are all here, your honor. Ms. Banks is an upstanding citizen with no history of drugs or violence, not even a parking ticket. In light of all this, and the overwhelming evidence that she is a target of a potentially threatening individual; your honor, I am asking that bail be set, and Ms. Banks released until trial."

The judge examines the papers, then takes a minute to make her decision. The minute feels like it's an hour to me.

The judge finally says, "Considering what is presented to me, bail is set at $5,000, a trial date must be set in thirty days, the defendant is to surrender her passport if she has one to the court." With that, she slams her gavel.

A sense of relief comes over me, and my hands stop shaking. Jacques walks with me to pay bail. I had to go back to jail to get cleared and retrieve my items. Jacques offers to take me home. I tell him that Sara is waiting for me. He smiles. "How's Sara? Still crazy?"

I smile and say, "She has graduated to insane."

We laugh as Jacques hugs me once more, "I will be in touch to prepare for the trial."

I sign the release papers, and the clerk hands me an envelope with my items. I quickly walk out of the facility, not giving them time to change their mind. Thank God Sara was waiting for me. I jump in her car and tell her to drive. She looks at me and asks, "Do you want to go and get something to eat first?"

I respond, "No, I want to go home and take a hot shower."

I want to wash the stench of the jail off me. Sara did not protest.

Once I arrive at my apartment, I go straight to the bathroom, strip off my clothes, and jump in the shower. As the hot water cleanses me, I cry out my frustration. I cry and cry and cry some more. I completely forgot that Sara was in the apartment with me. She must have heard me crying and wanted to know if everything was okay. I ignore her knocks and let my tears fall for a good ten minutes. I trip over Sara as I'm getting out of the shower. She's sitting by the door waiting with a sad look on her face.

She jumps up and asks, "Jazz. Are you okay?"

I respond, "I'm exhausted. I just want to go to sleep."

Sara continues, "Do you want me to make you something to eat?"

I explain, "Thanks, but I don't have an appetite. I just want to sleep."

If I go to sleep, everything will be fine when I wake up. It's still early in the day. Sara replies that she's going to the gallery because she has a meeting with a new artist. She gives me a big hug and says, "Everything is going to be all right. You just need to hang on." I give her an almost smile.

I put on my pajamas, turn off the phone and climb into my bed. I must have been in a deep sleep when I hear a knock from a distance. The knock becomes louder as I become fully awake. Suddenly, I panic because I'm unsure who's on the other side of the door. What if it's the police? What if it's the person who's trying to hurt me? What if.......

The knock did not stop. I look through the peephole, and here this jackass is banging on my door. Cobby must have told him about my arrest.

I fling the door open and scream, "Haven't you done enough, Michael? What the hell do you want?"

With both of his hands up, he replies, "Jazz, Cobby told me about the arrest last night. I am sorry. I am going to do everything to end this nightmare."

Still standing in front of the doorway, I reply, "Michael, your empty promises don't mean shit to me right now."

He pleads, "Jazz, please let me in. I promise it won't take long." I walk away, leaving him in the doorway. He comments as he makes his way inside, "I've been thinking of hiring a private investigator."

I turn with a disgusted look, "You wait until I am arrested to try to find out who is ruining my life? Do you have any idea what I just went through? The humiliation I suffered for something that I didn't do."

He rubs his head and then explains, "Jazz, I thought I could manage this. I am so sorry it took me this long to hire a professional to help us."

I yell, "Your I'm sorry, don't mean shit to me right now, Michael! My life is ruined! Who knows? I may end up in jail for a crime that I did not commit! You want to help me, Michael? Why don't you show me pictures of your girlfriends? At least I'll know who to be on a lookout for!"

Michael rubs his head and says, "Because I didn't want you to play the comparison game."

"What kind of bullshit answer is this?" I scream, "Do I look like someone who would compare myself to anyone? Just in case you did not know, I am immensely proud of who I am and would not want to be in anybody's shoes but mine."

Michael rubs his head and replies, "Jazz, I know you are a confident person. That's one of the qualities I love about you. I did not mean to upset you." He pulls me closer to hug me, "Jazz, I know that I am the cause of your troubles. I am going to do everything in my power to make this right. Please believe me."

I'm exhausted from spending the night in jail. I do not have the energy to deal with him. I pull away from him, then reply, "You know what Michael, you can go fuck yourself!" I walk back to my bed, leaving him standing in the living room.

CHAPTER 26

The Wrath

I wake up to someone yelling in my apartment. It takes me a minute to realize it's Sara. I jump off the bed, run to the living room to see who she is yelling at. She is in Michael's face with all her guns blasting. Oh God! My guess is that Michael never left last night. Sara has a key to my apartment. She must have opened the door and found Michael there. Sara never liked Michael from the first time she met him. I should have listened to her when she told me that Michael was trouble, and I should have left him alone. I should have never gotten involved with Michael. My gut was still yelling RUN!

Sara yells, "You have some balls showing your face here. It's because of your lying, cheating, manipulative ways that Jazz is in this predicament."

Michael shoots back, "Who the hell you think you're talking to?"

Oh boy! I wish he did not go there. I allow them to hash it out without interrupting.

Sara shouts back, "A man who would fuck anything that has a pulse. A man who's going around spreading his seed around without knowing how many children he has out there. A man who manipulates his way into a woman's heart with no intention of loving her. I have thousands more if you are interested to know who you are. You see, you may fool Jasmine, but I got your number the first time I met you. You're nothing but a shallow, lying, cheating son-of-a-bitch."

Michael rubs his head and clinches his fist, "Sara, I've put up with your shit because of Jazz. Today is not the day."

Michael turns and realizes that I was watching the show. He runs to me and says, "Jazz, I am sorry. I didn't mean to wake you."

Sara moves closer to me like a competing parent waiting to see who I will address first. I did not feel like entertaining either of them, so I walk to the kitchen to make tea.

Michael follows me to the kitchen. He whispers, "I'll call you later to finish discussing the private investigator." He kisses my cheek then leaves without saying anything else to Sara.

I look at Sara and shake my head. She starts, "Don't tell me that you're allowing Michael back in your life after all he put you through. Jazz, do you realize that your life turned upside down ever since you met this man? Why was he here?"

I open my mouth to explain to Sara that he wants to hire a private investigator to help me. But instead, I turn and go back to my room.

She follows me to the room, yelling, "Don't tell me that you're mad at me because I told that jerk off."

I look at Sara, "If you shut up and listen for a minute, you would know that he was trying to help me."

She screams, "I can't believe that you believe this man. Don't be stupid Jazz, if he wanted to help you, he wouldn't have waited this long to do so."

"You think you know everything," I yell at her, "I shut him out of my life many times. How was he supposed to help me? Sara, I am grown," I continue. "You need to stop thinking that you can control who I decide to be in my life." She looks hurt. I soften my tone a little and explain, "I understand that you have my best interest in mind, but I can take care of myself."

She did not say a word. She just sits on my bed, staring at the ceiling. I know that she's upset and pouting like a spoiled child. I have bigger things to worry about than Sara's feelings. I climb into my bed without saying anything to her. I'm physically and emotionally exhausted. I need rest, not a lecture from Sara.

She realizes that I wasn't about to entertain her, so she pokes me on my side and asks, "Are you hungry?" I don't answer, so she asks again like only she could, "Heifer! I said - are you hungry?"

I smile and say yes. To be honest, I have not eaten anything since I left jail. Sara jumps off the bed, runs to the kitchen, and comes back with two bags. She pulls out a bottle of wine, a tub of ice cream, and sushi, just what I need. Without a word, Sara hands me chopsticks, my sushi, and a glass of wine. I take a sip of the wine, and it could not taste sweeter. The difference a day in jail makes; you appreciate the smaller things. We ate in silence. I did not have the energy to try to defend my actions to Sara. She asks, "Do you want another glass of wine?" I gladly accept it.

"I am sorry," Sara confesses, "I really shouldn't have screamed like that when you were trying to rest. I am not trying to control your life, Jazz. You have a good heart, and you see good in everyone. Your heart is clouded by your judgment when it comes to Michael." She walks over and hands me the tub of double Belgian chocolate with two spoons, just like when we were roommates in college.

I know that Sara means well. I did not choose to love Michael. It was my foolish heart that decided to fall in love with him despite his transgressions. Instead, I tell Sara to chill with the attacks on Michael. She promises that she will try for my sake. We finish our ice cream and drink the rest of the wine.

Jokingly Sara asks, "Did big Bertha visit you in your cell?"

I give her the middle finger, and we laugh. Just like that, we are cool again. I can never stay mad at Sara. She is my ride-or-die chick, my BFF, and my partner in crime.

I finally confess, "I'm scared Sisi. I don't know what's going to happen to me from one moment to the next. I don't know who's doing this. The only person I could think of is Laycee, but why?"

Sara replies, "Jazz, I did not want to say anything but the last time you and Rico…I mean, Michael were in the gallery when his tires were slashed. I caught Laycee watching Michael with such hatred in her eyes. Do you think there's a connection?"

"Now that you mention it," I reply, "The last time she was in my apartment, she saw a photo of me and Michael on my nightstand. She kept asking about him. It was really uncomfortable."

Sara comments, "That's not a coincidence Jazz."

I did not want to sound paranoid, but Sara is making sense. I say, "Let's call Nadine and have her look into Laycee. The trial is in thirty days, and Jacques said that we must be prepared. I want to find who's doing this to me and bring them to justice."

Sara replies, "I am going to do everything to help, even if I have to be nice to Michael for a little while."

Sara decides to spend the night, and I welcome her company. A nightmare jolted me from my sleep. I forgot Sara was sleeping next to me. She jumps up, wondering what's wrong.

My dream was intense. I was strapped to an electric chair surrounded by many faces, some I knew, and some were strangers. Among the faces were Michael, Theo, Cobby, and Sara. They were all laughing, taunting me. Laycee was holding a switch device with a big red button and was getting ready to push it.

I tell Sara to go back to sleep, and that I had a bad dream. I go to the kitchen to get some water while pondering the dream. What does it mean? Are all these people involved in my demise? I shake off the idea that Sara would be part of anything that would cause me pain. She's sitting on the edge of the bed, waiting for me to enter the room. I decide not to tell Sara about the dream because I'm afraid that it may come true

CHAPTER 27

Logic Vs Reason

The next day I woke up with a bad headache. I let Sara know she'll have to open the gallery. I am going to stay in bed for a little longer to deal with my headache. She agrees that I should take the day off. Later that afternoon, Michael calls to say, "Come on, you need a spa day. I am taking you to Cobby's place for a massage."

A spa day sounds good right now, I thought to myself. I have not been back to Cobby's place since my sexcapade there with Michael. I think a good massage will cure my headache. He says that he is on his way to pick me up.

When he arrives, I ask, "You think a massage will get rid of my problems?"

He replies, "Probably not Jazz. But right now, I just want you to destress and relax. I'll take you to your favorite restaurant, then I'll bring you home."

It's been a while since I was in Michael's care. He hops in the driver's side then grabs my hand, "Jazz, everything is going to be okay."

I snatch my hand from him and ask, "How can you be sure?" He did not answer, and just like that, the conversation ended.

We finally arrive at Cobby's place. I hop out before Michael can walk around to open my door. I rush to go inside. Luckily Cobby was in the lobby. He practically ran over to give me a bear hug. I needed that hug. I feel like my world is crashing down, and there's nothing I can do about it. I stay in Cobby's arms for a little bit longer. He has become a great friend. Michael comes in while Cobby is still holding me. He clears his throat as if he did not want to interrupt the moment.

Michael finally speaks up," Cobby, will you please take care of Jazz for me for a couple of hours?"

Cobby replies, "Do you need to ask, man? Clearly, she is stressed and scared with good reason."

I sense a hint of judgment in Cobby's voice. Michael ignores Cobby's comment, walks over, kisses me on my forehead, and reminds me that he will pick me up within two hours. He leaves without saying a word to Cobby.

I ask Cobby, "Is everything okay with the two of you?"

He replies, "I told Michael the truth, and he did not like it. Don't worry about Michael right now. You need to focus on yourself."

Cobby calls the same massage therapist who took care of me the last time I was here with Michael. For two hours, this woman works every crevice on my body. I forgot that I may be going to jail and that my life is over. I push that thought out of my mind. I enjoy feeling like I'm on cloud nine. My massage therapist leaves the room once she finishes. I stay for a little longer, reminiscing on the last time I was here. Remembering how my body felt while making love in this place. It was mesmerizing.

A light tap on the door wakes me from my trance. It's Michael, he asks, "Are you ready?"

I stretch my arm out, I reply, "I'll be ready in five minutes."

As I hop off the table to get dressed, I notice Michael has a wicked smile on his face. He asks in a seductive voice, "Do you know where we are standing?"

I pretend I don't know what he's talking about. He pulls me closer and says, "This is the same room we were in the first time we came here."

His words send my body into a frenzy. I pull away. After all Michael put me through, he still has control over my body. I grab my clothes, go to another room to get dressed and head to the lobby looking for Cobby to thank him for the massage. He hugs me, "Call me or drop by any time you need a massage or someone to talk to."

I accept the invitation and kiss him on the cheek. Michael tenses up every time I show any affection toward any man, even his best friend Cobby. I ignore his childish gesture and continue to love on Cobby. If it weren't for him and Sara, I don't know where I would be right now. They have been my rock through this time of my life.

Michael comes over and pulls me away from Cobby and mumbles that we have to go. He has the nerve to be jealous after all his whoring around. It's already late in the afternoon, and I have had enough of Michael for one day.

I demand he takes me home. He looks at me and asks, "What about my other surprise?"

I'm not in the mood for any more surprises. I reply, "just take me home."

Michael did not argue. On the way home, he reminds me that he is coming back with food. At this point, I did not care; I just want to get in my apartment and go to bed.

My phone rings as I'm entering the apartment. It's Theo. I have not spoken to him since the fight with Michael in my apartment. I answer, "What's up, stranger?"

He laughs, "I should say the same thing about you. I stopped by the gallery several times; you were not there. I called and left you several messages, and you have not returned my calls."

Oh yeah, I have not checked my messages, and frankly, I have been keeping my phone off, fearing that Michael's crazy girlfriends could have my number and call to harass me. Instead, I tell Theo that my phone hasn't been working.

Theo replies, "I'm around the corner. Wanted to see if you're in the mood for company."

"I had a long day, and I'm about to go to bed," I comment. Well, that is the half-truth. I did not want him to come over because Michael would be back, and I was not in the mood for round two of their testosterone match.

Theo gives in but says, "Tonight, I'm picking you up because I have a surprise for you, and I will not take no for an answer."

I reluctantly agree, then reply, "It's a date. You can pick me up at seven p.m."

Shortly after I hang up with Theo, Michael knocks on the door. I take a deep breath before I let him in. He walks in with two brown bags, which I assume was dinner. Having Michael in the apartment reminds me of all my troubles, no matter how apologetic he is. No amount of spa days or dinners will make me feel better. As he places the food on the kitchen counter, I notice the restaurant logo. It's Jack's place.

Before we eat, I walk into my room to take a quick shower. I close my eyes and let the water massage my face and run down my back. As my eyes close, I can feel his presence standing behind me. My body tenses up as he slowly rubs my back. I stand still as if I'll become invisible. Once again, my body is ready to betray me. My body yearns for his touch. I close my eyes tighter, fighting with myself, knowing damn well that I cannot win this fight. Michael slowly turns me around and kisses me hard and deep. My legs tremble. Michael scoops me up without breaking our kiss. Oh, how I miss his kisses. I reciprocate the kiss to let him know that I miss him too. I straddle him. Before my brain could say, "What the hell are you doing?" my body was ready to receive the sweet pleasure Michael brings every time we make love. Electricity runs through my body as he enters me. It takes a special skill to have sex standing up. Michael's strong legs hold me steady as I move up and down to match his rhythm. He kisses me as if this were our last kiss.

Michael never kissed me like this before. His kisses are passionate and deep to my soul. My body no longer can take the sensation of the kiss and penetration. Minutes later, I explode. He takes the sponge to wash my body. It feels like my soul left me. He grabs a towel, dries me off, carries me to my bed. Without a word, he walks to the kitchen. Minutes later, he returns with the food on a tray with a single rose and a card. I look at him then the tray, to say, what are you up to. He lays the tray on the bed then carefully climbs in.

Michael comments with a wicked smile, "You need to eat because you need your strength for what I'm about to do to you."

Still emotionally torn, I muster enough courage, "There will not be a repeat. What happened in the shower was a mistake, and it should not have happened."

Things will never be the same between Michael and me. I still have to deal with another female being pregnant with his baby as he lay here.

Michael did not expect that reaction, especially after the sex we just had. He quietly gets up, dresses and leaves. I throw the tray in the direction of the bedroom door, causing food to spatter all over the room. My emotions turn to rage. The pain is unbearable. How could I love a man who's so damaged and so broken? I don't want to continue to put myself in harm's way because of my love for him. I must guard my heart and protect myself. I am tired of this emotional rollercoaster.

CHAPTER 28

Days of Reckoning

I feel like shit after I left Jazz's apartment. She sticks a knife through my heart every time she reminds me of my mistakes. On my way home, I call Cobby to talk. He and I have not been in a good space after Jazz's arrest. With anticipation, I dial his number. Cobby answers on the third ring, "Yeah," followed by silence. That's how I know that he is mad at me.

I reply, "Hello. Cob? Are you there?"

"Yeah, I'm here. What you want man?" He shouts back.

"Cob, come on man, don't you think this has gone far enough?" I reply.

"Damn you, Mike, why do you have to be so fucked up?" Cobby screams on the phone.

"Man, I'm not here to hear all that. I just called you to thank you for taking care of Jazz," I shout back.

He lets out a loud breath, "You don't need to thank me for helping Jasmine. That's the least I can do after all you've put her through."

Cobby gave me the same grief two weeks ago when I told him that a woman I slept with was pregnant. I tried to explain, "Cob, this was a one-night stand. Unfortunately, the young lady ended up pregnant."

"See Mike, that's what I am talking about. It's a miracle that your dick doesn't fall off due to your dangerous behavior," Cobby scolded me.

"It's just an excuse, man. There was no reason ... Jazz and I was not in a good space. I was at a bar sitting next to this beautiful lady with long legs and curvy hips. I strike up a conversation. The vibe was good. She invited me to her house to continue the conversation, and one thing led to another. I did not hear from her until she called to announce that she was pregnant. How was I going to explain to Jazz that I got someone pregnant while we were together?" I explained.

Cobby commented, "Mike, you should have come clean to Jazz as soon as you found out that this woman was pregnant."

"Cob, she was already going through so much, I didn't want to add more to her troubles," I replied.

Cobby said sternly, "That's bullshit, and you know it, Mike. Jasmine deserved the truth, including why she has not visited your place."

I arrive home not ready to end the conversation with Cobby. I ask, "How did I get so fucked up man?"

Cobby lets out a big exhale and says, "Sometimes life trauma can manifest differently, man."

"I put Chantae through the same thing back in Chicago. I still have nightmares of her shooting herself in front of me," I reply.

Cobby explains, "Mike, the nightmares are not going to end until you deal with the issues. Remember my post-traumatic stress disorder after Lau's death. It took me years of therapy to get to where I am. Good enough to be in a healthy relationship again."

I confess, "I realize that I need help. I can't keep hurting people that I love. Especially Jasmine. I am going to take your advice Cob and call a therapist."

Cobby chimes in, "Believe me brother, that would be the best thing you can do for yourself and Jazz."

I reply, "Yeah! For her sake, I need to change. She deserves so much more."

Cobby teases, "Oh shit! Is that a hint that someone has been bitten by the love bug?"

I let out a belly laugh, "Man, I think I was bitten the first time I saw Jasmine."

Cobby laughs, "Well, I'll be damn. Mr. Mike finally found someone worthy enough to make him go see a therapist."

I ponder what Cobby said. Yes, I am willing to turn my life around because of Jasmine. She makes me want to be a better man.

Cobby comments, "You know I only tell you the truth because I love you, man and want to see you finally at peace."

I reply, "Man, I love you too. That's the only reason I put up with your shit."

We hang up on a good note. I'm happy that Cobby and I are on speaking terms again. Besides Jazz, he is the only one I can talk to. I decide in the parking lot to go inside and remove all of Chantae's pictures and keepsakes from the house. I am going to redecorate and invite Jazz over. I am going to fight for her with my last breath.

CHAPTER 29

Fool's Heart

I must have fallen asleep during my crying session. I am awakened by a loud knock on my door. I make my way to the door with one eye still closed. Ugghh! It's Theo. I forgot that I told him to pick me up tonight. I was not in the mood to go anywhere or for company. I did not open the door. Hopefully, he will leave thinking that I'm not home. Theo continues to bang on the door. I give in and open the door. He looks perplexed and asks, "What are you doing?"

I explain, "I was sleeping and forgot about our appointment. May I have a rain check."

Theo replies, "Not a chance! You are going out even if I have to drag you out."

I roll my eyes and tell him to come in. He follows me to the living room then plops himself on the couch like a pouting toddler. I walk back to the bedroom to get ready. I step on something slippery and splat, down I go. I have food all over my bedroom floor. The loud thump startles Theo. He rushes to see if I'm okay. On the floor, embarrassed with food in my hair, on my face, and on my clothes. I reply, "Oh, I am just peachy."

He helps me up and looks around inquisitively. He says, "Let me guess," he points to the food, "your boyfriend? That's it! Go and get ready. I'll clean this up. I'm taking you out tonight. You are not staying in this apartment alone in the condition you're in." Theo demands.

My ego was bruised because Theo had to see my humiliation. I went to the bathroom, shut the door. With tears running down my face, I turn on the shower so that the water can bury my cries. I step out of the shower and see that Theo did, in fact, clean up the mess. I get dressed and step out of my bedroom to find Theo staring on the living room sofa.

He asks, "Are you ready for some fun?"

I give him a faint smile and reply, "I can use the distraction."

He takes a bow with his hand extended to me, then says in a soft New Orleans fashion, "After you, Mademoiselle," I take Theo's hand, and out we go. We drive to Bayou's Spot, where he had performed with his friend the last time we were together. It's a weeknight; the place is not as busy as before. The host finds us a table near the stage.

As soon as we sit down, the tall waiter with a ponytail comes to our table. He asks, "Would you beautiful couple like to order drinks now?"

Theo and I look at each other and start laughing. I am used to it now. People often think we are a couple. Theo orders a gin and tonic for him and a glass of red wine for me. A glass of wine is just what I need. He looks at me and says, "What's going on Jazz? What has you so down?"

I really did not want to talk to Theo about Michael. He and Michael are not friends, so I reply, "I'm fine."

He did not believe me but chose not to push the issue. The stage is empty, so Theo hopes on the piano and starts playing an unfamiliar tune. He is so talented. He grabs the mic and announces, "This next song is dedicated to the beautiful woman up front, Jasmine. You are more than enough."

Why he got to put me on blast like that. Luckily, the restaurant is not crowded. Theo sings a jazzy rendition of "I Want to Know What Love Is" by the group Foreigner. He sounds amazing. Wow! He really should think about doing this professionally. He sings that song so beautifully tears were rolling down my face. The song ends, and everyone in the restaurant starts clapping. He takes a bow then joins me back to our table.

I give Theo a big hug as he approaches our table. I comment, "That was amazing. That's actually my favorite song."

He's taken back by my gesture and replies, "I should perform for you more often if I am going to get this type of reaction."

I give him a playful jab. There's a chemistry between Theo and me. Unfortunately, Michael is the barrier. I ask Theo, "Why don't you pursue a career in music?"

He replies, "If I did, I wouldn't have met you."

I roll my eyes but say nothing.

He looks at me with a serious look and replies, "I would have given up the world if it meant I get to be here with you Jazz."

I feel guilty hearing Theo's confession. There's no doubt that he could have been a good lover, but unfortunately, the heart wants what it wants. Michael has stolen my heart, and there's nothing I can do about it. I was quiet for a minute, thinking about how ironic life is. This beautiful man is sitting in front of me, ready to love me and treat me how I deserve, but I am in love with a man whore. Tears roll down my face just thinking of how unfair life is.

He wipes my face with his handkerchief, then asks, "Jazz did I say something to upset you?"

I reply, "No, you did not do anything wrong. You're trying your best to cheer me up. I have a lot going, which I don't want to get into right now."

He pulls his chair closer to me and holds my hand, "Jazz, stop torturing yourself."

His observation makes me upset. Suddenly, I no longer want to be here. I ask Theo to take me home. He pays for our drinks, then we leave.

Once I arrive home, I fire up my computer to send Michael an email. I start with:

I made several attempts to write you this email, but my ego would not let me hit send. Many emotions stir in me every time you touch me. I was doing fine with the wall that I built around me to guard my heart. You used all the right words. You did everything right so that I could let my guard down. I must congratulate you on the game well played. They say that there's a thin line between love and hate, and I must tell you that I have experienced both for you. I am not sure you understand the pain you have caused me. I believe you every time you tell me that you want to change, and it is me you want and only me. I hang on to your every word. Now, I know that it is just another lie you tell all your women. All the sleepless nights and anxiety you're experiencing, it's nothing but karma knocking at your door. Your life is so fucked up because you are reaping what you have sowed. Why did you have to drag me into your mess?

You knew from the beginning that you were not serious about being in a relationship. To think that while we were together, you got someone pregnant when you told me that you were done with all of them. You're sick, and the sad part is you don't even realize it. I've tried to rationalize your behavior. Were you molested by a woman when you were little? Did you have mommy issues? All these questions you have to answer for yourself. I am so stupid and too desperate to have allowed you in my life and my heart. Stay the hell out of my life. Get your shit together and grow up.

After I hit send, I turn off my phone and computer in case Michael replies. I go to the kitchen and pour myself a glass of wine. I sit on my couch feeling drained and lost. I keep asking myself: How am I going to get out of the predicament? What if I go to jail for drug possession? How long would I go to jail? I was petrified spending one night in the holding cell; I cannot imagine spending years locked up, especially for something that I did not do. Tears roll down my cheeks as I think about my future. I am all alone in this. Sara can't even help me in this mess. My life is fucked up because I decided to let this man in my life.

Truth to be told, I cannot blame Michael or any of these women. I blame myself for being afraid of being alone and ending up with him. He showed me who he was from the beginning, I chose not to believe him. I pretended that I was the only woman in his life so that I could justify me being with him. I knew that being with him was wrong, and I was ashamed of the relationship. I kept the relationship hidden from friends and family for a while. I would have killed for Michael if he asked me to. He was my drug. I was willing to go to the end of the earth for Michael. He occupied my mind day and night.

I compromised my self-worth, values, and integrity to be accepted by this man. I am broken by his manipulations and exhausted by his apologies. He believes that he loved me and wants a life with me in his own sick and twisted mind. And I believe it too.

CHAPTER 30

A Woman's Scorn

It has been two weeks since I sent Michael the email. I keep myself busy at the gallery and with the poetry nights. Theo and Claude perform occasionally, and it's always a full house. One day Nadine shows up at the gallery to discuss what her investigation uncovered.

She makes her grand entrance in the office. "What's up heifer? Why haven't I seen you?" She scolds me as she hugs me.

"Girl, you know I'm being stalked," I reply while hugging her.

She takes a seat in the oversized chair. She says, "That's why I am here. I did a background check on your girl Laycee. I did not find anything on her."

I take a deep breath, relieved that Laycee has checked out. I ask, "So Laycee has checked out?"

"No, that's not what I am saying. The name does not exist," Nadine replies.

I frown. Sounding concerned, I ask, "What do you mean the name does not exist?"

Nadine slams the folder she was holding down and replies, "Jazz, Laycee is a fake name."

It feels like a ton of bricks fall on my chest. I walk around the desk to have more room to move around.

I ask Nadine "Could it have been Laycee all along?"

She replies, "I don't know, but I am going to find out. Do you have a copy of her identification documents from when you hired her?"

I walk back to my and desk and pull her file from the cabinet. I hand the file to Nadine. She says, "Her driver's license says that she's from Texas, but that could be fake too. I am going to call a friend from the FBI to run a facial recognition. I will let you know more details when I have them."

I am still shocked by the news that Laycee uses a fictitious name. Why would she go to such lengths to get close to me? My head is about to explode. I must get out of the gallery. Nadine promises to call as soon as she knows anything. She comments, "Jazz, don't worry, if Laycee, or whatever her name is, has been putting you through all of this stress. We will get her." I hug Nadine goodbye.

Theo and I continue to work on various art projects. We have developed a beautiful friendship. I'm happy that Theo finally let go of his infatuation. Theo called one afternoon, sounding far too excited, "Jazz, I found this new studio. It has everything I need. I want your opinion. I'm on my way to pick you up."

I explain, "Theo, you can't just call me and expect me to drop what I'm doing to go and look at a studio."

He replies, "Jazz, please this is important. I promise it won't take long."

"Fine," I reply,

The air is unusually chilly for an autumn afternoon. I put on a sweater and jeans. Minutes later, Theo knocks on my door with the same excitement in his voice. He asks, "You ready? I am taking you to eat after this." He continues, "We know how you love to eat."

Since drama and danger are my constant companion, I make it a point to tell Sara where I am going, who I am going with, and check-in with her when I am back. I send her a quick text to let her know that I am with Theo.

I jump in his car. As he races out of the parking lot, I yell, "Damn, Theo, why are you in a hurry?"

He replies, "Because I am excited, and I can't wait for you to see this place."

I roll my eyes, "Well, don't try to kill me in the process." He gives me a blank stare.

Theo's excitement got him talking fast. He says, "Oh Jazz, you're going to love your resting place."

I look at him and frown, "What do you mean, my resting place?"

He lets out a squeaky laugh, "Oh, you'll see what I'm talking about when we get there."

I've never seen Theo this excited. Thirty minutes into the drive, my phone rang. It's Nadine. I sure hope she finally has news about who Laycee really is.

In an urgent tone, Nadine asks, "Jazz, where are you?"

Her tone alerted me that whatever she found out meant I could be in danger. I reply, "I'm with Theo. We're going to see his new studio. Do you have news on Laycee?"

As I say Laycee's name, Theo looks at me strangely then starts driving faster. I hold on to the dashboard to keep myself from hitting my forehead.

"Will you slow down?" I yell.

Theo ignores my plea and continues driving erratically. I continue with my conversation with Nadine while holding on for dear life in the car.

Nadine replies, "Jazz, my friend from the FBI just sent me Laycee's information. Her real name is Mona Desiree Watts."

I scream, "Mona!" My stomach dropped.

Theo makes a sharp and sudden turn. My head crashes into the car door frame, hard. I must have blacked out. When I come to, I'm disoriented and have no idea where I am. I feel a sharp pain on the left side of my head. It's hard to focus, but I can see the silhouettes of a man and a woman standing in front of me. Trying to move my hands, I realize that they are tied to a chair. I am trying to make sense of this. The last thing I remember, I was talking on the phone with Nadine in Theo's car. I blink twice to refocus to see who's standing in front of me. No! This can't be. My eyes are playing tricks on me. Laycee and Theo are arguing about what to do with me.

This is not the studio Theo wanted to show me. It looks like an abandoned warehouse. Is this what Theo meant when he said that this would be my resting place? I am going to die in this dark, damp place, and no one will find me. The thought of dying here scares me. I yell out to get Theo's attention, but my scream is muffled by tape over my mouth. Laycee realizes that I'm alert and trying to speak.

She walks over and yells, "Surprise bitch!" She yanks the tape from my mouth. I wince from the sting of the adhesive. I stare at Theo, trying to make sense of this. So, many questions are going through my mind. I try to speak once more, but Laycee put a gun to my head and says, "You got something to say?"

Theo rushes over and yells, "MONA, you promised you're not going to hurt her."

Mona? Theo? Laycee? I don't care that I have a gun to my head; I need an answer.

I direct my questions to Theo, "Why are you doing this? Who are you to Laycee?"

Theo responds with a cold stare, "All will reveal itself once your boyfriend gets here."

I look puzzled, "Is this about Michael?" I turn and look at Laycee and reply, "I don't understand."

Laycee presses the gun at my head and yells, "Didn't you hear what he said? All will be revealed, so shut the fuck up."

I don't want to press my luck, so I keep quiet. Laycee, I mean Mona, dials a number, and says, "Michael, if you want your bitch alive, you better meet me at a warehouse on Forty-Fourth, and you BETTER come alone."

Minutes later, I hear someone screaming my name. It's Michael. I yell, "Michael, I am in the back!"

He reaches the back of the warehouse and notices that I'm tied to a chair. He rushes over, trying to get to me. Theo pulls out a gun, points it at Michael, and yells, "Don't do it, man." Michael stops and puts his hands up.

Laycee comes from the shadows, and Michael yells, "MONA, this is between you and me."

She fires back, "You made it about her when you decided to leave me for her."

"Should I tell her, or should you?" She asks aggressively.

"Mona, please let her go. I'll do whatever you need me to do. Just please let Jasmine go," Michael pleads.

"NOT UNTIL YOU TELL HER THE TRUTH," Mona shouts as she presses the gun harder against my head.

Michael rubs his head and starts, "This is Mona, My son's mother. She's the one that has been calling me."

Still in a daze, "Why do you keep calling her Mona? Her name is Laycee."

Michael shakes his head, looks over to Mona, then says, "Laycee! Really, that is your new name?"

Michael turns to me with fear on his face, then asks, "Didn't you tell me you had an employee at the gallery named Laycee?"

He turns to Mona, "It was you all along? The break-ins, the drugs," he yells. "You've gone too far, Mona."

Mona walks up to Michael, calmly grabs his face, and licks it, then she says, "Not far enough, lover boy."

Michael pushes her out the way. She laughs. She walks over to me. I can feel her breath to my right ear, "That's right bitch, he's the baby daddy I've been telling you about."

I look at Theo, trying to make sense of his connection to Laycee/Mona. I ask, "Theo, who are you?"

Before Theo can answer, Laycee yells, "Didn't I tell you to shut the fuck up bitch."

Theo rushes over and yells, "Mona, enough. You promised not to hurt her." Then with a pitiful look, he rubs my face and asks, "Are you okay, baby?"

I tilt my head to the other side out of his reach. Theo makes another attempt to reach for me. Michael yells, "Get your fucking hands off her."

Theo's face changes from Dr. Jekyll to Mr. Hyde as he stomps over to Michael then whoosh. Theo strikes him with the gun. Michael falls back. As Michael regains his balance, he surprises Theo with an uppercut sending him flying over my right side. Michael attempts to launch at Theo once more, a loud bang stops him.

With the gun in the air, Mona yells, "Enough! You take one more step, and I will blow her head off."

Mona's threat seems to work. Michael has his hands up and stands closer to me. He asks, "Are you okay?"

"What kind of bullshit question is that?" I yell through tears, "I have a gun pointed at me by this crazy bitch,"

The butt of Mona's gun crashes against the left side of my head. As I began to lose consciousness, Michael launches at Mona, then bang, another shot.

I am awakened by Michael's voice while tapping my face, "Jazz, wake up, wake up Jazz, please."

As I begin to gain consciousness, Mona comes over and kisses Michael. He pushes her away, calling her a crazy bitch. Theo smacks Michael across his face and yells, "Don't talk to her that way."

"You get the picture now, Michael?" Mona yells.

If looks could kill, she would have been dead from the way Michael was stabbing her with his eyes. It makes sense now. There's no way I could have put it all together. Michael has never seen Laycee at the gallery.

Still confused as to Theo's relation to Mona/Laycee, whatever the hell her name is.

I ask, "Theo, you're a part of this?"

Theo replies, "Chantae and Mona are my sisters."

His comment struck me like a baseball bat. "So, you were part of Laycee's - I mean Mona's - plan all along?"

He giggles, "It was so easy to play the role. You're so gullible Jasmine."

Mona starts laughing, "No, more like stupid. You should have seen her face when I told her some of the sad stories about my baby daddy, and all this time I was talking about her boyfriend."

This is too much to take. I ask, "Theo, WHY?"

He walks over to Michael, kicks him, and replies, "Because this son-of-a-bitch killed my sister."

Still dazed, "But I thought Chantae committed suicide."

Mona screams as she taunts Michael with the gun pointed in his direction, "ARE YOU STUPID? HE KILLED HER!"

Theo replies, "I made it my life's mission to go after this son-of-a-bitch for ruining my sister's life."

"Now that we are all acquainted, I need you to TELL HER now," Mona demands.

Michael begins his confession; the gun is pressed to his head. "It's true. Mona is Chantae's sister. Chantae and I dated for five years. She meant everything to me. I loved her."

"LIAR!" Mona screams as she hits Michael with her gun. He falls to the floor with a gash of blood seeping from the side of his head. My instinct is to run to him, but I can't move to help him.

Mona drops on the floor, grabs Michael's face, and licks the blood from his head. In a psychotic tone, she says, "Poor baby, I am so sorry, I did not mean it. Why are you lying to her?"

Michael crawls, trying to move away from Mona. Enraged by his action, Mona points the gun at me and says, "Hurry up and get to the good part, Michael."

Michael is on high alert, "Okay! Just stop pointing the gun at her." Reluctantly he continues, "I was sleeping with Mona while I was with Chantae. Mona wanted me to leave Chantae to be with her. I told her that sleeping with her was a mistake and I would never leave Chantae."

Mona chimes in, "I had to tell Chantae the truth to get what I wanted and what I got was a baby." She rubs her stomach.

Michael continues, "She tricked me into getting her pregnant and told Chantae everything. Chantae was devastated and committed suicide in my apartment."

Mona replies, "I guess the ultrasound pictures I left for her didn't help either."

This chick is batshit crazy! Why did Michael get involved with her? I can't believe what I'm hearing, and I don't want to hear anymore. I yell, "STOP! just shut up."

Mona urges him to continue, "No, I don't want him to shut up. This that next-level Jerry Springer shit."

Theo is laughing. He sounds as deranged as his sister.

I plead for Michael to stop, but Mona urges him to go on. He continues, "I lied to everyone because it was the only way I could justify her suicide."

Theo's face becomes unrecognizable. He looks at me, then replies, "And that's why he has to pay." His statement of judgment ends with a punch to Michael's gut.

Michael falls backward, and Theo uses the opportunity to continue kicking Michael in his stomach, ribs, and head. I yell, "Theo, stop!"

Theo looks at me with such rage. "You haven't seen anything yet!"

I try to rise from the chair to shield Michael but trip and fall over him. My action infuriates Theo. He drags me off, Michael still tied to the chair. He begs mockingly at Michael and yells, "GET UP!"

I've never seen such rage in Theo's face before. Theo fixes my chair upright. He gets in my face, with clenched jaws, as if he was ready to scold a spoiled child. "After all this man has put you through, you want to protect him?" He was about to say something else when sirens blared from every direction.

Mona points the gun at Michael, "I thought I told you to come alone."

Michael pleads, "I didn't tell anyone I was coming here, I swear to you, Mona."

Mona screams, "GET UP!"

Michael wrestles his way up and shuffles, imbalanced closer to me. The sirens are getting closer.

Theo says, "Good, more witnesses for when I put a bullet in his head."

Mona aims her gun in my direction, "Nothing is going to ruin my plan. If Michael doesn't want to be with me, he sure as hell is not going to be with you."

I hear an explosion from a distance. I am paralyzed by a bullet coming toward me in slow motion. When I regain consciousness, on the floor, a hand is pressing against my neck. Someone is screaming, "Ma'am, are you okay?"

Not fully understand what is going on, I manage to mumble, "Am I dead?"

The person replies, "No, you're not dead."

I ask, "If I'm not dead, whose blood is this?"

I remember a bullet from Mona's gun was coming straight at me before I blacked out. My head hurts. I squint to see it's a paramedic who's asking me questions. The red and blue lights flashing reminded me that something terrible had happened. I look around for Michael. Where is he? Did he run and leave me alone? I start hyperventilating as I notice a trail of blood. It stops by a man lying on the floor with his bloody shirt ripped open and paramedics trying to resuscitate him.

Remembering what he was wearing, I realize it's him. I lunge toward Michael, screaming his name, hoping he can hear me. I grab his bloody face screaming for him to wake up.

"WAKE UP Michael, wake up please, Wake up."

A paramedic tries to push me out of the way. I push him away from me and continue screaming Michael's name. Screaming and fighting with anyone trying to pull me away from him. Two officers swoop me up and carry me outside.

I scream as I point at Michael, "I don't need no fucking medical attention! He needs help."

Mona's body is lying at the entrance of the warehouse. Her eyes are opened. The right side of her face is shattered. I notice Theo in handcuffs as the paramedics usher me to an ambulance. I run over to Theo and punch him in his face, and scream, "You monster! You killed him! You killed him!" I keep saying it as the paramedics pull me in the opposite direction.

Cobby, Sara, Nadine, and Misha are all waiting outside of the warehouse. I try to walk over to them, but blood rushes to my head. As I hit the ground, Cobby runs and catches me. I whisper, "They killed him, they killed him."

Cobby asks, "They killed who?" I look at him, and without a word, he rushes toward the warehouse entrance to see for himself. The officers stop him at the door, yet he sees Michael's body on the ground. Through a blur, I see Cobby put his hands on his head, then drop to the floor wailing!

"Growing up in Haiti, my grandmother, Pierrecina Deshommes, was the best storyteller in the neighborhood." Author RVantaire would move to South Florida to be with her family at 12. Her love for books grew when she served as a student library assistant in middle school. Her creativity and affinity for words led to her professional career as a Senior Learning and Development Specialist. A crime story junkie, you can find her listening to conspiracy theories and true crime stories podcasts. RVantaire loves mysteries and exploring other genres to challenge her imagination. She is the mother of two amazing young ladies. Her love for travel to exotic places opens her heart and mind to create.